DESMOND WINTERS
IN THE REALMS
OF THE CAGED SUN

BY
LEA RYAN

ISBN: 0-9979599-0-8
ISBN-13: 978-0-9979599-0-1
Library of Congress Control Number: 2017900532

ACKNOWLEDGMENTS

A huge thank-you to my readers: Dee Crabtree, Rowan, Brooke, and Josette. An equally huge thank-you to the writers who made my childhood magical with their genius.

FORTES FORTUNA JUVAT
FORTUNE FAVORS THE BRAVE

CHAPTER 1

Desmond's strange day began with an intruder in his bedroom.

The first sound, the brush of something dragging across the floor, startled him awake. He remained still, hoping that it was his imagination or remnants of his dream, his mind playing a trick.

Without sitting up, he scanned his surroundings. His door was still closed. The window at the foot of his bed, however, was not. The pane stood open, the curtain parted just enough for him to see tree branches. He hadn't left it that way. He hadn't opened the window at all the day before.

A second sound, a clicking, chittering noise, sent his pulse racing. This thing in his room was an animal. It made a thump on the seat of the chair and then another on its return to the floor.

Desmond sat up and tracked its movements, claws clicking to his right. He kept quiet for fear it would vanish under a piece of furniture or into a vent, where he would never find it. Then he'd be in real trouble.

Mrs. Dunwiler, the live-in housekeeper, had no patience for animals in the house. She would have a conniption if she saw the window open. He didn't even want to guess what she might do if forced to hunt down errant wildlife *because* the window was open.

She had only just given him permission to sleep in the main part of the house while his parents were gone. All his assurances and promises to be careful were for nothing if she walked in before he could get the animal out and the window closed.

Worse, she would tell his parents. The work he'd done to prove that he had matured enough to travel the world with them would be wasted. He'd be stuck at home forever.

The claws clicked back toward the chair. It leaped from the floor, and the seat creaked.

If it were the size of a cat or a raccoon, its head would have poked up over the footboard. With this reasoning, his fear of being attacked diminished, unless of course, the thing turned out to be a rat. He shuddered at the thought.

A tuft of electric blue fur popped into and then out of sight.

He searched his groggy mind for an animal with fur that vivid a color. Most of the animals he'd seen near home had feathers or fur in shades of brown or gray, maybe a dash of yellow or red. He had seen blue jays but never one so bright.

Slow and steady footsteps thudded up the staircase down the hall from his room. Mrs. Dunwiler was coming to get him for breakfast.

He looked again at the open window. He leaned forward in bed, careful not to squeak the mattress springs, and peered over the edge.

The intruder was a blue squirrel with a bushy tail that twitched as the animal rifled through a pair of pants haphazardly folded on the chair. Pointy ears stood straight up from its head, ending in tufts. Its black eyes locked onto Desmond.

Mrs. Dunwiler knocked on the bedroom door. "Desmond?"

"Don't come in, please," he blurted out. "I'm not dressed."

"Sorry, dear. Breakfast in twenty minutes." She went on her way, humming.

He let a sigh of relief. His freedom was preserved. Now, he just had to deal with the furry problem in his bedroom. It had abandoned the chair, not for the window, he decided, judging by the sound of skittering.

He hung his head over the side of the bed and discovered the animal hiding underneath, peering back at him. Other than the strange color and the ears, it looked like any other garden variety squirrel.

He whispered, "What are you doing here?"

It turned on its small haunches and bolted the other direction, scrambling across the wooden floor. In a flash, it was bounding floor to chair, chair to the outdoors.

As he tried to go after it, Desmond tangled his legs in the blankets, and he fell. He stumbled to the window in time to see the squirrel scamper down the trunk of a tree and across the yard before disappearing behind a low, stone wall.

"Figures."

His one bit of excitement in months blazed for a glorious moment and then fizzled like a spent firework. He was glad the squirrel no longer posed a threat to his freedom, but he'd hoped for more than the sight of it running off.

The heavy clouds let loose their burden in a shower of rain. He closed the pane against yet another day of dreariness and turned his attention to the chair.

Clothes were piled there. A short-sleeve, button-down shirt, the kind his mother made him wear to casual social functions, was rumpled, the collar flipped up. Beneath that, he found a t-shirt and a pair of jeans. He was sure he hadn't put the clothes out the night before, just as he was positive he hadn't left the window open.

The housekeeper's humming neared the other side of his door again. An idea occurred to him, an obvious explanation. All he needed was confirmation.

"Mrs. Dunwiler?"

"Yes?"

He asked, "Did you lay out clothes for me?"

"No, I did not. You requested I not do that anymore. As I recall, you informed me that you were old enough to take care of it. Do you need assistance with selecting proper attire? My services as a stylist are always at your disposal, especially if I can prevent another orange shirt, green shorts debacle."

"No. No thank you. I'll be down for breakfast in a few minutes."

"Suit yourself." She chuckled at her own joke and headed back downstairs.

The squirrel arranged the clothes there for him. He didn't want to believe it, but he thought about the way it had looked at him, almost as if it wanted to tell him something, but that was impossible.

Squirrels didn't break, enter, and offer style suggestions. Squirrels gathered nuts and lived in trees, and they certainly didn't have blue fur. He grappled for a plausible explanation that didn't involve the possibility that he'd gone bonkers overnight.

"Ridiculous," he insisted to himself while he considered whether to actually wear the outfit.

What harm could come of doing so? They were his things. What if he were somehow meant to wear them?

Yes. He would wear what the squirrel wanted him to. One should embrace the opportunity to be assisted by extraordinary wildlife.

He got dressed, and as he closed his door behind him in the hallway, he felt an object in his pocket. His fingers found a coin his mother had given him a couple years before, a yellow Russian coin with a bear on it. She told him it was lucky, and he believed her.

He liked the gifts she brought him, but he would've preferred having her around the house more often. Desmond's parents were always traveling without him. Wherever they went, he was either too young or their destination too dangerous, or they had too much work to do. If he had his way, he would soon change their minds.

He stood in front of their door, the one across the hall from his. Their room was off-limits when they were gone, privacy and all that, but he still managed to sneak in from time to time. He was a step closer to them in there.

He felt a presence at his side and said, "Good morning, Rathbone."

The Irish wolfhound was a skinny, old man with his fur thinning in spots, but his bark was still powerful enough to intimidate. At night, he slept near the front door in order to protect the family. With morning in full swing, he wanted to be near Desmond.

Desmond patted the dog's head. "They come home tomorrow. Maybe we should make sure their stuff is in order." After another glance down the hall to confirm Mrs. Dunwiler wasn't coming up the stairs, he opened the door as quietly as he could manage.

Rathbone trotted in, happy to be in the room again. He sniffed the Persian rug in front of the fireplace and then proceeded to wipe his face and drop to a shameless wallow in the worn softness. He'd missed his favorite spot in the house.

The white canopy bed was perfectly made, throw pillows arranged so neatly that Desmond wondered if Mrs. Dunwiler had used a ruler to place them. His father's dark, wooden desk, while crowded with books, office implements, and souvenirs, was equally neat and waiting for its owner to return and write about what he'd seen while far away. The chests of drawers, the fancy full-length mirror, the books lined on built-in shelves, all was as it should have been.

"Guess everything's fine. Come on, Rathbone."

The dog whined.

"Don't worry. The rug will be back open for business tomorrow." Desmond turned to his mother's vanity in the corner, next to the door.

Among sparkling bottles of perfume and tubes of lipstick and the comb with the crystal handle, white powder was scattered, the lid to its container knocked askew. Four-toed footprints made a weaving line in the powder from the left side of the vanity to the right. They were big enough to be those of a tropical bird like he'd seen at the zoo. Just beyond the end of the tracks, a bright green feather was lodged in a cup of soft-bristled makeup brushes.

He checked his reflection in the mirror for evidence that he was losing it. What did crazy look like? He had no idea. All he saw was himself with mussed, brown hair. He hastily smoothed it down as if doing so brought order to the world again.

He searched the room, the ceiling, the canopy over the bed. No bird perched on the shelves. With Rathbone unconcerned but close by, Desmond bent to check under furniture. He found no bird.

He asked the dog, "Shouldn't you growl if a strange animal comes into the house? Can't you smell it?"

The dog answered with a lick of his chops. He cared more about the savory scent of buttered biscuits drifting up the stairs.

Mrs. Dunwiler's powerful voice rang long and loud from the kitchen. "Desmond! Breakfast!"

"Coming!" He answered quickly to keep her from coming back upstairs to get him.

Desmond hesitated at the vanity. Did he have time to clean it? His mother wouldn't want to come home and find it in that condition.

He remembered the squirrel in his room. A bright blue squirrel and a huge bird on the loose in the house had to mean something, not to mention the mystery of the clothes on the chair. He needed to know that his imagination hadn't sent his sanity off the tracks. He needed confirmation that at least some of what he'd experienced since he woke up had really happened. He needed to consult Gwen.

"Desmond!" Mrs. Dunwiler called again.

CHAPTER 2

"Coming!" he answered, louder than before.

He closed the door behind him and went downstairs, tapping the polished top of the banister as he reached the foyer. Portraits of his grandparents glared disapprovingly as he made the corner and hurried through a formal dining room used more for the storage of antique furniture than anything else. The Winters' house had many rooms like that, more museum than living space.

"About time. Your food is getting cold." Mrs. Dunwiler had set breakfast at the big table in the kitchen, where she could keep an eye on Gwen and him while she worked on the dishes and other chores. Gwen had not yet arrived.

He grabbed a biscuit for his plate and bypassed a bowl full of scrambled eggs for the honey pot.

"Eggs and sausage, too," Mrs. Dunwiler nagged without turning from the kitchen sink. "You haven't seen Gwen, have you?"

At that very moment, the door to the backyard burst open in a rush of wind and rain. A figure, a bundle of stringy, dripping hair in a plastic raincoat and galoshes, nearly fell onto the rug just inside. She fought to yank her red umbrella closed against the force of the wind.

"Good god, girl. Have you lost your mind? You're soaked to the bone." Mrs. Dunwiler snatched the umbrella away to bop her daughter on the head with it. "What were you thinkin', stayin' out in nature's wrath so long?"

The sky concurred with a rumble of thunder that trembled the clean dishes stacked on the counter.

"It wasn't so bad when I went out." She knocked a clump of mud from her coat.

The housekeeper's face reddened at the sight of dirt falling to the floor. "I just swept there an hour ago. Now clean it up, and then go clean yourself up."

"Aw, can't it wait until after breakfast? I'm so hungry." She clasped her hands together to beg dramatically. "Please, my lovely mother? Your fabulous cooking makes my stomach growl."

Her mother sighed. "Turn. Let me see you from the back. We can't have mud on the kitchen furniture."

Gwen complied with a ballerina spin, giving the kitchen a fresh sprinkle of water. "See? No mud on my bum, promise."

"Very well. Don't get anything on Desmond. We need to keep at least one of you looking civilized." She winked at him.

Gwen flopped into the seat next to Desmond. She filled her plate with the eggs, sausage, and biscuits and then drenched the lot of it in a thick layer of honey.

Desmond noticed movement in the pocket of her raincoat. Knowing better than to draw Mrs. Dunwiler's attention, he tapped Gwen on the shoulder and pointed in a silent inquiry.

She grinned through her bite of honey eggs, put down her fork, and reached her dirty hand into her pocket to pull out a drowsy toad. She held it under the table for him to see, a bumpy, wrinkled thing lounging on its back in the palm of her hand, its legs stretched out. She stroked the white belly with her finger and then gently eased it over onto its stomach to reveal a jagged, bright pink stripe like a lightning bolt down its back.

His mouth dropped open. Another of those strange animals found its way inside. There had to be some logical explanation.

His science teacher, Mr. Harrul, would've come up with theories about their weird coloring, like contact with pollution or changes in the animals' diets, bacteria or some other external factor, and Desmond probably would have accepted whatever Mr. Harrul came up with because nothing exciting ever happened around him, especially not at his house.

"Gwendolyn Henrietta Dunwiler, that had better not be what I think it is." Mrs. Dunwiler's stern countenance loomed over the table. She glared down at them from the other side of breakfast. Lightning brightened the sky in the window behind her, giving villainous flair to her anger.

Gwen stuffed the toad in her pocket. It protested this abuse with a flailing of legs and a loud croak. She grinned sheepishly.

"Out. Now." Her mother pointed. "And don't stand there with the door open like you did before. Go change your clothes, too. I've had enough shenanigans for this morning."

Gwen complied with a sulky trudge to the door. She knew better than to argue when her mother reached the breaking point. Animals weren't allowed inside, not even the injured birds and rodents she'd told Desmond she so desperately wanted to nurse back to health. If allowed, she would've filled the house, floor to rafters, with tiny habitats and beds and nests.

Once the toad was out and Gwen had gone around the corner to her room, Mrs. Dunwiler's chipper demeanor returned. She said, "I need you and Gwen to go into town to the butcher's shop and pick up a roast for your parents' welcome home dinner tomorrow night. I have too much to finish and not enough hours in a day. You can ride your bikes after the storm moves through. Shouldn't take long." She lifted a bowl to run a wet rag over the table.

"Really?" He could hardly believe his ears. They'd never been allowed to leave the property alone. "By ourselves?"

She smiled. "Yes, dear. I figure you and Gwennie are twelve now. High time you got some kind of experience out in the world."

"Oh."

Isolation in the old house in the country was the norm when he wasn't in class. Venturing outside the gates on his own, on their own, wasn't a scenario he'd planned for.

"Well, I thought you'd be more enthusiastic about it. If you don't want to go, 1 can have the gardener pick up the meat later. Given your recent pursuit of independence, I figured you might want to get out of the house."

"I do want to go." He crammed the last bite of his biscuit into his mouth to stall for enough time to make up an excuse that didn't make him sound like a coward. "Do you think the road is safe? There's no bike trail."

"Only a couple of cars a day take that road. You'll be fine and dandy so long as you keep to one side and pay attention. Charlotte is going along, so there'll be three of you."

"Ugh. Charlotte?" Gwen came into the room dressed in fresh jeans and a gray t-shirt with a bat on it. Her nose wrinkled with disgust at every mention of her cousin's name. "Are you punishing me for the toad?" Her hair was still wet but drying into tangled, brown locks that hung down to her shoulders.

"She's not so bad," Desmond said.

"Not so bad? You only say that because you aren't a girl, and she isn't your cousin. Besides, she *likes* you."

It was Desmond's turn to wrinkle his nose. "Does not."

"Does so. She wants to marry you. She told me when we were seven." She dropped back into her seat at the table.

As she'd done many times before, Mrs. Dunwiler encouraged peace. "I realize she can be difficult, but you need to try to get along. You could be close like sisters, you know."

"She makes fun of me," Gwen said. "You just don't see because she does it when grownups aren't around. She's a snob monster. A fake snob monster."

"That's enough, girl." Her mother motioned to the door with a wooden spoon. "You two go on and occupy yourselves in a clean, quiet manner. You can get the bikes from the shed when the rain quits."

Desmond snagged a biscuit to take with him. Gwen followed him out.

She said, "Did you see the pink stripe on the toad? I found him next to the wall, sitting there as fat as he could be without a care. He let me scoop him right up, didn't even try to hop away."

Because he wanted to get caught and brought in, Desmond thought.

"I have something to show you," he said. "Weird stuff has been happening all morning."

Thunder struck again as they reached the top of the stairs. It was an ominous scene, the dim lighting and the raging storm beating against the large window at the front of the hall. Even Rathbone seemed wary. He stuck close to them.

"The woman is cracking in her old age. This storm isn't letting up anytime soon." Gwen raised her voice to douse the eeriness of the hall. "The clouds have been here all morning. I barely saw the sunrise."

Desmond opened his parents' door. "First, there was a squirrel in my room, bright blue with pointy ears, and then I came in here."

"Blue? You must've been dreaming. How the heck would it get in?"

"The window was open when I woke up. Afterward, I found this." He pointed to the tracks and the feather.

"It probably came through your open window," she reasoned. "The bird, I mean. A squirrel got in. Why couldn't a bird?"

"The bedroom doors were closed. A bird wouldn't have made it this far unless it could turn doorknobs."

"I have seen some smart birds. Did you check the window in here?"

"No."

She went to the curtains behind the desk and opened them. The rainy day remained behind the glass. She checked the latch. It was secure.

"Speaking of intelligence, I noticed you cheating on the science test the other day."

"Don't say that so loud. She'll hear you."

"You really aren't very good at it. I could see you from a mile away, so could Madison. Let me know if you need some pointers."

"I don't need *pointers*. It was only once, and I needed the grade to keep my A." Desmond changed the subject. "Did you notice the color of the feather? The bright green?"

"I would call it more of a teal," she said absentmindedly.

Gwen bent to look under the desk and then scanned the surrounding shelves. She executed the same search beneath the furniture as Desmond, going to knees to peer beneath the chests of drawers, the bed, even the nightstands, which were too low for a bird with that size of feathers to fit.

"Birds around here aren't that color," he said.

"It's probably somebody's pet parrot."

He hadn't thought about that. "What about the squirrel and the toad?"

She ran out of furniture to search and planted her hands on her hips. "I don't know. Does seem weird. We ought to find the bird before we worry about them. It's not in here."

"What are you going to do with it?"

She shrugged. "I'll have to decide when I see it. Maybe Mom will let me keep it in a cage in our quarters."

"I doubt it."

She paused at the bedroom door. "You never know."

Gwen stepped into the hall, quieted him with a finger to her lips and then pointed to the ceiling further down the hall, where the panel leading to the attic hung open like a mouth agape. Darkness lurked beyond the edge of the ladder poking out.

"Just enough space," she moved closer to it, "for a big, naughty birdie to squeeze through."

CHAPTER 3

"We should tell your mom," Desmond said.

"Why?" She shot him a dirty look over her shoulder. "Are you afraid of a bird?"

"No. I don't like the attic. They sprayed for spiders last fall. Probably some big, dead ones up there, or other dead things. Chemicals, too."

"Now you're afraid of dead things? Because they're so threatening, yes? If I were you, I'd be more worried about ghosts." She reached for the long cord to pull the sliding ladder the rest of the way down.

"Ghosts aren't real." He glanced behind them to make sure Mrs. Dunwiler wasn't coming. If she discovered them getting into the attic, she would be furious, infinitely more fearsome than any poltergeist.

Rathbone had abandoned their investigation. Seemingly with no shame for his cowardice, he sat patiently near the top of the stairs. Desmond felt a twinge of envy. No one made fun of a dog for following his instincts.

"The kids at school say your house is haunted."

"No, they don't."

"Oh yes, they do. They talk about it every Halloween, and they dare each other to ring the bell."

"Is that why no one comes to trick-or-treat? I thought we were just too far from the neighborhoods in town."

Gwen put a foot up on the first rung but then hesitated. "You should go first," she told him.

"No way. This is your investigation. You go first."

15

Begrudgingly, she started up the ladder. "You're such a chicken. You say you're going to travel the world, but around here, the only kind of adventure you seem to want is in a book. You're never going to see anything with your nose in a bunch of moldy, old pages. Alright, I'm up."

"At least I'll pass the sixth grade." He climbed after her. The lightness of her face and the gray of her shirt were all he could make out in the dark. "There's a pull chain for the light, I think."

"It's not my fault all the teachers hate me."

The bulb clicked on, illuminating the rough finish of the attic. It was a dusty place, crowded with steamer trunks and large frames covered in old blankets. Dingy, porcelain dolls with painted smiles were gathered in the corner, a collection exiled to the attic by Desmond's mother once his grandmother passed on. A battered coatrack made a suitable place for a big spider (very much alive) to weave a web in which many moths and one unfortunate dragonfly met their demise.

"This is fantastic!" Gwen clapped her hands. She went to her knees in the inch of dirt on the floor to throw open the lid of the trunk closest to her. "Dishes," she said, disappointed.

"Fantastic isn't the word I'd use." He kept his attention on the rafters above them to watch for signs of the rogue bird.

She went to the next trunk. "Encyclopedias? Boring."

"What were you expecting?" He stepped over a glove, which he guessed had once been white. A thick layer of grimy fuzz clung to it.

"I don't know. Something exciting. A pirate treasure, maybe."

"I thought we were looking for a bird."

"This stuff is better than a bird. You should've told me this was up here." She shut the trunk.

"You're making it out to be more than it is. Why would we have a pirate treasure?"

"Your family had to get all that money in the first place. Poor people don't found banks."

"My grandfather was not a pirate." Desmond pushed by a rolled rug.

"How do you know?"

He spotted the bird preening itself in a shadowy section of the rafters. It was much larger than he would've estimated, given the size of the footprints and the feather, and it looked more like a hawk than a parrot and definitely not anyone's pet. He put his hand out behind him to warn Gwen to be cautious.

"Is that...? Whoa." She gasped. "What now?"

"This was your idea."

"I didn't think we'd actually find it."

The bird stopped preening. It stepped into the dim shaft of light coming from the bulb that now seemed very far away.

"We should go get your mom."

"Stop saying that. We'll get in trouble."

"Would you rather get ripped to shreds?"

The bird protested with a shriek that sent the children running and stumbling away, through a cloud of dust stirred by their flight. Desmond covered his eyes with his arm until he hit the wall at the opposite side of the room. He dropped to his knees under a window and huddled there with Gwen in anticipation of the avian monstrosity, but the bird hadn't followed.

"We should see if we can get to the ladder. I think it's that way." He pointed to the faint aura of the light bulb that was visible over the wall of junk.

"We can get the bird out through this window." She stood and worked the latch until it sprang open.

"Are you nuts? Did you see the claws?"

"All it did was screech at us. It's just scared."

"*I'm* scared."

"You're always scared." She eased the pane open as far as the rusty hinges would allow. "There. Now, all we have to do is get it to fly this way."

"The space isn't big enough."

"Of course, it's big enough." She went back the way they came.

"How will you get it to move?" he asked, but she'd already disappeared. He found her near the ladder. "Here, we can leave." He tugged her toward the exit.

"Stop it," she hissed. "Stop being so chicken." She jammed the spiderweb-infested coatrack into his hands. "You're going to be brave today."

"I'm not chicken! I hesitate to engage threatening wildlife. There's a difference."

"Go." She urged him toward the bird.

Desmond held the coatrack in front of him with both hands. His vision had adjusted to the dimness, somewhat, so the place itself didn't seem quite as scary. With the hawk on the loose, he no longer worried about dead spiders or breathing exterminator chemicals. There was only him and the bird and the supposedly brave girl hiding behind him. Desmond raised the coatrack so that the hooks hovered near the bird.

"Shoo," he said.

Gwen giggled.

"What's so funny?"

"Shoo? You sound like you're talking to a chicken or something."

Irritated, Desmond whacked the rafter and said in a deep voice he sincerely hoped sounded manly and threatening, "Leave this place, foul bird!"

Gwen nearly collapsed with laughter. "Foul bird? Like *fowl* bird?"

"Do you want to do this?"

"No, no. Sorry." She tried, unsuccessfully, to stifle her grin.

The bird was not as amused. It remained stern, unmoved by the presence of children, and it glared at them.

Desmond asked, "Should I poke it?"

"What if you hurt its wing?"

"I wish you'd worry more about us than it."

"Fine. Poke it, then, just not too hard."

The poke ended up being more of a sideways nudge. The bird gave its large wings a flap, puffed out its chest and let another shriek, the volume of which seemed to shake the very frame of the house.

Desmond and Gwen covered their ears but held their ground. He executed another nudge.

Wings spread impossibly wide, the bird tilted forward into a glide over the Winters family relics, on course for the window when it disappeared from view.

Gwen smacked Desmond on the back. "We did it!"

"We need to make sure it went out."

They made another dash for the window.

"Look! There he is." She pointed to a nearby oak, where the bird sat, watching them. "He's actually kind of pretty."

The rain had stopped, and the sun was peeking out from behind patchy clouds. Mrs. Dunwiler would come looking for them any minute. Desmond shut the window.

Gwen chewed on her thumbnail. "Aunt Nini says a bird in the house is an omen."

He closed the latch. "Isn't your Aunt Nini crazy?"

"Only every month or so when the moon is full, Mom says. Something unusual is going to happen today. I can feel it. Hey, look." She picked up a brass telescope from the floor. She extended it and put it to her eye to look outside. "I told you Grandpa Winters was a pirate."

Desmond shook his head as he walked away. "Was not."

CHAPTER 4

Down in the kitchen, Mrs. Dunwiler was mopping the floor. "I called for you two a while ago. Your cousin is ridin' over. Go get the bikes from the shed, and make sure your tires have air. I have too much scrubbing and dusting to do to come pick you up if you get stuck with a flat. The man is coming to fix the front step this afternoon, too. The house needs to be ready," she said, more flustered than usual. She got that way whenever Desmond's parents came home, not out of fear for her job but because she took great pride in what she did.

When Desmond and Gwen returned, Charlotte was there, sitting on the counter, swinging her crossed ankles. She wore a pristine, pink dress, and her sandy blonde hair was in curls. She chatted with Mrs. Dunwiler with the same enthusiasm she used with every adult.

"Your cooking is amazing, and I love your pot roast most of all. Would you teach me how to make it sometime?"

"Trying to weasel an invitation to dinner," Gwen muttered.

"Anything for my favorite niece," Mrs. Dunwiler said.

Charlotte jumped down from the counter. "Hey!" She smiled at Desmond. "I brought my bike for our trip into town. You'll have to try and keep up with me. I've gotten pretty quick."

"I'm pretty quick, too." Gwen sneered.

The two of them were always engaged in some competition that began with a proclamation by one and a counter-claim by the other. He hoped their ride hadn't just become a race.

In the front yard, as they prepared to leave, Mrs. Dunwiler gave Desmond money and strict instruction. "Go to the butcher shop on Fabor Drive. Do not go to any other store, and absolutely do not go to new downtown. The construction there is awful. The way has enough potential for disaster without addin' construction equipment to the mix."

"Yes, ma'am," he said as he put on his backpack.

Greenville was divided into two sections. It had begun with the original downtown, centered around Fabor Drive. All the older houses, the courthouse, the library, and of course, the original Winters Bank and Trust were built there, most of them before Desmond was born.

New construction was located just west, a right turn after the bridge, rather than the left that would take them to Fabor Drive. New downtown consisted of shops, a mall, and worst of all, a bank run by a corporation. As a show of solidarity with the Winters family, Mrs. Dunwiler made a point to avoid that part of town. Desmond didn't think his parents cared either way, really.

Desmond, Gwen, and Charlotte set off down the road. Farm fields and rolling hills surrounded the Winters' property on all sides, which kept them from having many neighbors. The closest house, belonging to Charlotte's family, stood two fields down and across the street. They passed the two-story, brick farmhouse as they picked up speed, and they rode for a while, and no one raced.

The trip went smoothly until Gwen skidded her bike to a stop at the beginning of the bridge. Fear took hold, then, and she stared straight ahead, seemingly unable to move. She had been afraid of water since they were small, specifically the river that ran under the bridge and behind the Winters house. No matter how much she loved nature, she refused to go near the water.

Desmond tried to coax her. "Come on. Cars go across every day. I don't think our bikes are going to cause a collapse. Just ride in the middle."

She stayed where she was.

Luckily, Charlotte knew just how to push her buttons and get her moving. "Come on, Des. Crybaby can find her way back home."

"I am not a crybaby."

"You look like one from where I'm standing." She went ahead, unconcerned.

Gwen's face set with determination. She clenched her jaw and furrowed her brow and rushed across, pumping her legs, passing Charlotte and Desmond. Seconds later, she was waiting at the other side, a look of triumph on her red face.

"Not a crybaby."

"Impressive." Charlotte rolled her eyes.

"I heard there's a candy store in new downtown," Gwen said to Desmond as they rode on. "I bet going over there wouldn't take too long."

"No way." Charlotte butted in. "We're supposed to go straight to the butcher shop and back home."

Desmond agreed. "We don't have enough time. Besides, I'm not getting in trouble for candy."

After the bridge came the fork in the road. A large tree had fallen there, completely across the road leading to old downtown, generally making a nuisance of itself to both Desmond and the crew involved in its removal.

A man in a hard hat fought with a pair of birds who seemed adamant about the idea that he had wronged them. The sparrows squawked and shrieked and flitted about, agitated at the loss of what Desmond could only assume was their tree. A trio of the man's fellow, more bird-free workers surveyed the damage. Desmond approached one wearing a red hat and holding a clipboard.

"Excuse me. Can we go around?" He addressed the reflection of himself in the lenses of the man's sunglasses.

"Can't go around here." He scribbled on the clipboard without looking up. "You've got the drop-off that way," he pointed with his pen and then moved it to point over his shoulder, "and the roots and poison ivy and thorny bushes that-a-way. Be about three hours 'til we get this clear."

"Okay, thanks." Desmond turned his bike around. The girls waited behind him. "We'll have to go back."

"No," Gwen stated flatly.

"He said we can't go around."

"This is another sign. We're supposed to go a different direction." She shifted her gaze to the turn to the right, the road leading to Admiral Parkway and new downtown.

"Oh, what are you talking about?" Charlotte asked.

Gwen ignored her. "Come on, Des. You know it's true. The universe wants us to go."

"You're so dramatic." He thumbed the brake on his handlebars while he weighed his options.

"This is an adventure. I just know it. Look, the streets all connect somewhere out there. All we have to do is follow them in the right direction. Do you want your parents to have the perfect dinner or not?"

Straying from the path wouldn't necessarily be their fault. They could call Mrs. Dunwiler from the butcher shop once they got there, tell her why they'd been delayed. The only risk involved was traveling through the unknown parts of town. He didn't know the way or which streets had sidewalks.

They could end up anywhere, in any situation. The more he considered the possibilities, the less desirable that particular course of action became.

"I don't think it's a good idea. We should probably go home."

Gwen hopped on her bike and rode off. "I'm not letting you wimp out this time. If I die, I guess my tragedy will be on your conscience."

"Wait!" He went after her, and Charlotte reluctantly followed.

At the beginning of a paved bicycle trail, the landscape shifted abruptly from wide expanses and trees to streets with houses gradually becoming newer and closer to one another. Further in, subdivisions with gates bearing names like Windfall Commons and Traders Grove divided that side of Greenville into bite-sized chunks of neighborhood.

Gwen kept up her pace, all-out pedaling far ahead of them until her attempt to brake at a busy intersection came so late that she overshot the sidewalk, slid between parked cars, and nearly collided with a delivery truck. The driver let a long, angry blare of the horn, punctuated by the passenger hanging out the window to yell back at her.

She giggled and waved. "Sorry!" She rolled backward to the sidewalk.

"You're an idiot." Charlotte was not pleased with having to chase her down.

The three of them took in their surroundings. Shops and cafés with gleaming windows lined a road filled with cars stopping and going with the turn of traffic signals. Colorful signs and grand opening banners hung on the faces of finished buildings, over the heads of pedestrians bustling about with shopping bags or small kids in tow. Charlotte, Desmond, and Gwen had stepped from quiet country life into a dynamic suburb where everything seemed to move at once like parts of a noisy machine.

"I smell," Gwen closed her eyes and sniffed the air, "donuts. Let's get one."

Charlotte said, "You don't have any money."

"You don't know what I have." She walked her bike.

"You never have any money."

They found the donut shop several stores down. A man stood outside with a plate full of free samples, pieces of donuts on toothpicks. Gwen made a point to turn around and eat the sample in front of her cousin. She closed her eyes, relishing the taste.

"Thank you so much, Mr. Donut-Man." Then she was on her way again. "I wonder what else we can find."

Desmond and Charlotte let her go ahead while they hung back, and she continued chattering about everything without seeming to notice they were no longer with her. Charlotte watched with an expression of disapproval.

She told Desmond, "I don't know how you can stand her. She's so rude."

"Funny, she said nearly the same thing about you earlier this morning."

"What did she say about me? I know she didn't call me rude, because that wouldn't even be true."

Gwen stopped beneath a construction scaffold to stare at the building across the street. Unlike everything else, it appeared old. The walls, rough piles of stone seemingly ready to topple, crumbled at the base. Thick glass in the arched windows didn't shine like the windows on the other shops did, and the slanted roof sagged mournfully. The sign over the door identified the place as Castle's Book Shoppe.

Gwen said breathlessly, "This is it. I can feel it calling me. We're supposed to go in."

"Looks creepy." Desmond squinted to read the street sign at the next intersection. They needed to head east to get to Fabor Drive; he was sure.

"What nonsense." Charlotte started to walk away. "We're supposed to go to the butcher shop."

"Come on, Des. Since when do you not want to look at books? It all makes perfect sense."

He'd never seen her so adamant about anything having to do with reading. She detested school. Her hours in class were spent gazing out the window or coming up with pranks to pull on the teachers. Reading was just about the last activity she would choose. He noted, also, that the presence of a nearby candy store hadn't registered. She zeroed in on this store for a reason.

He sighed. "Alright. We can go in for a minute, but then we have to leave."

Charlotte protested as they crossed the street. "I don't like this one bit. How can a place so run-down have anything good inside?"

CHAPTER 5

A brass bell overhead announced their presence with a ring that echoed in the cavernous interior. The ceilings rose high above them, much higher than the exterior of the building suggested. Birds nesting in the exposed wooden rafters flew and cooed as freely as if they were outside.

"Gross." Charlotte wore a look of horror. "Make it fast, Gwen."

But Gwen had already abandoned them to hunt for whatever adventure she thought a bookshop might hold. Desmond and Charlotte lingered near the front of the place, near a reading area bordered by a low shelf. Inside, chairs and tables were ready for readers but empty. Model skeletons displayed on the top of the shelf drew Desmond's attention. He went over to pick one of them up.

"It's a unicorn." He turned it over. From further away, he'd thought the model next to it was a dinosaur but on closer inspection, decided it was a dragon. Next to that was a fairy skeleton, a tiny human with wing bones affixed to its back. Then came some kind of insect with bones instead of an exoskeleton.

"Don't touch the models," a gruff voice barked from behind, almost causing him to drop the thing in his hand.

He turned to see a balding, Ebenezer Scrooge sort of character in a brown vest and a dingy white shirt. He glared from behind a pair of crooked bifocals perched on the long bridge of his nose. His back had a slight hunch to it, too many hours bent over some kind of work.

He went on, "No running. No horseplay of any kind. No talking. No laughing. No climbing. No spitting. If a book is out of your reach, it isn't meant for you, and stay out of the gated enclosure. Books in that collection aren't for sale." He turned and left them standing there.

Desmond placed the model back on the shelf and went after him, past shelves of paperbacks and a rack of ancient candy, to a counter. The shopkeeper lifted part of the countertop to go inside, promptly slamming it behind him.

"What is this place?" Desmond asked.

"If you can't read, you need to leave. This is a business, not a malt shop."

"What's a malt shop?" Charlotte kept her distance.

"We've been to bookshops. That's not what I meant." Desmond was about to ask how long the store had been there when he noticed a pair of paintings behind the counter, on either side of a door he assumed led to an office. To the right was a landscape of a wheat field with the bookshop at the center, nestled into the side of a hill. The building in which they stood was there long before anyone thought of new downtown. How had he never heard of it? Surely his parents knew it was there, or Mrs. Dunwiler.

A painting to the left featured a woman with her dark hair loosely pulled back. Her face was pretty and round, pale with rosy cheeks. She wore a formal, off-the-shoulder dress. With her hands folded in her lap, she smiled benevolently.

"Who is that?" he asked.

The old man snarled, "Mind your business. Get out or buy a book and then get out. Makes no difference to me." His head dipped below the counter as he rummaged for something.

"You have terrible customer service skills," Charlotte scolded.

"We'd better find Gwen and leave. Mrs. Dunwiler is going to have a fit if we're too late." He glimpsed a name engraved on a brass plate on the bottom of the portrait frame. Lucinda. It was a nice name; he thought.

The deeper they moved into the store, the older the books became. He could've spent all day in there reading and discovering. He decided, then, that he liked the place, the mystery of it, the creak of the floor, the old book and furniture smell. It was magical in a way, maybe just not the way Gwen hoped for when they came in.

At the main aisle that separated the two primary sections of shelves, an enormous mobile hung from the ceiling. Models of what looked like floating islands were wired together around a metal frame encasing a sphere, the surface of which swirled with painted shades of gold and flame orange.

"What is that?" Charlotte stopped to look up. "How can a sun be underground?"

"It's probably from a book or something." Desmond moved ahead.

"Shoplifters will be keelhauled." She read a sign affixed to a shelf. "What does that mean?"

"It means drag you under a sailing ship in water," he replied and then called for Gwen.

"Well, that's just rude."

He continued past a long table with a potted Venus flytrap as a centerpiece. Where the shelves ended, a section of open books displayed in glass cases began. The pages of the first one had an illustration of a baseball player riding a camel on a city street. After passing a book of owls wearing hats and one of music for marching hares, they came to the enclosure the shopkeeper told them about.

The wooden bars were like the decorative rails on a staircase but as tall as the shelves. The books inside were bound in dark leather, much like the books Desmond's parents kept in their room. Just ahead, the gate to the enclosure stood open, and one of those burgundy books, a thick one, was on the floor, half in, half out. He went to pick it up.

Charlotte asked in a hushed voice, "What are you doing?"

"Looking," he answered in an equally hushed voice. It was heavy in his hand, the size of the dictionary in his classroom.

He and Charlotte read the title together, "*A Guide to Curiosity.*"

Written in gold ink, the byline indicated that the book was written by Authors Unknown. He found no copyright page like all his other books had, no publisher or date or dire warnings against unauthorized reproduction. Instead, the first page of text consisted of a list of instructions for approaching the Authors Unknown.

They must be interrupted only in the most extreme circumstances, as their work is integral to the transcription of accurate histories. Tributes may consist of ink, paper, gems, jars of deceased insects, and/or cookies of the sweetest variety. No frosting or sprinkles will be accepted. Books by parties other than the Authors Unknown are not permitted in the Loft as the presence of such items constitutes an insult. Content in books by the Authors Unknown must never, under any circumstances, be called into question as their knowledge supersedes that of all others.

He turned a couple of pages to an inscription in golden, looping scrawls like the title. *Fortes Fortuna Juvat* with the translation *Fortune Favors the Brave* below it.

The first pages offered advice for adventure preparation. The supplies: a rope, a canteen, a multi-realm compass, a journal, and a pocketknife were recommended as friends to the intrepid.

"What's a multi-realm compass?" he asked.

Charlotte shrugged.

The text went on to describe camping equipment. It advised against carrying too much food due to the risk of a predator smelling it. A good luck charm was listed as an essential.

He read a section about choosing the right companions for an adventure and how the personalities of all involved should balance one another, a strength for a weakness and so on. From there, the book took a turn for the weird with a chapter on herds of giant buffalo children on the plains of a realm called Havestemm. They flew kites and gliders made of lightweight wood, and they had a tendency to trample smaller beings for their amusement.

He read a warning about cannibalistic fairies. They were willowy creatures, their pale skin printed with intricate patterns of swirls. Stranger still, thorns protruded from their forearms and elbows. Pictures showed them sitting on the ground next to a bonfire, looking savage as they feasted on meat.

He paused over a guide to birds of the Tabis Realm. On the page, an illustrated version of the bird he and Gwen had freed from the attic glared up at him, the detail too perfect to deny that it was the same.

CHAPTER 6

Desmond closed the book. "I want this."

"He said the books in there aren't for sale," Charlotte reminded him.

"Technically, it wasn't all the way inside. That means he has to sell it to us, right?"

They heard Gwen's voice nearby. "I see you up there, so you might as well come down."

Charlotte and Desmond found her standing on her tiptoes near the back wall, in front of a large window. She spoke to someone or something over her head, in the rafters.

"No use hiding, now."

"Who are you talking to?" he asked.

"Loony bird," Charlotte muttered.

"There's a boy in the ceiling." Gwen pointed. "He looks wild."

"I think the dust is getting to you. We'd better go," Desmond said.

She snatched the book from his hand. "What is this? *A Guide to Curiosity*. What does that mean?" She opened the cover. "Ooh, look at this picture."

An illustration of a banquet attended by foxes in scarves and buttoned jackets stretched across the pages. They drank from chalices and ate food from plates piled high with roasted bird legs and wings with feathers still dangling from the skin.

"You need this book," she said to Desmond. "This is why we're here. If anyone needs this, it's you."

"What's that supposed to mean? I'm plenty curious."

"Not enough to find any real adventure."

"We're here, aren't we?" he asked.

"This isn't real adventure. We're in a bookstore. Besides, I'm the only reason you didn't run back home."

"Charlotte and I could've just as easily let you go on your merry way alone."

The shopkeeper's voice boomed over the shelves. "No loitering! I know you're still back there. I can hear you whispering. Get what you need, and get out."

Charlotte shook her head in disgust. "What a crab."

"You're going to buy it," Gwen insisted.

"The only money I have is for the roast. The book is from that special collection, anyway. He's not going to let us."

She closed the book and held it to her chest. "This is the plan. We're going to march up to that horrible, old man and demand that he sell you this book. Then, you're going to pay for it with some of the money Mom gave you. We will proceed to the butcher shop, where you will 'accidentally' purchase the wrong and cheaper meat. She'll be very understanding, and we can get the right meat tomorrow before your parents get home."

"I'm not stealing from your mother."

She sighed in exasperation. "We'll pay her back. You have money at home, don't you?"

"A little. I don't know if I have enough to cover the book."

"Let's find out." She shoved the book into his hands and walked ahead.

Charlotte and Desmond went after her, back through the shelves, to the counter, where they found the man looking just as annoyed as ever. Gwen put on her best impression of a well-mannered child.

"Good afternoon, kind sir. Let me say that this is the loveliest bookshop I have ever seen."

He snorted and crossed his arms. "What do you hooligans want? You'd better not be spies from that developer company.

I already told them the only way I'm moving out of here is in a casket. You hear me?"

This statement threw her off her game for a few seconds, but she quickly recomposed herself. "My friend would like to make a purchase, but the book doesn't have a price tag. Can you tell us how much it costs?" She motioned for Desmond to come forward.

At the sight of the book, the shopkeeper's face reddened. "Forbidden! That book isn't for you. It isn't for anyone! Get out. Get out right now." He grabbed the book, dropped it onto the counter and then led Desmond by the shoulder of his shirt all the way to the front of the store. The force with which he opened the door flipped the bell so hard that it struck the wall. "Don't come back."

Charlotte and Gwen came out just as the shopkeeper slammed the door and turned the sign to Closed. The old man scowled at them before disappearing back into the shop.

"Horrible manners," Charlotte said.

As Desmond readied his bike to leave, Gwen approached him with her hands behind her back. He knew that look in her eye.

"Please tell me you didn't do what I think you did."

"Open your backpack."

He shook his head. "No way. You're going to get us all arrested. Take it back."

"I'm already outside with it. He'll call the cops regardless of whether we give it back. Hurry up."

Against his better judgment, he let her unzip the bag and stuff the book inside.

The door swung open, and the old man burst out, yelling, "Thieves!" He clamped a hand on Desmond's backpack and with surprising strength, dragged him inside.

Desmond stumbled backward, struggled to hold onto his balance and struggled against the straps on his shoulders. The man withdrew his property from the bag and keeping his iron grip, continued to the counter, where he slapped down the book and picked up a phone.

"I told you the collection was off limits. The police will know what to do with you, Winters boy."

"How do you know who I am?"

"You're just like your grandfather. You look just alike and apparently, you operate alike. I should've tossed you out the second you walked in."

Gwen got a hold of her own on Desmond's arm. "We tried to pay you for it. Why are you so mean?" She tugged but wasn't strong enough to free him.

Charlotte got in on the fight. "Let him go. You have your precious book back."

All of a sudden, the shopkeeper turned pale, and the scowl fell from his face, replaced by an expression of pain. He let go of Desmond to lean on the counter, then opened the gate and staggered through.

"Get…" the shopkeeper began but stopped. He wheezed, his eyes rolling toward the ceiling as breath refused to come.

Desmond told Gwen, "Call for an ambulance."

She nodded and went for the phone next to the cash register. "Not working."

The shopkeeper collapsed, and as he landed, a vibration coursed along the planks beneath Desmond's feet and spread like a ripple over water. To the counter and beyond, up the walls, shaking dust from the rafters, stirring birds from their nests, the disturbance grew until the building threatened to collapse on them. Then, it ceased.

Desmond, Charlotte, and Gwen looked at each other. They bolted for the exit.

The front wall trembled again, rattling the windows in their frames. A high-pitched squeal started from a corner and swept across the shop, swooped over their heads like a hawk descending on prey. The three of them clutched one another and cringed.

A low whir came from somewhere out of sight. Wooden shutters dropped over the windows, one at a time, clunking into place, blocking the view of the people on the street and snuffing out what little daylight found its way inside. The door suffered the same fate, a larger shutter knocking the brass bell from its bar. The bell clanged to the floor and rolled toward Desmond and the others. When all was finished, the front of the store had become a wall.

Charlotte left Desmond and Gwen to pull on the shutter. Gwen joined her and then Desmond, but it wouldn't budge.

They backed away from the wall to stare at it in disbelief. Every opening had closed. They were locked inside.

Charlotte wiped tears from her cheeks. "Was that an earthquake?"

"They'll find us. Someone will find us." He turned to go back to the counter. "The police will come."

In this fresh darkness, in the low, low light of some far off lamp, the model skeletons of fantasy creatures looked more ominous, more like the remains of things which had once lived. The creak of the floor became a warning to watch your step in the dark. Empty tables and chairs weren't just lonesome; they were forgotten, and shadows had overtaken the aisles.

Desmond rounded the edge of the shelves and stopped. There, kneeling on the counter, looking down at the shopkeeper was a stranger, a boy, maybe a year or two older than them. His hair was a mess of tangled, dingy blond that hung down in his face. His hands and arms were dirty. His clothes, a mottled gray shirt and a pair of ragged jeans, were too small for his scrawny body, and he wore battered, black boots he had barely bothered to tie.

"Hey!" Gwen said. She gasped as he turned to look at them and then she asked, "Did you lock us in here?"

He shook his head no and then dropped behind the counter without a word.

CHAPTER 7

"Mr. Castle?" The boy spoke, barely above a whisper. He waved a hand in front of the shopkeeper's half-closed eyes.

Desmond asked, "Is he dead?"

"I don't think so. I hope he isn't. Will you help me lift him? I can't carry him on my own."

"Who are you?"

"I'm Rasq." His face had an odd, long quality to it, and the corners of his eyes turned up toward his ears as if in a smile, but he wasn't smiling. He rose to his feet, taller than the rest of them. "The store shuttered itself because it sensed Mr. Castle was in distress. There's a bed in the office, where he sleeps." Rasq opened the door between the portrait of Lucinda and the painting of the bookshop alone in the field.

The four of them each took a limb, and they hauled the man into a small room containing a cot, a desk heaped in paperwork, and an olive green cabinet pushed against a wall. Dishes in pairs: plates, bowls, and glasses, were stacked neatly on a small cupboard. Other than the mounds of paper, the place was tidy. Rasq counted to three, and they lifted Castle onto the cot, atop wool blankets.

"Does he live here?" Desmond couldn't see how anyone would want to live in the place, as dark and depressing as it was.

"We both do."

"This is crazy." Unable to contain herself any longer, Gwen erupted. She asked Rasq, "Did you kill him?"

"From what I saw, if anyone killed him, it was you three. You probably gave him a heart attack."

"We most certainly did not." She didn't sound so sure.

Charlotte remained indignant. "I demand you open the door so we can leave."

He ran his hand over his hair. "I'll try, but I don't know if I can. The crank probably won't move. It gets stuck sometimes as it is, and with Mr. Castle unconscious, it probably won't let us turn it."

"Gets stuck? How often do you trap people in here?" Gwen crossed her arms. "Is this a regular thing for you? What do you plan to do with us?"

"Nothing." He went to a door next to the desk, and it opened to darkness.

Rasq stepped inside, flipped a switch. A fixture hanging from a chain at the middle of the room cast a spotlight on a big spool of rope topped with what looked like a ship's wheel with four bars protruding from it. A thick rope wound around the base and stretched to a deeper shadow and out of sight. Rasq positioned himself behind one of the bars to push.

"Come on," he said.

They joined in, their hesitation apparent. The four of them leaned into the effort. Desmond pushed hard with his arms and his legs until his muscles strained. Charlotte slipped in her shoes but gave her best. Gwen, growling, put her weight into it, even attempting different ways to grip the bar. The crank refused them.

"The rope is too tight," Charlotte complained. She gave up.

Frustrated, Rasq yanked on the section of rope connecting to unseen machinery. "This isn't going to work."

"What if we cut it?" Desmond looked around for something else to try, but shadows veiled the edges of the room. Nothing else was visible.

"That isn't what the shop wants."

Gwen let out an incredulous burst of laughter. "What the shop wants? What does that even mean? We're going to die in here. Of course, that's probably what you had in mind all along." Her outburst didn't faze him.

"Cutting the rope will separate the crank from the pulleys. I have to go." He went back through the door, into the office.

"Go where?" Desmond followed.

Rasq went to the green cabinet next to the desk, and with Desmond's help, he scooted it away from the wall. Behind it was another, smaller door, three feet tall with a shiny brass handle. Rasq opened it.

"Wait here. I'll get help."

"Wait," Gwen said.

"What?"

"You're just leaving us here? Does that lead outside?"

"Do you always talk in questions?"

She blushed. "No. I just think you leaving us with a dead body and no explanation is rude."

"He isn't dead. Mr. Castle told me that if anything happened to him to go find the Unknown. They'll help us."

Charlotte asked, "The unknown what?"

"You should probably wait here."

"Fat chance," Gwen countered.

"Fine. Don't blame me if something bad happens."

"Just out of curiosity, what could happen?" Charlotte asked.

He answered with grave seriousness. "Anything."

CHAPTER 8

Desmond, Charlotte, and Gwen followed Rasq into a
corridor lit by dim bulbs hanging by wires. The floor dipped,
ever so slightly here and there, taking them further underground, and the brick walls gave way to dirt. As Desmond
noted the change to himself, another realization dawned on
him. They had walked about the equivalent of a city block, too
far for them to be under or near the bookshop anymore.

They came to a ladder made of thick but brittle wood. Rasq took
to it with no hesitation, the steps creaking beneath him. Gwen went
next. Charlotte and Desmond watched the ladder shake.

He asked Charlotte, "Are you going?"

"Should we?"

"Either that or head back to the bookshop."

"The ladder doesn't look stable. Then again, I don't want to
stay behind in that creepy place, either."

"What are you doing? I'm not waiting for you," Gwen called
down from high above their heads.

He said, "We'd better follow. Want to go first?"

"Dress," she reminded him of her impractical outfit with a
shy smile.

"Right."

He went first, stepping onto the ladder. It felt as rickety as it
looked. Wood under his hands and feet shifted with every
movement the others made. Rungs bowed under his shoes,
and he wasn't sure how a thing so flimsy held up under the
weight of four of them.

They climbed up a tunnel that was narrow like a well, several minutes of up as the floor beneath them faded into darkness. At their destination, a round opening in the distance, the light shifted to pink, then to dark, then to pink again, almost as if spinning.

"This ladder is never going to end," Charlotte grumbled.

"We're almost there." Rasq was the first to reach the top. He poked his head up, into the light.

"What is this? Interruption!" a male voice bellowed.

"Interruption!" a second voice, that of a woman, squawked.

Rasq ducked back into the tunnel. "I think it's the Unknown."

"Go." Gwen pushed him.

With reluctance, he went, stepping over the side of the tunnel and out of sight. Then went Gwen.

Desmond took a deep breath of air that smelled sweetly of plants and something like spices. After his confinement in the bookshop and then the tunnel, he was eager to see anything but dirt and darkness. As he surfaced, the sunny day took on the rosy hue of dusk. Had they been in the bookshop that long?

They were in a wooden gazebo similar to the one in the town park, only this model had four enclosed walkways leading out. The central chamber into which they'd entered housed eight lecterns situated around and facing the tunnel entrance.

Behind each lectern sat a creature who looked almost but not quite human. Four were elderly. Four were young adults. Their seating arrangement alternated with their age: old, young, old, young.

Despite the obvious age differences, they looked similarly alien. They had long, tangled hair in shades ranging from white to ash to gold and pale green. Their eyes, cartoonish pools like colored ink, peered out over noses that pointed downward and hung just over their mouths.

Their clothes were even stranger. Upon their heads, each of them wore a cap seemingly made from the eyes and head of a big, brown moth. The wings, still attached, draped down their backs like capes.

The old man who had first shouted about the interruption pointed with his pen, which looked very much like the leg of a large insect. "Favors are required of those who dare to interrupt the work of the Unknown. You brought cookies."

Gwen snorted, and everyone looked at her. She stifled her giggle with a hand over her mouth.

Rasq replied, "No, sir. I'm sorry. I have no cookies."

"The Authors Unknown," Desmond said, more to himself than anyone. He hadn't meant to say it out loud.

"Recognition!" The old man raised his pen over his head.

"Recognition!" his cohorts repeated.

The sky suddenly deepened to night. A smattering of stars emerged and became constellations and commenced an orbit around the gazebo.

"If there are no favors, then you brought us a story." The engraved nameplate on the front of the speaker's lectern identified him as Alpha.

Rasq said, "Mr. Castle told me if anything happened to him that I should speak with the Unknown. He showed me the door."

"That is not a story. That is a fact. A story has three parts: beginning, middle, conclusion," a woman (named Beta, according to her nameplate) said. "Do you not know of books?"

"Yes, ma'am. I know of books." Rasq struggled.

Charlotte stepped in with a polite curtsy. She looked proper as always, despite being slightly dirty from the tunnel.

"Pardon my interruption. We are attempting to leave the bookshop. We just want to go home, so if you can point us in the direction of the exit, we would be happy to leave you."

"Still not a story," Beta declared.

A younger woman between Alpha and Beta entered the conversation. "What my elders want is a story in exchange for their assistance. I apologize for their lack of clarity." Her nameplate identified her as Gamma.

"Interruption!" Alpha hollered. "Mind your elders."

Dawn came once more, the sun flying in a hurried ascent. The sky whirled around them, churning through the hours on fast forward and disorienting Desmond. He needed to get out of there.

Rasq offered, "We have many books in the shop. I can bring you any book you'd like."

Alpha leaned forward. "Young man, are you implying we should plagiarize?"

"An original story." Gamma intervened before he started to shout again. "Travelers bring us their stories. We transcribe them into books."

"Please, can you help me revive Mr. Castle? That's why I'm here."

"Castle." Alpha tapped his chin with his insect leg pen. "I know this name."

"He runs the bookshop at the other side of the tunnel. He keeps a collection of your books."

"Doesn't let anyone buy them, though," Gwen said under her breath.

Rasq shot her a dirty look.

"And have you read any of them?" Alpha asked.

"I have. A little."

Out of the corner of his eye, Desmond spotted a blue squirrel on the railing, sniffing an acorn it held in its tiny paws. He wondered if it was the same one that had come through his window. It jumped down and scampered into the nearest walkway.

Desmond said, "I read some of *A Guide to Curiosity*."

All Authors Unknown bent over their lecterns in anticipation, the synchronized motion eliciting a unanimous creak from all furniture involved.

"What did you think?" Alpha asked for all them.

"It was brilliant. Was it real? I mean the animals in it and the other stuff. I haven't heard of any of the places."

"Of course, it's real!" Beta's mouth dropped open in horrified shock, causing her face to look even stranger than before. "We only write truth."

Rasq drew them back to the concern of the day. "Mr. Castle has collapsed."

"Yes, yes. The man who runs the bookshop at the other side of the tunnel."

"Wait." An Author Unknown behind them, on the other side of the tunnel entrance, asked, "That wouldn't happen to be Ms. Lucinda's Castle, would it?"

Rasq said, "She was his wife."

They all gasped and shook their heads.

Gamma scribbled furiously on the paper in front of her. "This - this is the start of a story if anything ever was."

The rest of the group nodded in agreement and scribbled as well. The sounds of pens scraping paper accompanied a fleeting afternoon and the songs of birds.

"How do we help him?" Rasq tried again.

Engrossed in their work, they ignored him, even Gamma, who had seemed to be the more rational of them. Gwen had picked up on the fact that Gamma was their best chance for getting information and went directly to her, placed a hand on the pen to stop its movement.

"Please help us."

Gamma blinked as though broken from a trance. "Yes. We'll help you in exchange for a story and also in gratitude for Lucinda's sacrifice."

"Bless Lucinda," Alpha said, and the others repeated his words.

"Only she can bring him back." Gamma nodded.

Desmond asked, "Where is she?"

"Dead but alive in a way. She gave her life to save the realms, gave her light to save Cosalis, the caged star."

Thoughtfully, as if he came up with the idea on his own, Alpha said, "Her light could bring him back. You would have to obtain it first, and that task, well, is much too impossible for children. You would have to travel through the realms, and that's dangerous."

"So, we're just supposed to stay trapped in a bookshop for the rest of our lives?" Gwen shot back.

"I think we should give them a chance. This could be a truly great story," Gamma told Alpha.

"And if they die?"

"A tragedy, then. Either way. Only one of them need survive for that."

"The vessel is too precious. We can't trust them to return it to us," Beta said, "especially given that one of them is a Winters."

The other seven of the Unknown drew back in their chairs. A carbon copy of the previous dusk settled in during the pause that followed. They stared at Desmond with new interest, apparently needing no confirmation as to which of the children was a Winters.

Alpha asked, "You are kin to Allos Winters?"

The name sounded foreign to Desmond. When the bearer of that name came up in family conversation, he was always father or grandfather, never Allos. He was a stranger, a face in pictures and a player in stories.

"He was my grandfather," he admitted and then hastily amended, "He died before I was born, though. I never met him," as if practically disowning the man might alleviate their concerns.

Alpha grimaced. "Allos was a scoundrel who plundered the

realms. We cannot trust his descendant with an object as precious as the vessel."

Gamma said, "We can't judge him based on his grandfather's crimes."

"Yes, we most certainly can." Beta slapped the lectern. "In fact, I wouldn't be surprised if he concocted this whole situation as a scheme to gain immortality."

"Immortality?" Desmond asked.

"Yes, dear. The light of the Cosalis is capable of that."

"We only want to go home."

"If he isn't meant to have it, the vessel will return to us before it can be used." Another Unknown spoke up.

"True." Alpha stroked his beard. "We should put this to a vote. Are we prepared to vote?"

The Authors Unknown indicated their readiness to vote by tapping their pens on their lecterns.

"Who says we entrust the vessel to the grandson of Allos Winters?"

"So that he may save Lucinda's beloved?" Gamma added.

All Authors but Alpha and Beta voted yes with another round of pen tapping. Alpha shook his head disapprovingly.

"So, it will be. We risk our treasure for the mere possibility of a story."

Gamma corrected him. "A great story."

The stars rose in the sky once more as Alpha rummaged behind his lectern. He tossed out metal cups and plates, a porcelain dog, which broke into pieces upon impact. He got down from his stool to put his head inside.

"Here." He withdrew from the lectern and plopped back onto his stool. "Here is the thing. Come forward, Winters boy."

Desmond wasn't sure how this task had ended up squarely on his shoulders. The only reason he was there was because Rasq brought him, after all. He'd only gone along so he wouldn't be left behind in the dark bookshop.

The object Alpha presented was a glass bottle encased in a slender, carved wooden frame. It was topped with a cork and a leather strap that made it a necklace. He held it out with both hands. Desmond reached for it. Alpha didn't release right away.

"Know that this object is among the most precious in the realms. Many people would kill to remove it from your possession. Be safe, and be true to your word. Be a better man than Allos."

"Yes, sir." Desmond put it around his neck. He glanced back at Rasq to see him glaring.

Gamma said, "The fastest route to Cosalis is through the Kelosian Veld."

"Will there be lions?" He'd read about velds before, grasslands in Africa where predators stalked.

"Of course. They'll be very helpful. A Keeper named Haelo will escort you." She waved off his concern. "Back down the ladder half the way you came. Take the door and the passage to Nola Junction and then the portal doorway to the veld."

"I didn't see a door."

"That's because seeing it at that time wasn't appropriate. Events must occur in order. Just think if you'd gone that way without seeing us first. Where would you be?"

"Come back with the story." Alpha reminded them as they stepped over the wall, back onto the ladder.

CHAPTER 9

They found the door exactly where the authors told them they would. It was a third of the size of a regular door and made of wooden boards lashed together. A piece of rope tied into a knot served as a handle.

Charlotte reached it first. "Here it is."

"Maybe you should let me go through before you, so I can make sure it's safe," Rasq said. He'd entered the tunnel right after her, nearly pushing Gwen out of the way to be next.

She climbed down several feet to give him room.

He reached across the space between the ladder and the door and across the sizable drop to the floor far below. He pushed, and the door opened slowly with a squeak that echoed.

"We'll have to jump," he announced.

"Jump? Are you a lunatic?" Charlotte said.

"You can still go back if you want." With that, he crouched, the best one could crouch on a ladder and leaped into the opening. He landed halfway in with his legs dangling and then climbed the rest of the way onto the ledge. "Come on. It's alright. Kind of warm over here, actually."

Desmond went next. The jump wasn't as difficult as he thought it would be, and he landed at the edge of the tile floor.

Gwen made it look easy. Days of chasing animals in the garden and generally running everywhere gave her great agility and the confidence she needed to clear the gap with no trouble. Charlotte didn't come as willingly.

"I can't make it." She looked down, never a good idea. "I'll fall."

"Figures." Gwen smirked. "Just go wait with the not-quite-dead man. We should get back eventually. You *probably* won't shrivel up and die first."

"I don't want to go by myself." She gazed longingly down the ladder. "Desmond?"

He certainly didn't want to go back. Gwen would never let him hear the end of it if he did. Besides, he was the one with the vessel.

"I have to go." He held it up to remind her.

"Oh."

"Come on. You can make it." He waved Gwen up to the opening so she could help coax Charlotte in. She rolled her eyes and joined him.

She snapped, "You called me a crybaby; now look at you."

"I am not a baby."

"Could've fooled me. You're blubbering like a baby." She made a mock crying noise.

Desmond stopped her. "Quit that." He moved her away from the doorway. To Charlotte, he said, "Come on. You won't fall. We won't let you." He held out his hand.

Her face set with a kind of pouty determination, she nodded. She adjusted her angle on the ladder, took a deep breath with her eyes closed, and jumped. She landed awkwardly on her knees, but she made it.

She laughed. "I did it."

"Goody for you." Gwen sneered. "Let's get on with this so we can go home."

On the other side of the door, Rasq, Desmond, Gwen, and Charlotte found themselves in a small chamber, the walls of which were covered in blue mosaic waves against a sky of white. Painted fish in shades of purple and green dove in an orderly, patterned fashion. The style of the artwork reminded Desmond of ancient Greek pottery he'd seen at a museum.

He smelled water, real water of the non-mosaic type. This was a gateway to some large body of it, probably a river, judging by the rushing sound. He could tell Gwen heard it, too, because she'd gone pale.

They emerged from the chamber on an expansive platform that ran along the edge of a wildly rushing river. A ceiling arced over them like the roof of an airplane hangar, propped up by an intricate network of rafters, much like the ceiling of the bookshop. They stopped to take in the view.

"This is the aqueduct," Rasq said. "I've always wanted to see it, but Mr. Castle never let me through the door, said it was too dangerous."

"Doesn't look bad from here." Charlotte fiddled with her hair, straightening her headband. "Pretty, almost."

"He keeps people from buying the books in order to keep this place secret," Desmond guessed.

"Yeah." Rasq proceeded toward a bridge leading across the river.

"Why put them out, then?" Desmond trotted after him.

"What do you mean?"

"If they're so secret, why not lock them up in a stockroom or something?"

"Our stockroom isn't big enough."

"Still, there has to be somewhere else he could— "

Rasq wheeled around to face him. "Mr. Castle knows what he's doing. Everything has a purpose and a reason. He doesn't need you to understand." He turned back toward the bridge.

"Well, aren't we testy," Charlotte said, "and president of the fan club, obviously."

Desmond said, "He's mad because they gave me the vessel instead of him."

"I don't see why that would matter." She gave an exasperated sigh. "Boys."

Made of the same kind of beams used in the construction of the roof, the bridge hung low, an invitation to the rushing water, and waves splashed into gaps and through the rails. At the steps leading up to the bridge, Gwen went from pale to green.

Her voice was barely audible over the sound of the water beast. "I can't."

Charlotte stopped on the steps. "Now who's blubbering like a baby?"

Rasq took Gwen's hands. "We don't have time to do this at every turn. We all have to be brave." Moving backward, he led her up the stairs. Her eyes bugged as they stepped onto the bridge.

"Come on. The bridge is fine." Desmond jumped up and down to show her it was sturdy.

"Not helping." Her voice trembled.

"Don't look down. Look at me," Rasq said. "We're almost there." He motioned to the other end of the bridge with a bob of his head. "The faster we move, the sooner we can get down from here."

Gwen saw how close the other side was and almost ran over Rasq to get down the steps. She stopped to catch her breath, grateful to be on solid ground.

"Way to cross a bridge, superstar," Charlotte teased.

Just ahead, they found the door to Nola Junction. Actually, there were two doors. One towered high above them, seemingly built for giants. The knob was too far for them to reach and too large. Luckily, a small door was built into the large, just the right size for human beings. Words were carved among the wooden vine and flower decoration.

Nola Junction
Take care
Beware
Pay your fare

A box with a slot cut in the top hung below.

"Who charges a fare to walk through a door?" Gwen had apparently recovered from her trauma. She tried the knob. It rattled and turned, but the door didn't open.

Charlotte asked, "Does anyone have money?"

Rasq shook his head no. "I might be able to find some in the bookshop. I could go back."

"How much do they want?"

Rasq inspected the box. "Doesn't say."

Desmond had left his backpack and the money for the meat in the bookshop. All he had was the coin in his pocket. He hated to give up his good luck charm, especially given that it was a gift from his mother.

"Don't look at me. I don't have any," Gwen said.

Her cousin retorted, "You never have any money."

"Where's yours, if you're so wealthy?"

Desmond sighed and removed the bear coin from his pocket and took a last look at it. "I have this. My mother gave it to me for luck." He held it up.

Rasq took it from him and plunked it into the box. Just like that, the coin was gone.

Gwen gave Desmond a light punch on the shoulder. "No worries. We'll get you another." She offered him a reassuring smile.

The door emitted a click and cracked itself open. Rasq went inside with the others close behind.

They lost the sound of the rushing river as soon as the door closed. A great and quiet Nola Junction rose before them, an arena dimly lit by a chandelier hanging from the highest ceiling Desmond had ever seen.

Rather than an audience, pitch-black portals in wooden door frames occupied the tiers, and each door frame had a plaque that probably identified the place to which it led. By Desmond's estimate, they numbered in the hundreds. It was a kind of dream for him, after feeling confined at home for so long, to have these new places so close. All they had to do was step through the right opening.

He turned in a circle, attempting to take in the full spectacle of the place. "How do we know which one? Are they in alphabetical order or something?"

Gwen ventured over to the nearest portal. "Farglen City." She read the plaque and then moved to the next. "Temple Stensalei. I don't think they're alphabetical."

"I guess we can start working row by row," Desmond said. He noticed Charlotte staring at a mound of dirty rags near the wall.

She whispered, "Something is in there. It moved."

He observed it with her while Rasq and Gwen went in opposite directions to search the first level of portals for the veld. They read each plaque aloud, strange names of strange places.

Desmond squinted in the dimness, focusing all his attention on the rags. There were enough of them to hide a man...or something larger. The mound shifted. He sucked in a breath to keep from shouting. Every hair on the nape of his neck rose. Gwen and Rasq continued to announce names, unaware of the danger.

"Cindar Valley," Rasq said.

"This is kind of fun." She sang the next name. "Tureky Yonder. That's a weird one. Hey, are you guys going to help or what?" she asked Desmond as she moved ever closer to the rags.

"What should we do?" Charlotte wrung her hands.

He wanted to call them back without drawing the attention of whatever was sleeping or hiding in there. He just needed a reason that didn't make his panic obvious. Nola Junction gave him one in the form of what, from a couple of yards away, looked like a drain directly under the chandelier.

CHAPTER 10

"Hey, come look at this thing. Maybe it's another tunnel." He struggled to keep his voice calm.

The four of them convened over the thing, which turned out to be a round door with a circular handle like he'd seen in pictures of submarine interiors. Made of copper, it was an odd find on a dirt floor. He motioned for them to move in close.

"We aren't alone." He pointed.

They turned to look. He swore the rags had parted, enough room for something underneath to peek out. The movement had become more distinct and rhythmic, inhale, exhale.

"What should we do?"

Rasq volunteered. "I'll talk to it."

"It? Why is it an 'it' and not a 'them'?" Gwen asked.

"The realms have different creatures. We need to be careful."

"What kinds of creatures?"

"Many different kinds. I'll handle it. I know the most about this place."

"Doesn't look like you know too awfully much to me," she said.

"I have a plan."

Rasq broke from the circle. He approached the pile with his hands up to show he meant no harm. "Hello? Do you live here? I was wondering if you could help us find the way to the Kelosian Veld. I would appreciate..."

He stopped talking as a being emerged. It rose to stand tall, taller than the children, taller than most humans, on a pair of long, hind legs that ended in white hooves with divisions like tree roots. It shook free of the rags, dropping them to the floor. A great, white stag with birch branches for antlers loomed over them.

He had bent posture and a tattered vest and pants that were filthy beyond recovery. His eyes were big and murky against his pale, fuzzy skin, and his lips curled in a smile that revealed blood-red gums and large teeth.

Charlotte clapped. "Ooh, how pretty! You're so much better than the moth hat people. They were gross. My name is Charlotte. What's yours? What are you?"

Everyone looked at her in surprise, especially the stag, who obviously hadn't expected this reaction. After a pause, he spread his arms and bowed deeply. He spoke his words smoothly, the undertone of his voice carrying a low rumble.

"Pleased to make your acquaintance. I hope you'll excuse my appearance. I don't get many visitors. My name is Elm. I'm a tree stag from Arbolettis."

Desmond, Gwen, and Rasq stepped backward to put some space between themselves and the utterly alien thing before them. Charlotte didn't back away.

Rasq pointed to a golden pendant hanging from the creature's neck. "That's a Keeper medallion, isn't it? Where did you get it?"

Elm cradled it in his palm. "I used to be a Keeper. I guess I still am, lifelong title, you know. I was on assignment far away when my realm fell."

"Fell?" Charlotte moved closer to him.

He showed his teeth in another sly smile. "Arbolettis. It was a realm of tree beings. We had no cities, only gardens for miles and miles. Statues and planters and fountains, so beautiful. You, my dear, would have loved it."

"How could you know what she'd like?" Desmond asked.

Elm patted her head. "She is obviously a child of refined tastes. I can tell by merely looking at her. How might I assist you this fine day? It is day, isn't it? I lose track in the dark."

Desmond asked Rasq, "Should we trust him?"

"He's wearing the medallion of a Keeper. They act as guardians of the realms. Something is wrong, though. He shouldn't be here."

Elm bent over so Charlotte could inspect the medallion around his neck. She held it close, her face inches from his.

She said, "Desmond, look how it sparkles. No light in here, and it still sparkles."

Elm leered at him. "Now, I see you have an interesting piece of jewelry yourself. We could make a trade, if you like."

"No thank you, but we would be grateful for some direction." He clutched the vessel protectively. "We're looking for the portal to the Kelosian Veld."

"You must be careful carrying such a treasure into the veld. They have lions there, you know."

"We're supposed to find a Keeper named Haelo."

"Mmm...Haelo. I know of him. Well, who better to get you to a Keeper than another Keeper?" He turned to the stairs behind him.

Desmond went along but kept a distance between them. "I wouldn't want to put you out."

"Oh, it's no trouble. I haven't had the privilege of helping anyone in quite a while, being realmless and all."

Charlotte held the stag's arm. "Please tell me more about Arbolettis. I wish I could see it."

"Certainly. Everyone had anything they needed: glorious light, water. The sky was deep blue, and our soil was the richest in all the realms. We had the most enlightened philosophers. Since they had no want of any necessity, they could devote their entire lifetimes to fully utilizing their genius. Every particle of their mental energy went to furthering the collective consciousness." He lumbered up the stairs to the first row. "Let's see. Kelosian Veld. I think I saw it up here. Stick close, dear. You never know who or what might come out of the doorways."

In frames embellished with the same vine and flower design as the main junction door, the portals themselves were impenetrable pools of blackness, the edge of which refused entry to the dull illumination offered by the chandelier. The multitude of those doorways, the openness of them and the possibility that other creatures as strange or stranger than Elm could emerge at any moment made Desmond nervous. They all stayed as far from the portals as space allowed.

"This way." Elm directed them down the fifth row. He gently removed Charlotte from his arm. "Lucky you found me. You could have been here all day." He stopped to study a plaque. "I really thought this was it. Perhaps it was up one more level. We'll have to go back to the stairs." He maneuvered by Charlotte.

Suddenly, he lunged forward, grabbed Desmond by the arm, and hoisted him into the air. Desmond kicked and shouted, and Elm switched his grip to an ankle, dangled him out over the drop.

Desmond's stomach lurched as the lower levels swung beneath him. He flailed for something to grab onto, arms pinwheeling, finding nothing. The pain, the hard grip on his ankle seemed to reach all the way into his marrow.

"No!" Gwen started to go after him. Charlotte stopped her.

"Put him down!" Rasq searched for some way to help without making the predicament worse.

"That would seem an inadvisable course of action, unless I want to severely harm your friend, which I do not." With Desmond thrashing at the end of one arm, Elm took the vessel. He looped the leather strap around his wrist.

"Give that back," Rasq demanded.

"Sorry, kids. I have an entire realm of lives to save." He flung Desmond into the others, and they landed in a heap. The stag crouched back on his white haunches and sprang forward, sailing into the center of the room, dropping to the floor, next to the submarine door.

Rasq was the first to get up. He scrambled to the stairs, practically tripped over his own feet in his desperation to catch the thief. The rest of them were on his heels.

Elm spun the wheel handle on the door and hauled the thing open with a groan of hinges. He hopped in before anyone else reached the ground.

Rasq, Desmond, Charlotte, and Gwen ran and stopped at the opening. All they could see inside was a wide tube leading downward at an angle and an orange reflection of what looked like flickering flames on the smooth, metal wall. There was a ladder, but it was mounted to the top side of the tube, and it would be difficult to hang onto, let alone climb. If they were to go after Elm, they would have to slide. Rasq prepared to lower himself in.

Desmond asked him, "Where does this lead?"

"Not sure, but I think it's an access shaft. A network of them leads out from Cosalis." He pushed forward and was gone.

"Wait!" Desmond called after him.

Gwen said, "I don't think he's going to wait."

"Thank you very much." Desmond went next, dropping into the shaft, feet first. Where the angle of it dipped, he picked up speed, accelerating with the rungs of the ladder whipping by overhead and the echo of Gwen squealing with glee.

The temperature and the humidity intensified until the shaft ended and dropped him onto a metal catwalk hanging by chains. He regained his wits in time to catch Gwen and drag her out of her cousin's way. Charlotte landed squarely on her rear with a squeak.

"What is this place?" Gwen rose. A gust of hot wind caught her hair.

Orange firelight seemed to come from everywhere and nowhere, below them, ahead of them. Rows of catwalks similar to the one on which they stood hung by chains, from hooks in the earthen ceiling, not connected to each other but close enough for someone to jump from one to the next. The place rumbled, a growl so deep, it was barely audible.

"Cosalis must be nearby," Desmond said. "The star. Do you see it?"

"If it's this close, why would the Unknown send us through the veld?" Charlotte put her hand to her brow to shield her eyes from the light. She pointed. "There's Rasq."

He was already three catwalks over, pursuing Elm, who was even further out, his long legs carrying him faster than any human could move. The catwalks shook with each jump, and the chains rattled.

"We'll never catch them," Charlotte said.

"It's no use, anyway. Elm is going to outrun him." Desmond gripped the rail. He looked down and saw nothing but light beneath them, no land. He also saw no way for them to get out. The ladder stopped at the end of the shaft, too high for them to reach. He saw no buildings or stairs, only rows of catwalks and occasional holes in the ceiling that he assumed were more access shafts.

A mechanical whine came from behind them. He turned.

Robotic spiders approached, running along the ceiling, jumping from rail to rail. Eight of them moved in with legs chugging at full speed, pistons at their joints releasing jets of steam. Their eyes were aglow, an angry orange-red.

CHAPTER 11

Desmond, Charlotte, and Gwen fled across the catwalk, jumped to the next one a couple of feet away, and it swayed. Charlotte screamed. He glanced back as one of the spider bots looped a leg around her waist and carried her up to the ceiling.

The next spider went for Gwen. She stopped running to kick its bundle of light bulb eyes, and it drew back, shaking broken pieces of glass from its face. Its cohorts abandoned it to go after Desmond.

He kept his focus ahead as he ran, not wanting to know how close they were. He kept his focus on Rasq and Elm and the catwalk shaking beneath his feet. Then he felt it, the metal arm around his waist, and he was flying. The robot's legs made poof sounds as the tips of them sank into the ceiling and withdrew and sank in again with lightning quickness. Steam pumping from the hydraulics reeked of sulfur and pollution.

Below, the spider robots swarmed Rasq, barreling over each other, fighting to get to him first. He kept running full-out after Elm, who had become little more than a sliver of white in the distance.

Desmond tried to shout a warning but lost his breath as the spider carrying him swooped into a hole in the ceiling. Metal claws ticking on the metal tube, it rocketed upward, causing his stomach to drop like he was on the first hill of a roller coaster. It went up, up, burst through a door.

All fell dark suddenly, and Desmond was on grass, free of robotic clutches. He rolled onto his back to drink in the air. A breeze cooled his skin. He sat up on his elbows as the spider climbed up a stone base and back into the access shaft.

Gwen and Charlotte were nearby, already arguing over who received rougher treatment from the spiders. Neither of them looked hurt.

The door popped open, and another spider emerged. It dumped Rasq onto the lush grass with the same lack of compassion as Desmond's spider bot had offered him.

Rasq wasn't about to take the insult lightly. He jumped up and lurched for the access shaft. Before he could reach the door, it slammed shut, and the wheel spun. Rasq climbed on top to tug at the door.

"Get up here and help me." His voice strained. "Come on!"

"He's gone. Even if we got back through, we wouldn't catch him," Desmond said.

Rasq growled. He pounded the metal in frustration. "Whose fault is that?" He hopped down and stormed over to Desmond. "I don't know what they were thinking, giving the vessel to you."

"So, it would've been safer around your neck?"

"Yes! Do you have any idea how long I've been studying the realms? How long I've begged Mr. Castle to let me apprentice as a Keeper? This place means nothing to you. Castle means nothing to you." He sat on the ground and hung his head in his hands. "We didn't even have the vessel for an hour."

"We'll get it back."

"Oh, really? Just how do you suppose that miracle will occur? What's your plan?"

Gwen put her hands on her hips (suddenly looking very much like her mother) and scolded him. "Well, you're a fine mess. One little setback and you fall apart at the seams. Is that what Keepers do? If so, you should be really good at it."

"Ha! If you were in charge, we'd still be back at that bridge waiting for you to quit your whimpering. And you," he addressed Charlotte, "How could any beast that looks him be anything but a monster?"

She pouted. "I thought he was pretty and magical."

"Many things here are pretty and magical. That doesn't make them safe. Do you other two hear me? We trust no one. In fact, now that you don't have the vessel, I don't think I need you at all." He brushed off his pants as he got up. "I'm sure some pretty, magical being can assist with getting you home. Don't follow me." He pushed into a nearby thicket.

"Good riddance," said Gwen.

"That was very rude," said Charlotte.

Desmond agreed, then took stock of their situation. The spider robots left them in a clearing, in a forest. Darkness blanketed the world around them, obscuring their surroundings and whatever beasties prowled within the dense foliage. Wind played among the tree branches, causing them to clack and groan.

"We should hide," Charlotte whispered and whipped her head in the direction of shifting bushes. "I don't like being out in the open like this."

"You'd rather go in there, where something can sneak up on you?" Gwen chewed her thumbnail, looking just as nervous as her cousin.

Desmond said, "She's right. We make easy targets out here. We'll find somewhere to take cover until morning. Then, we'll go home."

They moved to a spot where the forest wasn't as dense, and they ventured in. A trail cut through the vines and the brambles and the thick trunks of trees, and they followed it for a while, keeping close, searching for a suitable place to camp, despite the fact that none of them knew what a suitable place to camp looked like. They had never gone camping.

"What about that tree?" Gwen pointed out a promising oak, which had split open at the base. "No sneaking up on us there."

Charlotte cringed. "Probably all kinds of spiders in there."

"I've had enough of spiders for one day," Desmond said.

So they moved on.

After some more walking, he asked, "What about a cave?"

"I suppose that would be alright as long as it wasn't too deep, and it didn't have bats inside. I don't like bats." Charlotte glanced warily at the branches above them. In the night, they looked like complex configurations of bones, hands with fingers splayed.

Gwen said, "If we could just find, maybe not a cave, but a rocky sort of nook, a couple of walls we could huddle against. I would feel much better."

The others concurred, and they kept eyes out for this ideal formation of rock. They didn't find it. Instead, they came to a clearing with neatly-trimmed grass. The edge of the forest was cut back to create an open space of perfect roundness. At the center, on a slight rise in the earth, a pair of white chairs sat across from one another at a matching café table with legs made of white vines that coiled around each other.

The three of them hid behind a tree, with stalks, stems, and leaves scratching their arms. They'd been walking for an hour and were dirty and tired, and this bit of civilization looked enticing, especially so, given that the table held a gleaming teapot and therefore, potentially, food.

Gwen practically salivated. "What if there are scones, like the orange cranberry ones Mom makes?"

The other two mumbled in agreement. Scones would be lovely, but the problem with this idyllic scene was that they had no idea who this furniture was for. It was odd, its presence in the middle of a forest. Perhaps it was tea for wild beasts. Would an animal who took formal tea like a human still be considered wild?

Desmond's stomach growled for the fourth time in several minutes. "This hiding is ridiculous. If anyone is around, they'll be able to follow the noise my stomach is making right to us. I'm going to see if there's food."

"Wait." Gwen ducked, pulling him with her. She pointed to the opposite side of the clearing, where just beyond the tree line, a lantern moved along, bobbing as someone carried it. Desmond held his breath as a pair of creatures strolled into the clearing.

CHAPTER 12

The lantern one of them carried swung back and forth, casting slender shadows across the grassy hill: inhumanly long arms, legs, and necks, ragged wings on their backs. As they reached the table, the light hit their hair, which was woven back in tight braids. Their faces were almost canine, almost snout-like with pinched noses.

Dark swirl patterns and thorns marked their pale skin; Desmond didn't need to get close to know because he'd seen them before. The book back in Castle's shop, *A Guide to Curiosity*, had warned him about them, the menaces with a taste for fire-roasted flesh. Fairies were dangerous.

"Shall we practice introductions?" The one who looked slightly more masculine wore a shabby jacket closed with a couple of buttons in the wrong holes. "You'll need to get it right."

"I know, I know, Ogg. Quit being such a whinny," his female companion replied. Her dress was as battered as her counterpart's jacket.

"I think you mean 'ninny'," he said.

"Apparently, you don't know what I mean. Very well. Introductions, if it suits you."

"It does suit me, sister dear. I wouldn't want you to end up on the menu. You have to start over there."

"Can't we just pretend I already did that part?"

"Certainly. It's your life. Do with it as you will."

She groaned and tromped back down the hill, to the edge of the trees and said, "Begin."

"Presenting Nogg of House Flaquellyn. Now, skip."

Nogg skipped up the hill.

"Higher. Your arms need to swing higher."

"*Your* arms need to swing higher."

"We must be polite to the queen." He sang and then hummed a tune.

Nogg curtsied when she reached the table and then bowed so low, her head almost reached her knees. "Oh so very pleased to be invited, your Highness. Your grace is unparalleled among all realms."

"Boring." He yawned, dropped into the chair, and propped his boots on the table. "She doesn't care about grace or the other realms. She cares about how pretty she is, how powerful she is, and she cares about who's on the menu, and right now, I must say, you are looking quite tasty."

"Ogg! How can you talk that way?"

"I'm just offering you a peek into her mindset. If you aren't worthy of being her subject, at least you'll make a tasty dish."

Nogg sank into the other chair and buried her face in her hands to cry. "You're a horrible brother."

"Why? Because I want you to live? Try the flattery again."

"Do I have to do the bow?"

"Yes, you need to be able to recite with all your blood pumping into your brainpan."

"Maybe you should write it for me. What did you say, anyway?"

"I told her she could feel free to eat all the artists, because nothing they created could compare to her beauty, and they were, therefore, pointless."

"Ooh, that is good. Please do one for me, just a short bit."

"Okay, how about - the stars in the sky twinkle in the presence of one so awe-inspiring. They orbit the realms, drawn to you, my queen, brighter than Cosalis itself."

"That's overboard," Nogg stated flatly. "She'll think I'm being sarcastic. Are you trying to get me eaten?"

Ogg put up a finger. "Hold up. Do you smell that?"

Nogg raised her nose to the air. "I do. A gift for the queen?"

"A gift *is* much better than flattery. Anyone would agree." He jumped up to search.

Desmond drew back behind the tree. He held his breath. Charlotte was already there, pressing against the bark as if she could disappear into it.

Gwen pointed to the forest behind them, a silent suggestion to run, but if they did attempt to escape, the fairies would hear them. Desmond signaled they should stay.

Ogg and Nogg pranced around the clearing, whistling a melody they tossed back and forth like a tennis match. He whistled higher; she took the song lower with a certain malicious glee, and they moved closer to where Desmond and the others huddled in the shadows. Their song paused.

"Boo." A grinning Ogg appeared inches from Desmond's head.

He, Gwen, and Charlotte bolted without looking back. They made a racket, crashing through the trees in their haste. They didn't make it far.

Nogg's slender fingers clamped onto the back of Desmond's shirt. He shouted and tried to pull away from her, but she held tight, yanked him close for inspection.

"I think it's human!" she reported.

Ogg grabbed one arm of each girl and dragged them back. Gwen kicked him in the knee, so he switched his grip to her hair. She cried out.

He said, "These, too. Only three of them, then?"

"Three should be enough to fill Highness so that she'll move on to dessert before she eats me."

"True enough!" He laughed. "We might get a reward, too. Not many of these running around, I'd say."

"Thank goodness. They smell like onions, and they're missing parts."

Defiant as ever, Gwen snapped, "Parts like those poor excuses for wings? I bet you can't even fly."

Ogg leaned in close to her. "You'd be surprised the things I can do." He flicked his frog tongue onto her face, and she recoiled. "It tastes like an onion! A dirty onion, but an onion, nonetheless."

"Leave her alone." Desmond lunged.

Nogg reeled him back in. "Brave boy. Sad-when-you-die-for-it boy."

No one had ever called him brave before. He'd been called many names, mostly by Gwen when he'd refused to take some dare she gave him. Wimp. Chicken. Turkey. Why did people associate birds with cowardice?

After stopping at the table for Nogg to pick up their lantern, their party moved back into the woods, the way the fairies had come. The dirt trail there was wide and well-worn and provided ample room for Ogg and Nogg to keep a grip on their captives.

Desmond tugged. He squirmed in a futile effort to remove himself from Nogg's grasp, and the harder he did so, the more amused she became, smiling down on him and laughing. Her face was stranger up close. Her features, with the exception of that pinched nose, were too big, her frog eyes most of all.

Ogg whistled as they crossed a slumping, wooden bridge over a creek with almost no water in it. "Careful now, kiddies. You on the left, you try and bite me again, you get a toss. I realize the way doesn't look too far down, but that is an illusion of the optical variety. Then again, aren't all illusions optical? What is an illusion you can't see?"

"Truest," Nogg agreed. "Brother, dear one, you are quite the genus."

"I think you mean 'genius'."

"You can't possibly know what I mean."

CHAPTER 13

The trail took them down a tilting slope to a village lit by fireflies and lights strung across the road. Tall, narrow houses in toadstool shades of red and sickly, pale cream crowded together, their roofs sagging, their chimneys pumping trails of white haze into the air.

The place smelled of grilled meat, which simultaneously made Desmond hungry, then repulsed when he considered what they might be cooking.

Lanky fairies lumbered along, many of them making some kind or another of music. They filled the streets with sound, clapping, whistling, humming, even somehow laughing musically. Some paused to stare whenever Ogg and Nogg and their significantly shorter prisoners came into view.

A man in a cloak raised a handful of shiny, metal reeds to get Ogg's attention. "Last chance to change your wager," he said in a gruff voice.

"No worries. I'm a-okay. Appreciate the concern, though, Reg." Ogg caught Nogg glaring at him and asked, "What?"

"You bet on my life!"

"For you to survive. Otherwise, I wouldn't have been so eager to help." He winked at her.

She shot him a venomous look but let the subject go.

They continued down the street, past fairies dancing together, fairies gnawing on roots or bits of meat, fairies bickering. Had his life not been in immediate danger, Desmond would've found it a terribly interesting place to be, full of color and action.

At the end of the road, they came to a more finely dressed crowd. Fairies there wore sleeveless silk gowns, and their hair was twisted into more civilized arrangements than what Ogg and Nogg had. An enthusiastic swarm of fireflies had amassed there as well, landing on some of the fairies, in their hair or on their shoulders like pets.

Ogg said, "Part the waters, snooty snoots. We have gifts for Highness. I'd deeply regret having to inform her that you kept us."

The snooty snoots, not about to interfere with the presentation of any gifts, moved aside to present a clear path. They also sneered on the parade as it passed, as though hiding their contempt was just too potent a burden to bear.

An older woman sniffed Charlotte's hair and arched a thin eyebrow at Ogg. "They stink."

"I'm certain they think the same of you and your insect carcass breath."

Her lip curled into a snarl, and then she snapped her frog tongue to catch a firefly inches from his head. The sound of it crunching in her teeth turned Desmond's stomach. She grinned, her teeth aglow.

The building beyond the crowd was larger than the rest, taller than the rest with the thatched roof propped up by posts rather than walls. Strings of lights from the buildings along the road continued inside, where they split and formed a web overhead. And below that complex luminary, more snooty snoots had assembled around a long table. They stood in front of their chairs, striking various poses conveying superiority, boredom, or both. No one seemed particularly interested in the feast before them.

Gwen, on the other hand, was quite interested in the food. She didn't seem to care that none of the fruits or vegetables looked familiar or that one dish consisted of nothing but a steaming pile of grass. She disregarded the strangeness of the cooked boars equipped with too many snouts, the pie with six legs trying to walk away. All she cared about was pulling Ogg as close to the table as she could, and Charlotte helped with the task, tugging on his other arm. He held them both back.

Guards in brass-buttoned coats and helmets adorned with feathers and bones were stationed everywhere. Servers hurrying in with trays of food wore similar decoration, only their coats were plain, and their feathers hung from belts at their waists. It was all civilized and clean compared to the grungy village street.

Ogg led their party through a crowd of fairies who weren't important enough to have chairs, to the head of the table at the other side of the room. Music, violins accompanied by a flute, and the sound of a fountain gurgling nearby competed with the sly voices of fairies lavishing flattery upon their queen.

As Ogg made his errand apparent, the fairies backed away. Finally, after several rows of flatterers abandoned their positions, Ogg reached the queen.

Dressed in a mass of pink gown, she was rotund in form. Her hair was the most voluminous hair of all, a mountain of braids atop her head with a crown pinned to the front. Her nose and mouth protruded the same way as her subjects', that pinched snout, but hers was more pronounced, lending her an even more otherworldly appearance. Fireflies amassed, landing on her, fussing over her like they couldn't wait to be eaten.

She fed cookies to a two-foot long cricket on a leash. It snatched them from her hand, munched quickly, and looked to her for more with its mouth appendages working eagerly.

As the flattery from her admirers ceased, she looked around, seemingly startled by the relative quiet. "What is this? Who is this?" she asked of Ogg. Before he could answer, she announced to the room, "You will all be seated."

The fairies with chairs sat.

"Highness," Ogg began.

Her attention snapped to him, and he bowed so hastily, he nearly toppled forward into her lap. He shook the girls' arms to signal for them to bow. Charlotte complied. Gwen didn't.

"What is this?" she asked again in a light, quick voice. Her glassy eyes bugged at the sight of Charlotte. "How dare you." Her voice dripped with venom. "This creature wears my color. I alone may wear pink, for I am the Majesty." She was, indeed, the only fairy they'd seen wearing pink.

"The Majesty!" A chorus of her guests raised their glasses.

"Human girls are such repulsive, little creatures, anyway. Remove her at once," she snapped. "Fix this sartorial debacle. Bring her back so we may educate her on etiquette before I decide what to do with her."

A guard took Charlotte from Ogg. She cried and begged to know where he was taking her. He, nor anyone in the crowd, which had gone quiet, replied.

"Please. I didn't know," she said as she disappeared from sight.

Gwen fought against Ogg's grip to go after them. He held her tight, now with both hands. He thrust her toward the queen.

"Highness, we bring gifts."

"Where are they taking her?" Desmond spoke up.

The queen saw him. Her mouth fell open.

"Release them," she commanded.

Ogg and Nogg let go of Gwen and Desmond.

"Now, be off with the two of you. Leave the humans."

Their shoulders slumped at the dismissal. They'd expected something more for their trouble.

"Wait," the queen said, and they perked up. "What are your names?"

Ogg bowed again. "We are Ogg and Nogg of the House of Flaquellyn. Ever at your service, Highness."

She nodded slowly. "Nogg. Your test of worthiness was tonight, true?"

"Yes, my queen."

"Is this why you brought these children to me?"

"I would have brought them no matter the day, Highness."

The queen eyed her with suspicion. "So, you wouldn't have otherwise consumed them?"

"Never. I serve only you." She smiled, but there was fear as well.

"Very well. You have proven your worth. You are excused from the test of worthiness. Since you interrupted the proceedings, most improper, you shall not receive dinner."

Nogg put her hands together. "Thank you, Highness. Your beauty shines brighter than Cosalis." Still bowing, she backed away through the crowd, with Ogg executing a similar posture.

The queen shooed two very disappointed guests from chairs on her right and offered the seats to Desmond and Gwen. He sat next to her, and Gwen sat between him and the next fairy.

The queen noticed everyone staring. "You may eat," she told them and then turned to Desmond. "You're too young to be Allos, unless you've found a way to make yourself younger, in which case, you will be sharing your secret with me. Are you?"

"Am I Allos?"

"Yes. Clearly, you do not possess his quick wit."

"I'm his grandson. My name is Desmond."

She clapped her ring-laden hands together. "Grandson. You look exactly like him, only smaller. How many of you are there?"

"Just me, I think."

"I knew him," she nodded, "better than most, the scoundrel. Does he live?"

"He died a long time ago."

She sighed. "Humans. Such perishable fruit."

Gwen piled whatever food she could reach onto her plate

and scowled at Desmond when she saw him not doing the same. She filled it for him while he listened to the queen.

"He stayed here for a time. I kept him, actually, as he had something I wanted - that lion heart." She fed another cookie to the cricket. "If he wouldn't give it to me willingly in the form of his love, I thought I could eat the organ. He never did, and I never could bring myself to follow through with the eating. When he left after a year of being at my side, he took a sack full of golden reeds from the treasure room. Gold! A worthless metal. I only keep it to trade with the lesser realms. They seem to think it's worth something."

"Someone told me he was a thief."

"Oh yes, a very good one. Tell me, how did he end up? Where did he land when he slowed down?"

Desmond didn't know what their world was called there, so he ventured a guess. "The human realm. He opened a bank."

"Ha. Once a thief, always a thief."

Guards burst in from the side of the building, leading a dirty, thrashing form through the crowd. They tossed the boy to the floor, at the feet of the queen, on the other side of the table from Desmond.

"Let me go. I'm on official Keeper business," the voice of Rasq protested.

CHAPTER 14

Desmond and Gwen hopped up from their chairs. The queen motioned for them to sit down.

The guard said, "I found him at the edge of the village. He tried to steal food."

Highness spoke to Rasq. "Tut-tut, little mutt. Rise and tell me what you are. I see the human. What's the other half?"

Rasq saw Desmond and Gwen sitting at the table. He stared for a moment, confused by their presence.

He hung his head as he admitted, "My mother was a wood nymph, I think."

"You think? That means she abandoned you somewhere. Typical nymph behavior. What is this lie about being a Keeper? I was a Keeper before I inherited the throne, and I find your claim offensive. Speak true, now."

"I am a Keeper." He stood taller.

"Show me your medallion, then."

"Haven't got one."

She chuckled, pleased with her deduction. "I didn't think so. Now what to do with a lying, would-be thief?"

Desmond said, "Excuse me."

Gwen jabbed him with her elbow to tell him to be quiet. Desmond ignored her.

"He was with us. We got separated in the forest."

"Does this mean a second Winters intended to steal from me?"

He felt Gwen glaring at him.

"No, ma'am, I mean Your Majesty. We didn't even know this village was here. We were lost and trying to find our way home."

She patted her cricket's head thoughtfully. "I suppose that

seems likely." She told Rasq, "You may sit and eat. Should you attempt to steal again, our beloved chef has an enticing recipe for creamed flesh flambé I've been meaning to try."

Rasq went pale.

The queen waved away the fairy on her left, and he relinquished his seat, sulking, toting a handful of boar meat for his trouble. Rasq sat and practically drooled on the full plate before him, but he hesitated.

She asked, "What's wrong? Food doesn't taste good unless it's stolen?"

He decided her offer was sincere, and he became an eating machine, snatching rolls from a nearby basket and cramming them into his mouth until his cheeks were full.

The queen said, "So, young Winters, humans don't often grace us with their presence. I'm rather interested in knowing how you ended up at my table."

"We were in Castle's Book Shoppe, and he collapsed. The Authors Unknown say the only way to revive him is with the light of Cosalis. They gave us a vessel."

An intensity came over her, a shadowy eagerness that made Desmond's heart beat faster and reminded him what she really was. She had been gracious to them, but in an instant, she could become a murderous creature. She sipped from a gleaming chalice to compose herself.

"You carry the light of Cosalis?"

"The vessel was stolen before we could reach the star."

"Who took it?"

"A Keeper named Elm."

She groaned. "I've heard of him. After Arbolettis fell, he pestered everyone in the realms about finding a way to bring it back, an impossible task if ever there was one. Once a realm has fallen, it's gone forever. Poor, delusional soul. Where is he now?"

Rasq chimed in between bites. "He escaped through the access shaft in Nola Junction. The spiders threw us out before I could catch him."

"You planned to return to the human realm without completing your mission." She directed this accusation at Desmond.

"We have no idea where he went. Chasing him is pointless. He's too fast."

"You don't sound like a Winters at all, not like Allos. He was many things but not a coward."

"I'm not a coward."

Gwen said, "Yes, you are. This morning he was afraid of a bird."

"I didn't see you jumping at the chance to deal with it."

"Enough." The queen stopped them. "You cannot return home without the vessel of light. The problem has not been solved. You have no choice but to continue."

Rasq paused in his eating. "I was trying to continue."

"Good. At least one of you has some sense. I suppose they expected you to do all the work."

He shrugged.

"Get used to that if you want to be a Keeper. Everyone expects us to solve all the realms' problems while they sit around and twiddle their thumbs. Whose apprentice are you?"

"I have no master, yet."

She laughed. "How can you expect to be a Keeper with no one to teach you?"

"Mr. Castle didn't want me to train. He said the realms were too dangerous."

Charlotte returned, escorted by a guard. They had dressed her in commoner fairy clothing, effectively dashing her spirit in the process. Her tear-streaked face didn't brighten at the sight of the food or her friends. She only stood there, clutching part of her shirt where a button hole had torn. Her trousers were haphazardly chopped off the bottoms to accommodate her much shorter, non-fairy legs. Gone were the Sunday shoes. They were replaced by a pair of boots as battered as the rest of her clothes.

Gwen snickered at the sight of her proper cousin diminished.

The queen had a higher opinion of the change. "Ah, there is some more respectable attire. Always consider the needs of your host when you travel. You'll fare much better." She waved away the fairy sitting next to Gwen, and he departed with a roll of his eyes.

Charlotte took her seat without looking directly at anyone.

A man in a waiter uniform appeared next to the queen. "Pardon me, Highness. Would you like to begin the test of worthiness? We are overdue for commencement."

Her mood darkened. The waiter glanced toward the exit as though he considered bolting from the building.

"Have you not noticed that I'm chatting with guests? If you insist on being a nuisance, I shall have you for dessert."

He swallowed his terror. "M-m-my apologies." He fell forward in a bow. "I deeply regret the interruption. I was only concerned with ensuring the evening meets your expectations."

"I find your reasoning acceptable. Tell me, what is your name?"

"I am Sentrilc, Highness."

She addressed everyone at the table. "Anyone who is not human, halfling, guard, or Sentrilc will exit the building. The test of worthiness is canceled."

The crowd rose from their chairs, murmuring as they filed toward the exit.

CHAPTER 15

With trembling hands, Sentrilc refilled the queen's chalice.

She said to Desmond, "I know that name, Castle. Is he Lucinda's Castle?"

He nodded.

"Saint Lucinda. She gave her life for all of us." She closed her eyes in reverence. "Of course, you must go on your way. This cause is nobler than you know, not something to be cast aside or abandoned, young Mr. Winters. All three of you who planned to go home will proceed, and you'll assist this halfling all the way to the end."

"We don't know where to start. We don't know where Elm is," Desmond said.

"Such complaints. How could you ever expect to be a Keeper with that attitude?"

"Rasq is the one who wants to be a Keeper."

"No. This is the kind of quest a Keeper takes on. Nothing like learning on the job. You'll find a master along the way. I feel it in my bones."

He nodded.

"Now, let's talk about where you'll go from here. In the next realm, a realm called Ashfall, there is a seer named Bensai. He can find anyone in the realms. My guards will escort you to the passage. From there, you should have no trouble finding him. The village is just on the other side." She waved the nearest guard over. "Erul, saddle the hares. You will transport these children to the passage. If you can't get them there alive, don't come back."

Erul bowed and hastened from the room, taking three other guards with him.

"Mr. Winters, before you go, I feel I owe it to Allos to talk with you about this urge to give up. It's as unbecoming as it is unacceptable. You are much braver than you think."

Desmond felt his face burn with embarrassment. Gwen calling him on his weak moments was one thing, but a queen he'd just met, that was different.

"Are you familiar with the expression 'fortune favors the brave'?"

"That was the inscription in the front of a book in Castle's shop - *A Guide to Curiosity*, by the Authors Unknown."

"An appropriate place. It's also the Keepers' motto. It's engraved on our medallions, in our hearts. Fortune favors those who are brave enough to persevere when the situation appears hopeless. Some might have called your capture by my people a hopeless predicament, and yet you sat here, eating dinner with me. We had sensible conversation when you should've been running for your life. You've inherited a piece of your grandfather's lion heart, whether you believe it or not. No more of this quitting business."

"Yes, Highness."

"You'll have to be cautious in the meadow. The wolves are out this evening. They'll be hunting."

Desmond thanked her, and the others seconded the sentiment, even Charlotte, who seemed to have rallied. She'd filled her plate and sensing her opportunity to eat had nearly ended, was devouring everything she could get her hands on.

Two of the guards returned to inform her they were ready. The queen had one final warning for Desmond and the others before they left.

"Do not pass this way with the light of Cosalis. The prospect of immortality is powerful, and I couldn't be held responsible for my actions. When you carry the light, the danger to your lives will increase exponentially. Take care, and tell no one you have it."

He nodded. "We won't."

"Good boy."

The village had all but shut down during their dinner with the queen. Dirt roads had emptied. The strings of lights had dimmed. Most of the fairies and fireflies had gone home, leaving the chimneys to stand vigil over the narrow houses.

Where Desmond and company made a left onto another dirt road, small trees with their roots in burlap sacks were gathered close to the front of a nursery. Across from that, cured meat hung in a window. The village was a surprisingly organized place for such savage people.

They walked beneath an arch made of woven vines, and then an orderly forest replaced the houses and shops. Slim trees with high branches reached for the stars, shedding leaves every so often in their yearning for the sky.

"This night must be forever," Gwen said, "Feels like the sun is never coming up."

A guard walking in front of them glared at her over his shoulder.

"Friendly bunch," she added.

No one else spoke as they moved down a hill, toward a stable. Light from the open doors poured onto the path leading up to the entrance. Desmond squinted while his eyes adjusted.

He'd been to a stable with his parents. He remembered being in awe of it, the size of the horses, the extensive space and all the equipment needed for them. This setup was similar, the stalls arranged on both sides of a long aisle, tack hanging from hooks, but there was one significant difference.

Open stalls housed massive hares in place of horses. The coloring of their fur varied from black to white to tan and a shade of gray bordering on lavender. They sniffed when the children entered, their big nostrils silently working. Charlotte approached the first stall on the right, where a snow-white hare poked its head into the walkway.

"Careful. They bite," Erul told her.

She ran her fingers down one thick whisker. The animal pulled away, twitching its nose.

She smiled at Desmond. "Amazing."

A female guard prodded them on. "This is a royal stable, not a petting zoo. Move along."

Gwen snorted. "What a grouch."

Erul's face twisted in irritation. "If you knew the danger, you wouldn't be so cavalier."

Near the end of the walkway, saddles hung on a wall, their decoration ornate yet primitive with strings of beads, feathers, and leather straps. They were considerably longer than horse saddles with enough room for two or three people to ride together.

On the other side of the open door, between them and the meadow beyond, four hares waited in a line with three fairies. The latter stood at attention, none of them looking particularly happy about the late-night assignment.

"Telk, the two girls will ride with you." Erul spoke to a man with white braids looping out from beneath his helmet. He then turned to a bald man, who towered over his comrades, and said, "Sefan, you take the boys." Erul tilted his head to listen, then lowered himself to the ground, placed his palm on the soil.

The meadow went eerily still, the breeze, the weeds. In the distance, so faint they almost couldn't hear it at all, a wolf howled.

CHAPTER 16

"They're coming. We should wait," Sefan said in a gravelly voice.

"They'll only get closer." Erul made a circle with his hand, a signal to the others, and then he got onto a black hare with a narrow, white stripe from nose to tail.

Telk heaved Charlotte onto his gray hare, into a saddle with three seats. She giggled as the animal shifted beneath her. Telk put Gwen in the seat right behind his.

"Hold tight." He lifted himself up with a practiced grace.

Sefan's mount was a brown hare with black specks. It was more tolerant of the additional passengers and remained steady.

He said to Rasq and Desmond, "Lean with the hare, not against him, unless you want to end up on the ground or in the belly of a wolf."

"If the hares are this big, what does that say about the wolves?" Desmond asked.

"Trust me. You don't want to know."

Erul pulled a sword from a sheath hanging at his side. The fairy on the hare next to him, a woman with orange braids down her back, locked her boots in copper stirrups, drew a bow, and nocked an arrow. The blade of an ax in Sefan's hand caught the starlight and gleamed. They looked like they could handle anything.

Erul spoke to the woman with the bow. "Lysann, to the rear of the group. Cover our backs. I'll take the lead. Keep low. Stay quiet. Break formation only if we're hunted. Regroup at the mouth of the passage. Mind the creek." He pointed to the meadow with his sword.

The hares stood in unison, the sudden shift throwing Desmond off balance, and he gripped the handle in front of him to keep from falling. The four animals crouched, only for an instant, and then they were off. Through tall weeds and the blur of night-soaked green, they flew, paws barely touching the ground. They veered left.

Desmond tried to lean, but the turn happened so quickly, he barely had time to react before the thing darted another direction. He gave himself over to the will of the ride, letting gravity have its way, and he focused on his hands, holding on as wind rushed into his face.

Another howl passed over the meadow, closer, the precise direction of the sound lost in the sway of the weeds. Sefan steered the hare down a hill, and as they tackled the following incline, the saddle lurched.

Desmond lost all sense of direction. There was only forward and faster in the dark and the fluid motion of the world and all within it, and in that place, the quiet chaos of a brewing storm, he was helpless to do anything but hold on like his life depended on it.

His stomach did a flip as they dropped from ground level into a shallow ravine with a creek running through the middle. Sefan's hare slid sideways to a halt next to Erul. Next came Telk, Charlotte, and Gwen, followed by Lysann.

They gathered near a fallen tree covered in moss. The hares put their noses into the air, sniffing and turning in circles in search of a safe path, their paws splashing. Erul patted his mount on the neck.

"Easy," he soothed in a low voice.

A new round of howling began. Lysann held up fingers, pointing a different direction with each wolf voice joining the chorus. Five in all and the meadow became still once more.

"Hang on, boys," Sefan told them. "We're about to move."

On Erul's signal, they launched from the ravine, back up to ground level, where they were surrounded by mountainous shadows on all sides. The meadow dissolved into chaos. Growling. Drooling. Flashes of white teeth and glowing eyes broke the impenetrable darkness of their fur. Steaming breath perfumed with blood stifled the air, infecting Desmond with a terror that roared into his veins.

The hares scattered between boulder-size paws. Sefan veered sharply to the right. Desmond caught a glimpse of Gwen's and Charlotte's terrified faces as they disappeared into the weeds. And then the fairy guard and the boys were alone in the wild night, with a wolf on their heels. Desmond didn't turn, but he felt its presence there, its ravenous hunger radiating like heat from a sun.

Out of sight, an animal screamed.

Sefan grumbled under his breath, spurred their mount faster. He cut a wide circle, darted between the legs of a wolf in their path. It let an otherworldly yelp and spun to give chase.

The fairy tucked the ax behind him in the saddle. He leaned sideways at a dangerous angle and held his free hand out. They met resistance, and the hare kicked hard into the ground to keep its balance and its speed as Sefan heaved a fourth rider onto the saddle meant for three.

Lysann landed awkwardly, in a crouch over Desmond and Rasq. Bow in hand, she stepped between them, as easily as if the hare weren't running at breakneck speed, to a spot behind the saddle, and sat down.

She loosed an arrow. The monster on their tail hit the ground, rolled to a stop, and receded into the distance, no longer a threat.

They shot up another rise in the earth, where the weeds crowded close enough to whip their arms, and when they reached the top, a stone doorway came into view. Desmond had expected a cave, something small like the tunnel they'd taken out of the book shop, but the stone wall through which the passage cut was several stories tall.

Erul appeared at their side. Without any need for a command, Lysann jumped to his hare and dropped into the seat behind him, and they turned back to the meadow.

Another animal screamed, and the four remaining wolves howled, all at once. The sound of it sent a chill through Desmond. They hadn't let a victory howl with the first hare they'd gotten, which meant this prize was greater than the first.

Sefan stopped near the passage and said, "Wait inside. The wolves are too big to fit through the entrance."

Desmond and Rasq dismounted clumsily, landing in the dirt at the edge of the weeds. As soon as they were clear, their escort sprang back into action. He charged back into the meadow with his battle ax raised over his head.

CHAPTER 17

Desmond followed Rasq to the passage, and they waited there, just inside the entrance as they were told. They watched from the edge of danger, feeling the tremble of battle in the ground beneath their feet, seeing nothing but a starry sky over a meadow.

Desmond asked, "Do you think they're alright - the girls?"

He shook his head. "No way to tell."

Growling reached them, a guttural, furious sound escalating to a shriek. Then came the swish of weeds, an animal bolting from left to right, a fleshy thump, the scream of a hare down the wall from them.

Or was it a hare? It could've been the scream of a girl; Desmond thought. The idea gnawed the edge of his raw nerves. What if the scream had come from his friends? What if they died because he decided to remain in safety like a coward?

He plunged back into the night, in the direction from which he thought the sound had come. He stuck close to the wall.

"What are you doing?" Rasq followed.

"They're out here. I heard one of them scream," he whispered back.

"That was an animal. You're going to get us killed."

"I didn't tell you to come after me."

A wolf the size of a house trotted by. As it stopped to sniff the air, the boys flattened themselves against the wall. They froze, scarcely daring to breathe. It put its nose to the ground.

An arrow struck its left haunch. It jumped, scattering the dirt at its feet, and fled. Erul and Lysann flew by after it.

"Too close," Rasq said.

Desmond nodded. He heard crying and ran ahead, forgetting his worry about the wolves in his haste. He found Gwen and Charlotte, no hare, no Telk. Charlotte sat in the weeds, sobbing into her hands, while Gwen stood nearby, looking out into the meadow for signs of danger.

"Shut up. You'll draw them right to us," she hissed at her cousin. She saw the boys. "Des!" She ran over to hug him.

He asked, "Where's Telk?"

She spoke quickly. "One of the wolves knocked us off. Telk managed to stay on, but they chased him away."

"We know where the passage is. Come on." He held his hand out to Charlotte to help her off the ground. "It's this way."

Rasq stopped them. "Hold on."

He parted the weeds and stepped in. Seconds ticked by.

"What's he doing?" Gwen started toward the wall. "Come on."

A large shadow leaped from the meadow, over Desmond, knocking him onto his rear in the dirt, landing between him and the wall. Rasq sat astride the hare Telk had been riding.

He almost lost his balance in the saddle. "I found a ride." He grinned. "It was hiding."

Gwen asked, "Did you find Telk?"

The grin faded. "No."

Gwen and Charlotte climbed aboard. Desmond went last. He tried to situate himself just behind the saddle as Lysann had done, but there was nothing to hold onto.

"You can put your arms around me," Charlotte said. "I'll hold on for both of us."

She was pretty, then, in the starlight, despite the dirt and the remnants of tears on her face. He took her up on the offer, putting his arms around her waist and locking his hands together. He'd never felt quite so awkward before.

"We're ready?" Rasq asked.

Before anyone could answer, the head of a wolf burst from the shadows, teeth bared. The hare squealed, and they were off, scrabbling in the weeds. In its panic, their ride swerved right, then hard left, nearly colliding with the stone wall.

"You're going to miss the tunnel." Gwen shouted the warning to Rasq.

"No, I won't."

A second wolf jumped into their path. Rasq pushed the hare faster. He steered between the wolf's legs as he'd seen the fairies do, but the beast was ready. It snapped. The hare dodged sideways into the predator's leg as the first wolf caught up. They became a tangle of three animals, clambering, biting, squealing. The hare was thrown backward, and Desmond slipped forward from the saddle.

He caught the handle in front of Charlotte, and she grabbed his sleeve with one hand. In the midst of claws and teeth and the ground rushing up at him, she refused to let go.

The hare kicked free. They emerged on the other side of the fray, Desmond still hanging perilously close to the powerful hind legs. Rasq yanked the reins, and they turned left into the passage, leaving the wolves at the entrance.

The hare kept running until they were halfway through the tunnel, then, at Rasq's persistent command, it slid to a halt, claws raking the dirt. Everyone froze in place for a moment, paralyzed by fear of the next pounce. It didn't come.

Desmond released the saddle and dropped to the ground. He lay on his back in the cool dirt, staring up at the stone ceiling while his pulse returned to normal. He did a quick self-assessment. His arm, fingers to wrist to shoulder, burned and ached. His head spun, but he was in one piece.

"I can't believe we're alive." Gwen eased out of the saddle, to the ground next to Desmond. She sat with her back against the wall. Her face and arms were scratched.

Desmond asked, "Is anyone hurt?"

"No worries here," she said.

"I'm fine, except for some bruises," Rasq replied. "The hare has bite marks, but they don't look deep." He dismounted.

Charlotte said, "I'm more worried about Telk and the others."

Rasq unbuckled the bridle to remove it. "They look like they can take care of themselves just fine."

"We should stay here tonight. Camp out." Desmond couldn't bear the thought of standing again, let alone walking, until he had some sleep.

Once Rasq had the saddle off, the hare lay on its side.

"I agree." He sat next to the hare and rested against it.

"I couldn't walk another step if I wanted to." Charlotte did the same, nuzzling into the fur on the hare's stomach.

Desmond joined them. "Our parents have probably noticed we're gone by now. I wonder what they think." He noticed Rasq looking dejected. "Sorry."

He muttered, "Nothing to be sorry for," and turned over.

"Rasq?" Desmond felt his eyes starting to close. He was thirsty, but that wouldn't stop sleep from coming.

"Yeah?"

"How did you end up in the bookshop?"

"Someone left me in the tunnel to the human realm. I guess they figured I'd want to be there because I'm half human."

Gwen yawned. "If it makes you feel better, I didn't notice you were anything but human."

"It does."

Charlotte said, "I feel more sorry for you having to live with that man. He's horrible."

"Mr. Castle is better than he seems. He took care of me when no one else wanted to. Can you imagine him with a baby?"

They laughed.

"He's just protective because of what happened to Lucinda. If he wasn't afraid of cutting himself off from her completely, he would've closed the tunnel. He says people from our realm don't belong here."

Desmond agreed. If the other realms were as dangerous as the one from which they'd just come, they would be lucky to get back alive.

CHAPTER 18

To Desmond's surprise, night ended. Darkness in the fairy realm seemed an eternal thing, a persistent state. Dawn pressing into the passage from both ends was like a miracle. He woke before the others and decided to let them sleep. They looked peaceful there, Charlotte and Gwen snuggled up together like they'd never argued.

He went to the side of the tunnel bordering the next realm and warmed himself in the light of the oncoming day. It came from all around, a glow with no discernible source in the sky. It was strange, the absence of a sun.

Aside from that, the place looked somewhat normal. A road led from the edge of the passage, up a long hill of short grass to a village of small, white buildings. He hoped the residents were as mild-mannered as their village made them seem.

He turned at the sound of footsteps behind him. A pair of silhouettes approached from the fairy side of the passage, a man and a hare moving slowly together.

Desmond ran back to the others. It was Sefan, covered in cuts and bruises, holding his side with one strong arm. He and his mount limped.

"What happened? Did the others make it?" Desmond asked.

Charlotte, Gwen, and Rasq sat up, rubbed their eyes, and stretched.

Sefan smiled wearily. "We're alive, except for one hare. Telk has a broken leg. He's already being a pain about it. Thank the gods you survived. The queen would send us off to the chef if you weren't safe." He swayed on his feet but remained upright. "I'm here for the hare."

Gwen threw her arms around its neck. "Can't we keep him? He's so good and fast."

"Sorry, girly. We're down one already. They're hard to come by and even harder to train."

Rasq heaved the saddle, which was almost as big as he was onto the animal's back and pulled the straps tight. Desmond took care of the bridle. He patted the hare on the nose.

"Thanks, bunny," he said to it.

Gwen pressed her forehead against the hare's. "He saved us and kept us warm. We don't even know his name."

Sefan tightened a strap on the saddle. "They don't have names."

"That's not right. This boy deserves a name. From now on, he'll be called Henry."

Desmond and Rasq laughed. Sefan looked as amused as a serious warrior can look.

She asked, "What's so funny?"

Charlotte answered, "Henry? I expected you to come up with something more creative than that. Why not just call him Charles or Bob?"

Gwen narrowed her eyes. "I suppose you could think of a better name?"

"I certainly could. He can be Henry, though." She patted the hare's side. "It's a good name."

Gwen had expected more of an argument. Her cousin's concession threw her off, and she became flustered.

"Well, good."

They walked Sefan to the fairy realm side of the passage, where the meadow had become a cheery place. With the wolves gone, birds sang. Big butterflies flitted among the flowers.

Sefan got onto Henry's back, looping the reins for his hare around a handle on the saddle. He made an even more imposing figure above them, a mountain of muscle with an ax hanging at his side.

Desmond said, "We didn't get very far. Seems like we could've just waited for morning to come."

Sefan shook his head. "Not with the queen's appetite and her temperament. Who knows what she might've decided to do with you if she changed her mind. She knew herself well enough to send you off."

"Well, we're grateful, anyway. Thank you. Will you please thank the others for us as well?"

"Aye. Be careful. The realms aren't a nursery."

Gwen planted her hand on her hip. "We've noticed, and we aren't babies."

Still amused, he turned the hares around and disappeared into the meadow.

At the other side of the passage, Desmond, Rasq, Charlotte, and Gwen paused to take in the village. It sat at the top of the hill, eerily still in the bright day.

"It looks too well-kept to be abandoned," Charlotte said.

"Maybe it's some kind of trap." Rasq started toward it.

Gwen trotted after him. "What kind of trap?"

He held his hands up like claws. "Maybe giant lizards." He growled.

"That's not funny," Gwen said matter-of-factly, "especially after the wolves."

Desmond and Charlotte trailed behind them up the hill.

He asked, "Are you okay, you know, after the whole dress thing? They didn't hurt you, did they?"

"No. The guards weren't mean, actually. The queen was the only one who was unreasonable about it. They had a little house set up for people in unacceptable attire to change, so I wasn't her first victim. They even had a rack of hideous clothes for me to choose from." She laughed. "I was more embarrassed than anything. I'm just glad no one from home is here to see me like this."

"It's not so bad."

"Oh yes it is, but honestly, I'm glad the dress and the shoes are gone. They weren't exactly functional. They were ruined, anyway."

The two of them caught up with Gwen and Rasq at the edge of town, near a sign welcoming them to Quillet Village. The one-story buildings on either side of the street were a mix of shops and houses. White walls trimmed in dark wooden beams reminded Desmond of pictures of traditional Japanese homes he'd seen in his geography book at school. Roofs were flat, giving the line of perfectly-spaced buildings a neat and tidy appearance as if the village were manufactured in a factory.

Like the road, the covered porches were empty. A few odd looking roadsters, cars with exposed copper pipes, sat abandoned.

Desmond asked the others, "Do you hear anything?"

All was quiet. No conversation. No machinery. No sounds of movement anywhere. Even the birds, assuming there were birds in Ashfall, were silent.

"No. That's too weird," Gwen said. "Look, a bakery."

It was the first building in town and one of only two they could see which did not have a porch. A sign hanging over the door featured a picture of baked goods in a pile.

Gwen and the others gathered in a line to stare at the window display of breads, cakes, and cookies. The treats looked very much like human realm treats: caramel-colored rolls, cupcakes, big cookies.

Rasq put his hand to his forehead to peek inside. "It's dark. I don't see anyone moving around."

Gwen went for the door. "Oh, for Pete's sake. We'll never get any breakfast at this rate." She pulled, and it opened.

CHAPTER 19

"Wait." Charlotte reached for her.

"What?"

"We don't have any money."

She thought for a moment and then said, "We're starving children, lost and alone in the cruel, cruel world." She folded her hands beneath her chin like she was begging. "They can't just turn us away. Everyone put on your pitiful puppy dog eyes. Charlotte, cry like your mom refused to buy you new shoes."

"What's that supposed to mean?" She crossed her arms.

Rasq replied, "It means cry if you want to eat."

Charlotte commenced rubbing her eyes.

"Maybe I should go first. Let me check it out, I mean." Desmond moved by her. "The door should've been locked if they're closed."

"Just so you know, if the food is plastic or something, I'm going to cry for real," Gwen said.

He stepped inside. "Hello?"

He scanned racks of bread loaves, tables of goodies in cellophane and ribbon. He relished the smell of the food baked in the not-so-distant past. Gwen lunged forward, but he stopped her.

"Hold on," he said. "Let me make sure no murderers are lurking in the shadows."

She pushed by him. "I dare a murderer to come between me and that cinnamon roll." She ripped the wrapper off and began eating. "Little stale but okay."

Charlotte followed her cousin's lead, going for a loaf of bread on the next table. "This is so good." She spoke with her mouth full. "Nothing has ever tasted this good. This is way better than that weird fairy food."

Rasq wasn't so quick to dive in. He ventured through a doorway leading to another room.

Desmond checked behind a counter made of rough stone and found no sign of a threat. To the left of the front door was a dining room with chairs and tables, clean and neat like everything else they'd seen so far in Quillet Village. The tables were set with ordinary plates and silverware.

"Creepy, isn't it?" Gwen startled him.

"It's all so...human. This could easily blend in with our world. I guess I expected it to look stranger, like the fairy village."

"The fairy village looked human enough. They just built their buildings with different stuff."

"And their food was different. The food in here is exactly the same as what we'd eat at home."

"Good, too. You should eat some while you can. You don't know when we'll see the next."

He agreed and went back to the store part of the bakery, where Charlotte was still eating.

She said, "I wish we had a bag. Maybe they have one we can take."

"Go easy. I think we're stealing," Desmond said.

Rasq returned. "If we are, there's no one to catch us. I checked the kitchen. We're the only ones here."

Desmond pulled apart a small loaf of something that smelled like banana bread. "I hope we can find the seer. This place looks abandoned."

Rasq finally picked up some breakfast as well. He said, "Sure seems like they must have left in a hurry."

Gwen opened a door behind the counter. "This looks like a refrigerator. Ooh, milk!" She pulled out a glass bottle, drank from it, and promptly spat it out. She wiped her mouth with the back of her forearm. "Not milk."

Desmond chuckled. "I guess not everything is the same. What does it taste like?"

"Bitter. Like that time we tried to eat flowers when we were little."

"I think you tried to eat flowers. Is there anything else?"

"Juice? It's pink." She pulled out a pitcher and smelled it.

Charlotte went to the counter. "I'll try it this time."

Rasq carried his breakfast to the door. He stood there, eating, glancing up and then down the street.

"Why would they leave?" he asked, unable to let the question go.

Charlotte finished and wiped her hands on the front of her pants. "Our grandmother had to evacuate for a hurricane once. She stayed with my uncle for a while until it passed. Maybe the people here evacuated."

Desmond stood in the door next to Rasq and said, "That would explain why they left quickly. Of course, when the lady on the news predicts a storm back home, the first thing everyone does is go to the grocery store."

"The shelves would be empty." Rasq nodded.

"Unless they didn't have time to..." Desmond detected movement to his left and pulled Rasq back inside. "Look." He pointed.

A shadow spanning the width of the street passed in front of the bakery. It moved in silence, gliding in a straight path, directly over the road and toward the base of mountains beyond the edge of the village.

"Was that an airplane?" Charlotte ran to the window.

Desmond checked to make sure nothing else was coming and then stepped into the street. "It looks like a giant bird."

"Whatever it was, it's gone for the moment. We should knock on some doors. Maybe we can find someone who knows where the seer, Bensai, is," Rasq suggested. He told Gwen, "You and Charlotte take this side of the street. Desmond and I will go across."

The cousins headed toward the first porch on the building next to the bakery.

Charlotte smoothed her messy hair. "Maybe I should do the talking if someone answers the door."

"Why? You think I can't handle strangers?"

"I think you're too quick to argue, cousin dearest."

"You're crazy. You argue way more than I do." She kept her tone cheerful.

"I don't know what you're talking about," Charlotte said.

"Oh, yes you do, and so does that boy who always offers to carry your books for you in school. He told me you were late to class the other day because you wouldn't leave Mr. Fariss alone about his ties."

"The last one had cartoon dogs printed on it. I was just trying to help him get a date."

Rasq looked both ways before crossing the street. "Do those two ever quit?"

"I actually thought they were getting along better."

Down the row they went, house to house, shop to shop. They knocked on doors. They peeked into windows. Every building was abandoned. Near the end, Gwen came to an unlocked door. She turned the knob.

"Don't do that," Charlotte said. "You'll make them angry."

"No, I won't."

Desmond and Rasq overheard the conversation and joined Charlotte on the porch. Gwen ventured a couple of feet inside the door, and when nothing bad happened immediately, they went in after her.

"Is anyone home?" she called out.

No reply.

They were in a house, which appeared, perhaps, a little off to the left of human. It contained furniture, chairs, tables, and a sofa, a brass lamp next to the window. While that was all well and cozy, certain elements didn't fit with the human aesthetic. The carpet was grass trimmed to a half an inch long. Rather than wallpaper, paint, or family photos, a garden of vines and tiny bunches of flowers grew in planters mounted to the wall.

"Smells nice." Charlotte still seemed wary of the place.

"My house is going to look exactly like this," Gwen said. "It's brilliant. I'll never have to be inside, even when I am inside."

They went back outside.

CHAPTER 20

"Should we wait and see if they come back?" Desmond asked.

"There." Charlotte pointed past the edge of the building. "A sign pointing away from the village."

Shaped like an arrow, it leaned in the dirt, angled toward the edge of a nearby forest. A dirt path ran by it, into the trees. After another search of the sky, they left the porch.

Rasq read the sign aloud. "Old Quillet Village."

The word "Old" had been scrawled onto the wood in blue instead of the black used to paint the other words. The sign itself looked old as well, faded by the weather, except for the newest word addition.

"Where better to evacuate Quillet Village than Old Quillet Village?" Desmond asked.

"The name sounds weird now. You've gone and said it too many times." Gwen set off down the path.

"Excuse me. I didn't know there was a limit."

The tree canopy was thick, making day in the forest look more like a shadowy dusk. It was quiet, with only the occasional small bird or animal rustling in the brush. A cloud of shiny dragonflies hovered just off the trail.

"Ooh, so pretty!" Gwen started toward them.

Rasq stopped her. "Wait. You don't know what else is out there."

The carpet of plant life grew thick and tangled, vines and stems, leaves competing for meager shafts of daylight. The forest floor was completely concealed.

Charlotte added, "Could be snakes."

"I like snakes," Gwen said but decided against pursuing her communion with dragonflies, just the same.

Desmond, Gwen, and Charlotte followed Rasq, who plowed ahead as if he knew where he was going. Deeper in the forest, where giant ferns grew like prehistoric jungle plants, they walked without speaking to one another, which was alright with Desmond. He was tired of hearing people argue and just tired in general.

After a while, they came to a solid bridge made of wood. Beneath the bridge, a ravine ran from as far as they could see left to as far as they could see right, and it was packed with enormous but wispy, white spiders, moving like ghosts among the fern leaves.

"They look like they could blow away on a breeze. I wonder what they eat," Gwen said.

"They filter nutrients from the air as they breathe." A voice came from further down the bridge.

It was a man dressed in a straw hat and a dark robe with a belt. His features were amphibious, pale green skin glistening with moisture, enormous frog eyes. Leaning hard on a white walking stick, he was almost as tall as Rasq but hunched over. He moved to a spot next to Gwen at the railing.

He pointed with the stick. "They migrate along the floor of the ravine, miles to the west. There, they lay eggs and journey back here to die."

Charlotte sighed. "That's so sad."

"Not sad. Just life." He shrugged. "I'm Bensai. Might I inquire what business you have in our fair village?"

Rasq answered for the group. "My name is Rasq. This is Gwen, Charlotte, and Desmond. The fairy queen said you could help us find someone."

Desmond said, "We're looking for a tree stag called Elm. He stole something from us. We need to get it back."

Bensai rubbed his chin thoughtfully. "You're human, aren't you?"

Gwen replied, "Yes. What does that have to do with anything?"

"Well, you see, my people aren't very fond of your kind right now, especially the situation your ways put us in."

"What does that mean?" Desmond asked.

Bensai sat on the bridge and dangled his frog feet off the side. "It's your influence that's a risk to us. Your very presence is a risk to all the realms through which you pass."

Desmond said, "We have no intention of influencing anything. We plan to get what we came for and leave."

"Intentions and consequences don't always align, do they? If you are unable to go on, no more seers will look on visions of your world and feel the envy I did. We modeled our village after what I saw through another human traveler, and look what it got us. We went against our nature and were nearly eaten by the molebat."

Charlotte said, "Wait a minute. You're blaming us because you made a mistake?"

"He's bonkers." Gwen walked away. "The fairy queen was wrong. He doesn't know anything. Let's go."

"I know about your predicament with the bookshop. I dreamed of Castle, the way he sleeps. He's trapped in darkness," the frog man called after her.

"If you refuse to help us, what you know means nothing."

"I might be persuaded by an apology."

Desmond asked, "An apology?"

"If you want my help, you'll do as I request."

Rasq held up his hands. "Alright, alright. Whatever you need. Just get on with it."

Bensai stood once more. He hobbled to the far side of the suspended far above the forest floor and connected by bridges and swings. More amphibious people were there, cooking in big pots over fires or carrying big baskets of leaves. Children chased one another between the houses.

Bensai cupped his hands around his mouth and yelled, "Citizens of Quillet Village! Kindly assemble."

The five of them waited as the people assembled. Young, old, every age between, they arranged themselves in a group at the bottom of the steps leading down from the bridge, and Desmond suddenly felt very much on display, elevated above the rest of them on a kind of stage. And no one in the audience looked particularly happy to be there.

Bensai spread his arms wide. "My wonderful brothers and sisters! I realize you haven't been happy with me the last few days."

A collective grumble passed through the crowd.

"Ambassadors from the human realm have come to apologize for our situation. As you can see, they are very remorseful." He waved at the humans behind him, a plea for them to play along. They did so with a round of halfhearted nods.

Rasq stepped forward and without bothering to hide his irritation, announced, "People of Quillet Village, on behalf of the humans, I would like to offer our deepest apologies for the hardship we've caused with our influence. We had no idea the power we possessed."

Bensai applauded, and slowly, the crowd did as well. Desm-ond wasn't sure the seer accomplished what he'd set out to with this little show, but Rasq had done what he requested.

Bensai said, "They have also personally assured me, they will never influence us again." He nodded at Rasq, and Rasq agreed. "Good boy. Good boy." He addressed the crowd once more. "You may all return to whatever you were doing."

The crowd dispersed, still grumbling, still clearly not happy with almost being killed by the molebat, whatever that was.

Bensai turned from the village. "I'm so glad you four came to me. They might forgive me now that you've apologized. Let's get you back the way you came."

"Now that you've conned us into taking your blame," Charlotte said.

"Oh no, sweet plum, you can't see it that way. For proper perspective, see it thus. You helped me as much as I could be helped, and I shall help you. A fair exchange, wouldn't you say?"

"As long as we get what we came for." Desmond doubted the seer could help them much at all.

"Tell me, how accurate was the village? How close to human did we get?"

"Close. The food was spot-on."

"Good. I suppose this is far enough." He clapped his webbed hands together once. "Now, let's find this Elm character." He closed his eyes and tilted his head back. "Mmmm...he's running in the fire but tiring, and they're gaining. What's that he's got?" Bensai drew a long breath. "Treasure. Priceless. The vessel is dangerous cargo, even while empty."

"How could he possibly still be running?"

"They've kicked him out twice, but he goes back down. It is the fastest route to the star. Not the smartest or the safest but definitely the fastest. Soon...," Bensai trailed off.

"Soon, what?" Gwen threw up her hands. "Get on with it, already. I want to go home."

Charlotte, Desmond, and Rasq shushed her.

"Gaining, gaining. Let's try and see where they'll meet." He grimaced, swiveled his head back and forth as if trying to hear. "There. Just about there, the access shaft that opens in the glacier jungle." He blinked. "Why, that's not far at all, just on the other side of the mountains. You got lucky."

"That doesn't sound very lucky," Rasq said. "How are we supposed to climb a mountain?"

"Mountains. Plural. A range of them lies to the west. You'll find help on the first, assuming you get that far. A Keeper lives there."

"Elm told us he was a Keeper. Why should we trust this one?"

"You have two options: trust him or attempt to navigate the mountains in a rather impossible span of time. Can you fly?" He laughed. "You should know Elm's intentions are good."

Desmond asked, "What about Mr. Castle? Can you see him now?"

"Castle. He's in a place of deep darkness but alive. Rasq, he wants you to take over the archive when he's gone. Did you know?"

"No." Rasq stared at the ground.

"Why such disappointment? It may not be an adventurous role, but the archives are very important. Memories die, but records, as long as someone cares about them, live on for centuries, maybe longer." His smile faded. "Another thing. You can't let Elm talk you out of finishing this quest. Arbolettis was a lost cause the moment it crumbled into the abyss."

"Why did it fall?" Charlotte asked.

"Only the caged star knows for sure. I can't see everything, unfortunately." He took a deep breath. "Now for a dangerous part. Take the ruins of the labyrinth up the side of the mountain to the windmill. The Keeper there, his name is Vincent. He will help you find Elm and the vessel." He directed the last part to Rasq who no longer seemed sure about Keepers in general.

He nodded, his reluctance still evident. Apparently, Elm had damaged his notion of what he'd thought a Keeper was. Turned out, they could be just as flawed as everyone else.

Bensai wished them luck. He had one final and terrifying warning for them. "Beware the molebat. She's likely hunting."

Desmond, Charlotte, Gwen, and Rasq left Bensai and his village behind. With darkness coming on quickly, they ventured from the woods and beyond, past the new Quillet Village in all its stoic glory, to the open plain, where the sight of the next leg of their journey struck fear into their hearts.

CHAPTER 21

The mountain angled up from the earth sharply, with no foothills, no gentle swell of the land. It cleaved straight through flat grassland to reach for the darkening sky. The labyrinth ruins Bensai told them about began at the base of the mountain and led up the rocky side, cutting corners, dividing into intersections, and stair-stepping in a jumble of ascending walls.

A mass of shadow, the molebat climbed along the tops of the walls that were still intact. She spit fire like a dragon, big clouds of flame that billowed into the air when she lost patience and long lines of slower burning fires that seemed to cling to the stone in veins of illumination. The fiery place radiated like some terrible sun, the heat of it riding the breeze she made when she beat her leathery wings.

Desmond and the others maintained a silent and horrified awe for most of the way. He worried the molebat would see them before they got there, worried that it would swoop down on them as they moved along with no cover, but she went about her business, and they went about theirs, ever closer, ever hotter among the dry weeds.

They reached the point where direct light fell on the ground, and they ran for the shadow of the first wall. They found a gate ajar.

"No need to lock the door to certain death." Rasq's voice was drowned out by another explosive burst from the molebat. The ground shook under the force of it.

Gwen asked, "What could it be hunting in there?"

"I'm not sure I want to know." Desmond peered inside.

The visible section of the maze was dark and still. He waved the others in after him. They had two options: straight ahead or to the right.

"Which way?"

Rasq pointed to the ground. "We should follow the upward slope as much as possible. We'll know we're heading in the right direction."

"Good idea."

A gust of wind carried a wave of warm ash over the wall next to them. It fell, landed in their hair and clothes and sprinkled the ground with a sound like rain. They crouched, covering their heads with their arms until the shower of ash died.

Charlotte shook blackened pieces from her hair. "I hear it," she whispered.

Desmond could feel the mass of the thing moving on the other side of the wall, heard it sniffing. It exhaled, and its hot breath traveled down the passage, around the corner to where its human quarry remained perfectly still. The molebat rose up, spread its great wings over the tops of the walls and leaped into the sky. It flapped straight above them to look down on its maze.

Desmond flattened himself against the wall, motioned for the others to do the same. He figured the thing probably couldn't see well, given that it was a mix of two animals not known for having stellar vision, but when its beady eyes fell on him, his heart raced, just the same.

The face was more bat than mole, large ears, the snout turned up and the fanged mouth seeming to grin. At the tops of its wings was a pair of thick claws made for digging.

Firelight revealed the brown color and the singed tips of its fur. Its mouth opened and before Desmond could warn the others, it let a series of potent screeches, the force of which loosened pebbles from the passage wall.

They slapped their hands over their ears. Desmond closed his eyes tight. The molebat paused and then unleashed another onslaught of calls.

The wind died, and the heavy presence dissipated. He looked up to see that the monster had moved on.

"Is everyone okay?" he asked.

"Just dandy." Gwen brushed soot from her shirt.

Around a corner, a pile of sticks burned and around the next, embers were dying. Heat seemed to come from all directions, ahead, behind, above. Desmond led the way along the paths, up the side of the mountain. He kept to Rasq's plan of following the incline. With the exception of an occasional pass by the molebat, their way was relatively easy until they came to a part of the labyrinth that had broken.

"Looks like something hit it," Charlotte said.

The walls had crumbled, and the slope was battered into a jagged pile of rubble. They would have to climb it.

"We'll be too exposed. The bat will see us." Gwen kicked a broken piece of stone. "Maybe we should try a different way."

"What if this is the only way? The only right way, I mean." Rasq put his foot up on the first rock to evaluate the surface.

They looked up at their destination, Vincent's windmill. They had come quite a distance and were close enough, then, to make out the details. The building was mounted at a slant so that the top angled out from the mountain rather than straight up. The sails turned slowly, unaffected by the sudden bursts and shifts of wind.

Above the destruction, only four walls lay between Desmond and what he hoped would be the entrance. How could a destination be so close and seem so impossible to reach? It might as well have been miles above.

A fox with the tip of its tail blackened emerged from the rubble. It slunk past them, low and fast, with bigger worries than four human children and then disappeared at the junction from which they'd just come.

"He's got the right idea. I'd love to leave." Gwen looked longingly after it.

Rasq agreed. "Smarter than us, that's for sure."

Desmond said, "Okay, we need to move. Let's take a vote. Climb through or go around?"

The other three voted to climb, though Gwen did so with considerable hesitation.

He assured her, "We'll move as fast as we can."

Rasq said, "The rocks look loose. Watch for sliding. I'm going to stick to the bigger ones."

"Now I'm really glad I'm not wearing the dress and shoes." Charlotte stepped onto a chunk of a wall. "I should thank that fairy queen."

Desmond scanned for signs of the molebat. He found it in a passage several walls down from where they stood, rummaging in the dirt. Small fires burned on the walls.

"We should go, now. It looks busy."

They set into the climb with all the urgency it warranted. Rasq tackled it easily. He was at the top before any of the others got close.

"You're going to have to show me how you do that, sometime," Desmond said.

Rasq remained serious as he watched the molebat. "Coordination requires a different kind of focus. You concentrate more on the outcome, where you want to land, than on the effort needed to get there."

Desmond, Charlotte, and Gwen clambered up the side of the mountain with less grace, shoes sliding on the rocks, hands grasping for pieces that tumbled. Rasq waited patiently and offered his hand to help them up at the top.

The labyrinth continued, with passages leading to their left and to their right. They proceeded to the left and made a turn, which led them closer to Vincent the Keeper's house. They paused at the next junction, while they decided which of the three upward sloping paths to take. All appeared to lead in the same direction, toward the windmill slowly turning above them.

"They can't all be the right way," Charlotte said.

"Thanks for that obvious bit of info." Gwen crossed her arms. "That's kind of the point of a maze."

Her cousin ignored her. "How do we choose this time?"

Desmond replied, "We'll just have to try one. Take a chance."

"Do you hear that?" Rasq raised a hand to quiet them.

Aside from the crackle and sizzle of the fires in the various passages around them and the creak of the windmill, the mountain had gone quiet. No explosions. No echolocation or the flap of great, leathery wings.

He said under his breath, "It's coming."

The molebat burst up from behind a wall, bringing a fresh gale down on them, the corresponding ash an assault in itself. The beast seemed taller, perched upon the wall, more demonic with those piercing eyes and its claws working eagerly.

Desmond grabbed hold of Charlotte's hand and dragged her down the nearest passage. They no longer had the luxury of time to make a conscious choice of paths. There was only away, away from the snapping jaws and the fireballs flying at them from behind and banishing shadows wherever the flames landed. The molebat dropped into the passage.

Desmond made a corner, and found a tall, metal door embedded in the mountain. Without looking back to see who or what was behind, he ran for it, pulled the handle. It didn't budge. Rasq, Charlotte, and Gwen joined him, knocking and pounding and shouting.

The molebat squeezed around the corner. When she saw nothing lay between her and tasty human morsels, she let a fire-laced screech that left streams of flickering flames in lines down the walls. She clawed along the ground, dragging herself by the mole claws.

The door opened. A lanky man about the same age as Desmond's father emerged from the darkness. He started at the sight of the monster and began to close the door. Rasq caught it.

"We need to come in."

The man yanked him inside and grabbed Gwen by her sleeve. Desmond and Charlotte pushed through next. They helped the man slam the door. He grabbed a big lever with both hands and spun it.

The molebat struck the door with enough force to rattle Desmond's teeth. She drew back and hit again.

CHAPTER 22

The man stepped away from the door. "I think that should do it." He nodded. "Probably."

They all moved back, jumping as the molebat threw her weight against the metal again. An explosion rocked the side of the mountain. Rocks crumbled from the ceiling and the walls of the tunnel.

"You're lucky you came tonight instead of tomorrow. Tomorrow, Chirpy will really go all out." The man Desmond presumed was Vincent brushed his shaggy brown hair back from his forehead. He wore a dingy white button-down shirt with the sleeves rolled up and dark trousers.

Charlotte repeated the name in disbelief. "Chirpy? Is that what you call it?"

"What would you call her?"

"Demon," Gwen replied.

"Aw, she's not so bad, just hungry, really. Wait fifty years to eat and see how crabby you get."

The molebat attempted to break through again.

"We'll be more comfortable upstairs in the house." He wheeled around. "A wizard friend of mine put it together for me. I didn't mean for it to end up here, though. I guess when I requested a nice view, this was the locale in his mind, and it does have a nice view when Chirpy isn't running amok."

They moved further into the mountain, into a section dimly lit by small torches, to a set of rickety, wooden stairs. Echoes of the molebat's attempts to break in subsided, much to Desmond's relief.

"My name is Vincent, by the way." The man stopped as he reached the top of the stairs. "What shall I call you?"

"Desmond. And this is Gwen, Charlotte, and Rasq."

The interior of Vincent's house was packed to the gills with machine parts and science equipment, beakers and tubes, Bunsen burners. Furniture was plain but solid, reddish wood with tables in abundance, some holding books with papers jammed inside. Patchwork fabric draped from the ceiling, pinned up here and there and ripped in more than a few places.

"I don't see many of my fellow humans in the realms." He continued into a living room, which was just as cluttered. He dug a couch from beneath bundles of wire and boxes of small, copper pipes, piling the items atop the machine parts on a neighboring coffee table. "Please, have a seat." He batted dust from the cushions. "I'm sure you need to sit down after that ordeal. Would you like some tea?"

Gwen glanced warily back at the doorway. "Are we safe?"

"Ah, yeah. We're safe for tonight, probably. She won't really lose control until tomorrow. That's when the frenzy starts."

"Frenzy?" Charlotte paled and sank onto the couch.

"The last day before she goes back into hibernation is the most dangerous. We'll need to leave in the morning when she's the least active. You are staying, aren't you? I mean, you can go if you want, of course, but it isn't safe to leave." The chain leading down to the Keeper medallion under his shirt shone in the light. "If I may ask, how did you find yourself in this particular corner of the realms?" He started to leave the room and then paused. "That was a yes on the tea, correct? I'd want tea. Actually, I do want tea. I'll just put some on and then whoever wants it can have some."

"Tea is fine. Thank you," Desmond said.

"Do you have any food?" Gwen asked.

Vincent answered her from the other room. "Sure thing. We might as well clean the place out. The molebat will destroy the house once she gets worked up properly. I don't have much, but we'll eat it all." He banged around in the kitchen.

"He seems crazy," Rasq told Desmond in a low voice. "Look at all this stuff." He nodded to a broken clock leaning against the front of a chair. "Some of it isn't even useful."

Charlotte picked at a burnt piece of her hair. "Well, he obviously can't get out much. He lives on top of a mountain. Maybe he just keeps whatever he can get in case he needs it in the future."

Gwen raised an eyebrow. "Since when are you so understanding?"

"I just think we shouldn't be judgmental."

"You judge everyone else."

"That was the old me."

"The old you? That was like two days ago." She frowned. "I think. Has anyone kept track of the time?"

Rasq said, "Don't bother. It's all screwy here. It seems linear while we're in a realm, but the second you cross a border, it can change. You can go from Wednesday back to Monday or morning straight into midnight. In the shop, we have a book called *The Physics of Realm Time*. I tried to read it once, but it was too complex and boring."

Gwen added, "Anyway, don't act like it was a million years ago."

"Let it go," Desmond told her. "We haven't decided whether we should stay here."

"I vote no," Rasq said.

"Do you have somewhere better we can sleep?" Gwen asked, and then she turned to Desmond. "I'm not going out there again, not until tomorrow, at least."

"Me neither," Charlotte agreed.

"We stay, then," Desmond said.

Vincent returned with a large tray weighed down by cups, a teapot, and slices of bread and cheese. "I was quite pleased when the frog people down the way decided to copy human food. I had always wanted to know what it tastes like." He sat in a chair next to the sofa and popped a piece of bread in his mouth.

Desmond asked, "Aren't you human?"

He smiled. "Around here, inquiring about one's race isn't the most polite line of conversation."

Rasq tensed but said nothing. Rather, he took food from the tray, apparently deciding to trust the Keeper well enough to eat. Gwen and Charlotte followed his lead.

Vincent continued. "I am human. I've lived in the realms since I was a toddler, so I haven't had the pleasure of experiencing what our people have to offer. But you didn't come here for stories, did you? May I assist in some way other than offering shelter from our molebat friend?"

Desmond spoke for the group. "Bensai, the seer from the village at the bottom of the mountain, sent us to you. A Keeper called Elm stole something from us. We need to find him. It's a matter of life and death."

"I've never heard of anyone named Elm, but I haven't kept up with my fellow Keepers in some years. What did he take?"

"A vessel–"

Vincent said, "Wait. *The* vessel? As in, the one that can hold starlight?"

"Yes."

"Where did you come across that?"

Rasq said, "The Authors Unknown loaned it to us so that we can save Mr. Castle."

"Castle. He preserves the archives. That would be a priority for them, protecting their work, but why would they entrust a mission so important to a bunch of kids?" He said this more to himself than to his guests.

"Hey! I think we've done pretty well up until now, aside from the theft, which was not our fault," Desmond said.

"We made it through the fairy realm and past that molebat." Charlotte sipped from her cup. "We're fully capable is what we are."

"Fully capable of getting roasted by a molebat. Why you and not a Keeper?"

"I'm his son." Rasq silenced everyone in the room with this declaration.

They stared at him.

CHAPTER 23

Desmond wasn't sure if Rasq meant he was literally Castle's son or if his saying so was just a way to ensure his continued involvement in the rescue. Regardless of his meaning, he'd made his feelings known. If Vincent thought, even for a moment, that he might take over the task, he knew now that wasn't an option.

Vincent cleared his throat. "Well, yes, I guess that would give you an emotional stake, then. What has happened to Castle, exactly?"

Rasq answered, "We don't know. He collapsed. The doors and windows in the bookshop shuttered themselves, so no one can get in or out."

He considered and then said, "I'll help. Of course, I will. I'm obligated as a Keeper." He looked down into his tea. "I met Castle a long time ago, through Lucinda. Her sister and I...we were quite fond of each other. He's a strange soul, appropriately so for his work, I suppose."

They finished eating, and Vincent showed the girls to a room near what would have been the top of the windmill had the building been in its correct, upright position. Like the rest of the place, it was cluttered. Machine parts and books were all over everything, including a spacious but slanting bed, the headboard of which was made of metal scraps welded together. Charlotte picked up a jar of coils from the patchwork quilt and turned it over in her hand.

Gwen went to the window. No pane of glass shielded them from the outside. A breeze tousled her hair as she looked fearfully on the burning labyrinth below.

"This is not safe."

As if in reply, an explosion rocked the base of the mountain. They all ducked.

"She won't come up into the sails. Got herself caught up once. That was excitement enough for both of us. She won't do that again, I think," Vincent said.

"You think." She eyed the bed, likely deciding whether it was far enough away from the window.

Vincent took Rasq and Desmond to a room next door. It was mostly dark and had no bed, only a collection of mismatched chairs and a big desk in the center of the room. Jars hung from clotheslines strung from one corner of the ceiling to the other in rows. Vincent picked up a cane that was leaning against the door frame.

"I've been experimenting with luminary moths." He prodded the hanging jar closest to him.

The moth inside flapped and flickered. It lit up in a pale blue-white glow, and the jars down the line did the same, one at a time, until the room was bright.

"They can charge their internal batteries from the small light bulb in the corner. I've been giving them different plants to eat to see if I can change the color of their light. The only plant that worked was a fog lily. It made them go lavender."

Gwen walked into the room and gasped when she saw them. "Cruel! They're going to die in here." She tugged on the end of the clothesline closest to her, over her head. The jars swayed, clinking together.

"No, no, no, wait." He eased her fingers from the line. "They hatch in small tunnels below the ground. They like small spaces." He steadied the swinging jars. "I suppose I should let them go before we leave tomorrow." He reached up. "There's a hook and a latch. Just flick it to the left. The jar comes loose." He brought it down for them to see. "We'll take the jars out to the balcony. They can fly from there."

Gwen found this solution acceptable. They set to work, each carrying two jars at a time through the cluttered living room, to the small balcony at the back of the windmill. They opened the lids, and the moths crawled to the top and lifted into the sky, silent and vivid in the darkness.

As Desmond and the others worked, the pile of empty jars grew, and a river of light formed in the sky, over a vast body of water at the center of a ring of mountains.

When they were finished, Charlotte leaned on the railing to watch the moths. "Will the molebat go after them?"

"She prefers meatier prey. Even if she didn't, she's on the other side of the mountain in the maze."

The five of them stayed on the balcony for a while, keeping each other company in the comfortable silence they all seemed to need. Even the molebat calmed down. She ceased her explosions, and with that, the mountain cooled and grew still in the night, the way mountains are supposed to be.

Finally, Charlotte stretched and yawned. "I'm sleepy. Gwen?"

"I'm coming."

They shuffled off to bed. Rasq went shortly thereafter, which left Vincent and Desmond alone together on the balcony.

"Bensai told us we'd find Elm in the glacier jungle. Do you know where it is?"

"I do." He pointed over the water. "The mountains on the far side of the lake are made of ice. Beyond them, a conduit brings the heat from Cosalis into this realm. It melts the glacier and generates humidity, which creates an ideal environment for the wilds on the other side. I've only seen the jungle once, when I first came here. It's a dangerous place on a bad day. We'll have to be careful." He studied Desmond for a moment and then said, "Allos Winters. You look like him. Are you his son?"

His grandfather's legacy was going to follow him around like a shadow. People would continue to judge him for the grandfather he didn't even know.

"Grandson," he admitted.

Vincent repeated, "Grandson. Time in the human realm must move fast. I only met him in passing when he was in the midst of being banished from the Realm of White Sails. They accused him of thievery."

"A lot of people have accused him of thievery."

"Don't worry too much about what people say. Everyone has their motives, and no one can truly understand why another person does anything. Others can claim to know or think they know, but deep down, we're all vast and mysterious. Why did you come, grandson of Allos? Castle isn't your father."

"I can't go home until the bookshop opens, and the shop won't open until Castle wakes."

"No. That may be the reason you ended up on this excursion, but it isn't the entirety of your motivation. There's a certain look in your eye. It reminds me of myself when I was your age. You would be here, regardless, because saving him is the right thing to do. You have the spirit of a Keeper within you."

Desmond hadn't thought much about the doors in the bookshop in a while. He hadn't questioned whether he should keep going or return and wait for someone to save him. Since his dinner with the fairy queen, he'd only really thought about how to move forward. There was no going back without the vessel filled with starlight, not even if he knew he could escape the bookshop, not anymore. He had changed.

"You don't have to go home, you know." Vincent tossed out the idea. "The realms have more than enough adventure for our lifetimes."

"Stay in the realms?"

The possibility hadn't occurred to him. He considered what going back meant, the school day routines, Mrs. Dunwiler fussing over every little thing for him, the house seeming so much emptier when his parents were off having their own adventures. How much would they really miss him?

"I couldn't."

"Yeah, yeah you could." A smile crept across Vincent's face. "The Keepers, we're an old order. Even before I left on hiatus, our numbers were dwindling. Devoting one's life to heroics has fallen from fashion. We need people like you and your friends."

"I'll think about it." Desmond didn't really have a choice but to think about it with the idea planted in his mind. "Why are you on hiatus?"

He sighed. "My last assignment took a lot out of me. I failed, actually. Four of us were assigned to escort a dignitary from his realm to Pandresian City. Our caravan was attacked. We did manage to get him back, but he and the Council of Elders were none too pleased with us. Our group scattered after that, and I ended up here. It was a nice enough spot until the molebat emerged from hibernation."

"I'm sorry." Desmond wasn't sure what to say to make him feel better.

Vincent looked out over the water. "You should go get some sleep. We have running to do in the morning. At first light, we embark." He made a motion with his hand like an airplane flying over the water.

Back in the moth room, Rasq was curled up in a chair, under a pile of blankets. He removed one of them from himself and tossed it to Desmond.

"Did you mean what you said, that Castle is your father?" Desmond moved the junk from the seat of a battered armchair so he could sit down.

"No. I've suspected, though. Why else would a nymph leave

her kid at his door? And why would he bother taking me in? You've seen him. He isn't exactly the parental type. Doesn't matter, anyway. He's enough father for me." He paused. "I heard what Vincent said to you, about having the spirit of a Keeper. He should've said that to me. You wouldn't even be here without me. You wouldn't even know the realms existed." He spoke these words not with anger but with a kind of disappointment.

"I didn't ask him for his opinion."

"You just don't deserve the comparison is all I'm saying." Rasq nestled into the chair and closed his eyes.

CHAPTER 24

A tremendous slam startled Desmond awake the next morning. He shot up in the chair. He was alone in the room. Legs tangled in the knitted blanket, he fell forward onto the floor, kicked it away to free himself.

Gwen appeared over him. "What are you doing? Get up!"

A hard hit rattled the windmill down to its frame. Machine parts and papers avalanched. The floor creaked, a discontented sound of a thing about to snap.

Desmond ran after Gwen into the living room. At the center of the floor, the rug had been thrown back to reveal a large trapdoor underneath.

Vincent in a pair of tinted goggles popped up from below. "Good morning. She got started earlier than expected. I'm glad I decided to stay up all night to get the air canoe ready."

The windmill took another hit, and the floor tilted dangerously, driving Desmond to his knees. Glass shattered. Plates crashed. Charlotte shouted. She and Rasq were with Vincent, in a deep cart equipped with various mechanical apparatuses inside and out.

Rasq offered his hand to Gwen, and she took it and hopped down next to him. Desmond made a significantly less graceful entry, falling into the cart, landing hard on the wood.

Before Desmond could get up, Vincent said, "Ready? Good, then, we're off," and yanked a long lever. "Hold on, kids. This might get rough."

They gripped the sides as the cart clattered down a rail, sloping, angling sharply as if it might toss them out. They crossed into daylight, and the track hooked up into the air, into the bright of dawn glaring on the windshield and wind coming from over the water. They flew until gravity took hold. Time seemed to stand still. Then, quick as Vincent could discover his next lever had decided to be stubborn, the plummet began. The nose of the cart dipped, and the sparkling surface of the lake rushed toward them.

Vincent propped his foot on the wall to get leverage. Gwen, who was closest, helped, and Desmond joined the effort. They pulled until the lever flipped and locked into place.

Wings fanned out from the sides. A patchwork balloon that looked suspiciously like the fabric that was previously draped from Vincent's ceiling shot up from the front end and inflated over their heads.

He whirled around to press a series of buttons, which caused something, somewhere on their vehicle to sputter to life. Steam hissed from the rear of the cart. He went back to the control panel, grabbed hold of a steering stick and pulled back, rocked back on his heels in his strain against their downward arc. The wings shook violently.

"Come on," he growled through clenched teeth. "Work."

The nose of the cart raised, then hesitated, then leveled, and they were shooting across the water, close enough to carve a wake and startle several ducks. Vincent coaxed the machine higher and higher until their situation seemed, as such, that they might not plummet to their deaths that morning.

He tapped a few gauges. Satisfied with the altitude, he turned and grinned. "That went better than it could have." He rested his arm on the steering stick.

Gwen, her face a pale, celery green, vomited over the side of the cart. She wiped her mouth with the back of her hand.

Vincent added, "I probably should've installed seat belts. I didn't expect that rough of a ride."

The compartment in which they rode had the depth of a hot air balloon basket. It had no seats, only control panels, levers, and other machine parts. The more Desmond evaluated their ride, the less safe he felt. It seemed too heavy a thing to stay in the air, too incomplete.

From behind them, a great crash echoed over the lake. The sound drew itself out into a series of explosions, the breaking of wood and stone. Rubble flew in all directions. They all paused to watch Vincent's home dissolve into oblivion.

He sighed. "I really liked that house."

The molebat clawed up from the debris, a monster of the most gargantuan sort, worthy of a movie in which civilians ran screaming in the streets.

"Did it get bigger?" Charlotte asked with horror.

The creature let open its maw and unleashed a screech, an echolocation call, only this one could be the death of them. Over the water, in the air, they had nowhere to hide.

"It's looking for us," Desmond told Vincent. "We need to go faster."

"I am aware of both those facts. However, the air canoe isn't built for speed or maneuverability."

Gwen asked, "What is it built for?"

"Holding us aloft, my dear, which reminds me. We've probably exceeded the optimal weight limit. I built this for me and some scientific equipment." He put the goggles on top of his head and squinted at his altitude gauge. "If I had known you were coming, I would have planned accordingly."

Another shriek tore across the water. Chirpy climbed higher on the rubble and spread her wings. She bowed her head, and fell forward, caught the wind and flapped. She soared, slightly higher than the air canoe until another echolocation call gave her a better bead on their position.

"Rasq, man the bellows at the back," Vincent ordered. "It won't give us a big boost, but at this point, I'll take what I can get."

The bellows looked like the one hanging above the fireplace in Desmond's parents' room - a pair of spade-shaped boards with an accordion in the middle and a nozzle at the opposite end of the handles.

"How do I work it?"

Desmond showed him. "Like this."

Charlotte asked Vincent, "What else can we do?"

He thumped the altitude gauge with two fingers. "We're too heavy." He looked around. "Lose anything that isn't a part needed for flying. In a duffel bag in that corner are a hammer and a mallet."

A fireball whizzed by them on the left, missed them by only a few yards. A second fireball followed on the other side. Vincent pulled hard left on the steering stick. The canoe complied with a wheeze and a chorus of snapping sounds that did not inspire confidence.

Desmond rummaged for the tools and handed the mallet off to Charlotte. Gwen snatched it from her.

"I'm stronger," she said. "I'll pound. You pull."

Together, they loosened a wooden box with a hinged lid. It broke free and tumbled down into the water.

Desmond went at a folded umbrella, the base of which was bolted down. He bent the thin metal bracket and then twisted and gave it a firm hit with the hammer. Rasq broke from the bellows. He snapped part of the umbrella handle, and it took flight, twisting and springing open before spinning away.

Another fireball shot over their heads, sprinkling hot embers onto the balloon. Then came another shriek from the molebat.

The air canoe passed into a thick fog, a vapor with equal parts moisture and chill. The temperature dove.

Vincent's breath steamed in the air as he spoke. "Here we go. Yes!"

"I think the molebat is slowing down," Rasq announced.

Chirpy faded from view as she gave up the chase and stopped spitting fireballs. The mountains behind them and the lake, too, disappeared behind a gray veil. In the instant Desmond relaxed, he also realized they could see nothing around them. The world became featureless.

CHAPTER 25

Desmond went to Vincent's side. "Do you know where you're going?"

"Yes. Roughly. There's a ridge ahead. On the other side of that is the glacier jungle. Oh no." Vincent stepped back from the console.

"What?" Charlotte leaned around the windshield.

Desmond looked around the other side. "A beach?"

"A snow beach with women on it," she added.

"Let me see." Gwen pushed by Desmond. "Why do they look so mad?"

Vincent backed further away, to the rear of the air canoe. "Oh dear. Guess that means they saw me."

Gwen flinched away from something hitting the front of the air canoe with a clink. "They're throwing shards of ice at us," she reported.

Desmond looked again. A group of four women with silvery hair, pale-as-snow skin, and deep, dark eyes glared up at them. Enraged, they pelted the flying machine with shards manifesting in their hands. The hull took a beating from an assault that swelled into a hail storm from below.

"What did you do to make them so angry?" Desmond shouted to be heard over the barrage.

"Ice nymphs." He grinned sheepishly and shrugged. "They can be a bit over-sensitive in matters of romance."

The nymphs chased them, running across the ice and snow. A howl from one of them began as mournful only to climb into a rage-fueled scream. Vincent winced.

Desmond asked, "A bit over-sensitive?"

Charlotte pointed. "Should this light be blinking?"

"We're falling again," Rasq said.

Desmond pulled back on the steering stick, growling. Vincent took over, but the canoe refused to deviate from the gradual descent. The lower they sank, the faster it moved, accelerating toward the white-on-white below.

"The ice crystals are sticking." Charlotte plucked one from the outside of the boat and held it up for them to see.

"To the back of the canoe, all of you. We're going to crash." Vincent pushed Desmond back. "Get low. Hold on."

Desmond crouched with the others. He closed his eyes and listened.

There came a swish of the hull across snow.

Vincent saying, "Come on. Just make the ridge."

The crash as the full weight of the canoe came down.

Icy ground grinding the hull, splintering the wood.

A crack followed by the windshield breaking free.

The gust of wind as it sailed over their heads.

And then, weightlessness, falling.

The floor receding from beneath him.

Air left his lungs, and he thrashed. He clawed to the surface of water, thinking, curiously, how he didn't remember the splash as he landed there. He gasped in the humidity, his head spinning. The smell of the place was a mix of spicy greenery and moss.

He turned in the lukewarm water. Against a lavender sky, a waterfall poured from the top of a sheer ice wall, into a lagoon surrounded by blue vines and lush trees. A few feet away, the canoe was sinking, about to disappear forever. Gwen and Charlotte were close to the muddy beach. Vincent towed an unconscious Rasq in the same direction.

Desmond paddled over. On land, gravity weighed him down, and he resisted an urge to lie in the mud and rest.

Vincent dragged Rasq, who was very pale, onto the beach. He hovered over him, saying his name, patting his face. The girls were there, too, wearing similar expressions of worry.

CHAPTER 26

Vincent put his ear down to see if Rasq was breathing. "He seems okay. He'll come around if we give him a minute," he assured the rest of them and himself. "What about you three? Anything more than bumped or bruised?"

They confirmed they were fine.

While they waited for Rasq to come to, they cleaned themselves up the best they could. Desmond rinsed the mud from his shirt and wrung it out. He shook the water from his hair. He found a couple of scrapes but no substantial injuries.

Gwen dabbed blood from a cut on Charlotte's head. Vincent lay back on the beach next to Rasq and closed his eyes. They had gotten lucky; Desmond thought. The crash could've been much worse.

After he felt sufficiently recovered, he went to Vincent. "I'm going to walk around a little and see if Elm has been here."

"I don't think that's a good idea. If we get separated, I can't help you."

"I'll stay within earshot."

Vincent relented. "Come back if you see or hear any wildlife. This jungle has some nasty snakes and a cat beast with too many claws for its own good."

"I'll go with him," Gwen volunteered.

The two of them parted the foliage and stepped into the wild. Tangles of vines carpeted the jungle floor, twined up the trunks of trees to sprout lilies in shades of orange, red, and white with specks of brown. Bushes, roughly the size and shape of men, stood watch like green guardians, startling

Desmond whenever he caught one he hadn't seen before out of the corner of his eye. The canopy of tree leaves swayed in a breeze. They found no trace of Elm.

"Des?" Vincent called after a few minutes.

"We're over here," he replied.

"Rasq is awake. We should be able to move on shortly."

"Got it."

Desmond sensed a kind of apprehension in the atmosphere, like a storm was brewing, however, the day remained bright and serene. He ventured further into the wild through a row of grass taller than him.

"I don't get it. Why is it so warm here when we're right next to the ice?" Gwen asked.

"Vincent says there's a heat vent close by. A pipeline of sunshine, sort of."

What he saw on the other side of the grass wall stopped him.

Nestled in a depression in the earth, several meters away from them, was a square platform made of brick. A spire of light traveled from the earth to the sky in a great and silent tower, shimmering, twisting, tiny stars shooting along the stream. It was pure radiance, and he knew, he saw the miracle capable of bringing Castle back from the brink of death.

"Cosalis." Desmond managed to whisper the name. He tilted his face toward the sky where the starlight spread like fire, a tree of life pouring its energy into the realm.

"Pretty," Gwen said, awestruck.

"Very pretty."

"Desmond?" Vincent called. "Gwen?"

"Over here."

Vincent, Charlotte, and Rasq emerged from the wall of grass. Rasq's face was red, perhaps with embarrassment.

"What is that?" Charlotte asked.

Vincent smiled. "That, my dear, is a conduit. It channels the light and warmth from Cosalis into the realms. I would bet this is where we'll find your rogue Keeper." He started down the hill.

Desmond had an idea. "If we get the vessel back from Elm here, can we fill it at the conduit?"

"Wouldn't that be convenient?" Vincent said. "Unfortunately, no. The star energy here is diluted and relatively weak. Otherwise, it would blow the realm apart. You need the pure stuff, only available at the star itself. Sorry. Good thinking, though."

Charlotte trotted up from behind them. "So, if this is diluted, the star is even stronger and hotter. How will we get close enough to draw the light?"

"Pandresian City. An order of monks there used to care for Cosalis. They lived around the star and worshipped it. The tunnel they used to transport supplies down to their home is in the heart of the city. We'll have to head that way and hope for the best."

"Well, that's not very assuring," Rasq muttered. "There's an access shaft over there." He motioned to the left of the platform, to a much more modest structure. It looked just like the one from which they'd been ejected, the round door and the stone base.

"Bensai told us Elm was being chased," Desmond said.

"Those spider robot things." Gwen grimaced at the memory. "I bet that's where they'll kick him out."

They took up a position on higher ground to wait. Several minutes passed, and then a half-hour went by with no movement at the access shaft. The day grew warmer. Everyone began to lose patience.

Gwen asked, "How long do we have to stay here before we decide he isn't coming?"

Rasq shushed her.

"Well, that was very rude."

"You talk too much. Always an argument."

Unwilling to prove him right, she crossed her arms and resigned herself to pouting.

Not long after that, the ground shook, the tremble traveling from the bottom of the hill to the access shaft, where the heavy, metal door burst open. A flailing streak of white popped straight up into the air, howling, and tumbled across the ground. A robotic arm pulled the door shut.

Elm heaved himself awkwardly up to stand. He scanned his surroundings, clenched his fists, and roared. He kicked a rock at the base of the access shaft and then pounded on the door.

"You don't know what you've done." He laid his head with its wide rack of birch branch antlers on the door. "You just don't know."

"I'll go talk to him." Vincent started to stand.

"Wait," Desmond said. "Let me do it."

"Why you?"

"I can do this. Just trust me."

After dealing with years of conflict between Gwen and Charlotte, he knew how to defuse tension. He'd broken up fights between other kids at school before they escalated, worked out compromises with his teachers on the rare occasions they didn't like his work. He could handle this.

Vincent warned him, "Be careful. He might be dangerous."

Desmond approached Elm slowly in order to show he didn't mean to rush him, not that an unarmed and smallish human had any hope of overpowering such a large creature. A feeling of vulnerability took hold once he'd left their hiding spot behind. He gathered his courage.

The tree stag gave up trying to get back into the access shaft. He turned and sat with his back against the base. He didn't notice anyone else was there until Desmond had reached the bottom of the hill. They stared at one another in silence, at first.

"How did you get here so fast?" Elm asked. The strap attached to the vessel was looped around his wrist.

"You know time in the realms. It feels normal and linear, and then you cross a border and find that it isn't." He felt Rasq glaring at his back. Now Desmond was stealing ideas and lines. He might be a thief, after all. "Will you please return the vessel to us?"

"No."

"It can't bring back your realm."

Elm buried his face in one long-fingered hand. "This was my only hope. I have to fix it. I failed all of them. I failed Arbolettis. You can't understand."

"You're right. I really don't understand. No one could, but we need the vessel to save someone's life." He remembered the clout Lucinda's name carried in the realms. She had saved Cosalis. He said, "Lucinda would– "

"Lucinda. Lucinda didn't save Arbolettis. Why would I care about her?"

"She saved you."

"My life is nothing. I am nothing."

Desmond switched tactics. "Do you know of Castle? What he does?"

"No."

"He keeps the archive. The Authors Unknown write books about the realms, including Arbolettis, I'm sure."

"Words on paper are worthless to me."

"Arbolettis is alive in those books, the memory of it, and if Castle dies, the memory of what was written there is lost."

That was true, in a way. Without anyone to care for the books, they would get separated, sold (assuming the bookshop ever let anyone in or out), and classified as fiction.

"But if there is hope for my people, I must keep going. To give up is to condemn my world a second time. Do you know how many souls an entire realm holds?"

Elm was tired of running, tired of clinging to the glimmer of hope the vessel had become. He held on because it was the only reason he had to keep going, because he felt obligated to make up for his failure to protect his own realm. Desmond had to give him a better reason to let go.

He eyed the Keeper medallion. "Did you swear to protect all realms or just one?"

Elm stated flatly, "The rest don't matter to me."

"They mattered to you, once. You would sacrifice this man, one who serves all the realms, for nothing."

He growled. "Arbolettis isn't nothing."

He jumped to his feet, loomed over Desmond with his considerable height. He curled his fingers into fists. The dark pools of his eyes shimmered with new rage. He dipped his head to threaten with the wide rack of antlers atop his head.

Desmond didn't remember them looking so sharp back in Nola Junction. He held his ground, and then, remembering his friends hiding nearby, he made a subtle motion with his hand behind his back, a signal for them to stay where they were. He didn't want them scaring Elm off.

"Arbolettis is gone. Nothing can bring it back, not even Cosalis."

The Keeper's fiery rage died as quickly as it had come on. "I know."

"Please. Let us save Castle and the archive. The memory of Arbolettis is still there."

Elm looked away, into the jungle with its thriving trees and blue vines. He turned to the tower of starlight streaming into the lavender sky.

He let the leather strap fall from his wrist, and he handed over the vessel. "You should know, drawing the light from Cosalis is no easy task. This heat is nothing compared to the full power of the star."

Desmond put the strap around his neck. "We'll figure out a way. We have to. You could come with us."

Despite what Elm had done, there was something heroic about him. He could be an asset if they gained his loyalty, and they needed all the help they could get.

"Why? You can't trust me. You must know if I see the faintest possibility of saving my realm, I would do whatever is necessary, including betray you."

"What would you rather do? Go back to Nola Junction and rot in a pile of rags? You're a Keeper. You should be helping us."

Elm sneered. "And you are a child. You should remember that. Elders do not appreciate lectures from younglings."

Vincent, Charlotte, Gwen, and Rasq left their hiding spot. With Vincent at the lead, they descended the hill toward Desmond and Elm.

"I see your little group gained a member."

Vincent stopped in front of Elm and put out his hand for a handshake. "Always nice to meet a fellow Keeper."

Elm didn't take his hand. "You should have come instead of sending a small boy to negotiate."

"Hey, I'm not that small."

Vincent said, "He wanted to come himself. He's capable of making his own decisions."

"You're a coward."

"And you stole from them, which makes you worse than me."

Elm's face twisted into a snarl. "I did it for the good of Arbolettis."

Desmond planted himself between them. "Which way to Pandresian City?"

"That direction." Vincent nodded toward the other side of the clearing. "A long walk."

"We'd better get moving, then."

CHAPTER 27

The jungle was interesting, at first. Desmond spent an hour or so of their walk to Pandresian City pointing out oversize toadstools or flying squirrel creatures playing among the tree branches, their long, feathered tails streaming behind them. It all looked familiar yet simultaneously alien, perhaps a distant cousin of what constituted nature in the human realm. Leaves looked like leaves, but the colors or sizes or shapes weren't quite like the ones back home.

Gwen took delight in their surroundings as well, exploring this new world with all the curiosity it deserved. She plucked a lily from a vine and stuck it in her hair, only to have her stomach turn at the smell of it. Later, she knelt before a puddle. Before she could put her hand into what she thought was water, the liquid solidified into a coiled snake, which snapped at her fingers. Another incident involved a rose that burst into flames when skin made contact with its petals.

They waded through deep patches of foliage, hid when they thought a large animal wandered close. The day grew more oppressive as it went on, apparently creating an optimal condition for biting gnats to engage in feeding frenzies.

In the afternoon, all Desmond could think about was a cool glass of water. He even lost the desire for food, which was strange given that they didn't have any breakfast or lunch. He attempted to keep himself cool by picturing the glacier wall and the snow beyond. This strategy worked for a minute or so at a time, until his need for hydration smothered the daydream.

All they had was plants, forever blue vines and flowers. The bushes that looked like men became an irritation. They taxed his senses, their presence and their size. He avoided paying them any attention.

Elm was the first to give an outward indication of his discomfort. As he passed a tree, he reached out and yanked a vine from it, and tossed it aside in disgust.

"This is taking too long. Does anyone have any water?" he asked.

"We didn't have a chance to gather supplies," Vincent replied.

"Fine bit of a mess."

Charlotte trotted ahead. "The end of the trees!"

Gwen went after her. "Wait for me!"

Desmond didn't have the energy to try to stop them. Whatever they found beyond the jungle had to be better.

"Are you alright?" Vincent asked.

"I'll be fine." Admitting that he was light-headed and desperately thirsty only would've made him feel worse.

Rasq didn't look well, either. Judging by his slack expression, the day had worn on him as well.

Elm pushed back the last of the branches between them and an open field. "Thank the realms."

Various shades of mud ranging from a cream color to a deep, ruddy orange striped the ground. A farm field. Not far ahead, between them and a city of thin towers rising in the distance, the girls had met up with a group of several people. Except for the cotton candy tones of the strangers' skin and a certain oddness about their facial features, they appeared human.

Several women there wore flowing dresses, and their long hair was tied into intricate formations of loops. They waited with baskets of food and canteens.

Behind them, five soldiers in uniforms complete with chin-strapped helmets made an imposing line. The spears and shields at their sides were gilded with coppery floral designs.

"Tuck the vessel under your shirt," Vincent advised and then gave the group a friendly wave.

As Desmond did as he was told, he detected movement to his right. A toad with a pink lightning bolt down its back, the same kind of toad Gwen found in the yard at home, wiggled up from the mud.

He knew, then, the realms had called them to this destiny. They were meant to be in that strange place, and the presence of the toad was a sign that they remained on the right path.

He caught up with Vincent and the others, and a soldier with pink skin handed him a leather canteen. He hesitated to drink from it until he saw Gwen sitting on the ground, devouring a strange fruit and Charlotte gulping from a tin cup. Rasq, too, was handed a bottle of some liquid while a woman in a long, brown dress tilted his face up to look into his eyes.

"He has no head injury," she reported. "He must have fainted."

Gwen snickered.

He eased the woman's hand away. "I didn't faint. I'm fine. Thank you."

"Welcome, welcome!" A long-faced man with pale green skin stepped through the line of guards. The crown on his head was a golden framework with what appeared to be feathers from the flying squirrel creatures woven throughout. "Are you feeling better? Not much longer and you would have keeled over, I suspect." He wore a glittery, burgundy cape and equally gaudy sandals that were too big for his feet.

"Greetings, Your Majesty. We thank you for the refreshment. The jungle was stifling." Vincent gave a polite bow, and the Keeper medal tumbled out from beneath his shirt. "King Jacquess, I presume?" As he straightened himself, the king reached for it.

"I see you're a Keeper. Did you train here?"

"Yes, Highness. Many years ago. I am Vincent Graynell."

"Funny. I've never heard of you."

"I'm afraid I was never an exceptional student."

King Jacquess went next to Elm. "You're also a Keeper."

"I was," Elm replied in his rough voice.

"And I'll bet you trained in Arbolettis. They always thought their way of doing things was so much better than everyone else's." The smile remained plastered on his face.

Elm paused to check his temper before saying, "Perhaps that's true."

"What shall I call you?" the king asked.

"I'm known as Elm."

"Elm?" He snorted. "You look more like a birch. I'll call you 'Birch' because that will be easier to remember."

Elm's mouth opened as if to speak, but he swallowed the words.

Jacquess moved down the line to Charlotte and Gwen. "Hello, ladies. I don't suppose you'd like a proper meal, perhaps a bath and some clean clothes?"

"What do you get out of the deal?" Gwen, who was sitting on the ground and munching a rind, asked. "And what are you doing out here? Where I come from, kings don't hang out in fields."

"Gwen!" Charlotte poked her. "Be nice."

"Smart girl." Jacquess patted her on the head. "We should all be nice. All answers in due time. Pandresian City is a lovely place filled with joy and plenty for all. Well, look at this strapping, young fellow. What about you, halfling? How would you like to feast?"

Rasq said simply, "Yes, sir."

"What sort of nymph was your mother, anyway?"

His face burned a deep red. "I don't know."

"Mmm...never could depend on a nymph. They're so flighty. That's what you get with an all-female race, I suppose."

Charlotte put a hand on Gwen's arm to keep her quiet.

The king went on, oblivious to the insults he'd just lobbed at his guests. "I would guess a wood nymph, my favorite. They always smell like pine needles and sage." He scratched his chin. "We can train you to be a Keeper if you decide to stay. How would you like that?"

Rasq perked up, and then he apparently remembered his need to return home. "I'd like to," was all he said.

Jacquess landed lastly on Desmond. The king eyed the bulge under his shirt where the vessel hung.

"You pique my curiosity most of all. What is your name?"

"Desmond Winters."

"Well, Desmond Winters. How does a human boy end up in the glacier jungle with Keepers from two different realms, a halfling, and a pair of girls? And let's not forget that shiny bauble hiding beneath your shirt."

Desmond glanced toward Vincent in a silent plea for advice or assistance and received nothing but a look of dire concern.

Jacquess prompted him, "Well?"

"It's kind of a long story."

Seconds that passed in the pause that followed knocked by at a sluggish gait. He hadn't refused to answer, but he hadn't answered either, and if the king really pressed the issue, Desmond wasn't sure what he would say.

With a stern expression on his face, Jacquess clasped his hands behind his back and bent forward. "Long stories are best told over a meal. Wouldn't you say?"

Terrified, he answered, "Yes, sir."

CHAPTER 28

The king said, "Well then. If you've recuperated well enough, we should return to the city." He spread his arms. "I would've brought transportation, but the day is so lovely. I thought a walk was in order."

"So lovely," Gwen hissed under her breath as she stood.

"If you had come last season, we could've enjoyed the orange pepper crops. The seeds make a fantastic seasoning."

The soldiers positioned themselves between the king and everyone else. He kept prattling on about something or another, but his words were lost in the clatter of armor and the breeze blowing across the field.

Desmond nudged between Elm and Vincent. "What should I tell him?" he asked both Keepers.

"Nothing," Elm said.

"He's going to expect me to tell him something."

Vincent suggested, "You could lie. Make up some story."

One of the soldiers shot a glare over his shoulder. Desmond decided they'd be better off talking about it later when fewer ears were around.

The city entrance, though narrow, was open with foot traffic moving freely in and out. People transporting fruits or vegetables in wagons bowed to the king and moved aside when he got close. A pair of guards at the entrance stood at attention when they saw him approach.

Jacquess moved back through the procession to walk with Desmond. "We trade with a neighboring city not far from here. They provide coal and building materials." He tousled the hair of a small child running by. "We send harvests from our land."

The buildings rising tall around them were made of smooth, pale stone. The architecture was simple, straight lines and flat surfaces, with the only ornamentation being large, kaleidoscopic windows and decorative boxes filled with herbs. Crops grew in patches of soil throughout the city, in fenced yards between the buildings, on balconies or up walls so high, the people used hanging scaffolds to tend them.

The king's party crossed a bridge over a wide canal packed with rafts and turned the corner into a bustling marketplace, where music seemed to come from everywhere, the roadside, the alleyways bending and twisting away. Musicians strummed, clacked, sang songs, or beat on small drums, their songs blending together to create a discordant but somehow pleasant melody.

The snacks offered by the women in the field hadn't done much to fill the void created by their hike through the jungle. If anything, Desmond was even hungrier than before, the pit of his stomach having dropped from beneath the fruit and the water to some unknowable depth in his bones. The smell of meat cooking over a fire reached into this gaping emptiness and squeezed and made him dizzy.

His friends, too, stared at the food carts. Even Elm and Vincent seemed to have trouble restraining themselves. They craned their necks to take in the scents, to get whatever glimpses of food they could.

King Jacquess took great pride in his city. Voice booming over the music and the rumble of the crowd, he conducted their group like it was a tour. He pointed out the various plants and people of note, like the local crop inspector who held his clipboard to his chest as he bowed.

"It's a very important position," the king informed Desmond. "He inherited the title from his father before him. And here, nestled at the foot of the palace steps is our Academy for the Protection of the Realms. We are proud to house many such integral pieces of the machine that is our universe."

They stopped at the open doorway, the arch of which reached high above their heads to nearly touch the edge of the domed ceiling. A plaque next to the door was emblazoned with the Keeper motto - *Fortes Fortuna Juvat.*

In the large, open room he could see from the entrance, a group of kids around Desmond's age sat on the floor. An elderly instructor with a white beard pointed to a map affixed to a rolling stand.

A girl in the front row answered, "Dragon Realm."

The instructor applauded, delighted. "Yes, yes. Very good."

Vincent said quietly, "This brings back memories. I guess I was wrong. I don't have to worry about becoming an endangered species anytime soon."

Jacquess said, "On the contrary, we're growing quite the army. The school did shut down for some years due to a conflict between our city government and the Council of Elders. However, we missed having the Keepers around. They made wonderful protection. We reopened the academy with new instructors, Pandresian instructors." He raised a finger to punctuate the fact.

"Army?" Vincent shook his head. "We aren't soldiers."

"Yes, of course, we realize that." He patted the chest of the soldier closest to him. "That's why we have these fine warriors, but having Keepers around doesn't hurt."

"I suppose not," Vincent conceded.

"Any of you younger ones are welcome to enroll in the academy. We're always on the lookout for new recruits. You must be made of the right stuff if you made it this far from the human realm." He moved on.

Desmond lingered at the doorway. He belonged in that place. It tugged at him, like some gravitational pull toward adventure.

Vincent urged him on. "That's not for us."

The steps leading up to the palace ran the full width of the building. They were made of the same smooth stone as the smaller, residential towers but emitted a shine as if painted with a thin coat of gold.

Like the rest of Pandresian City, the place teemed with activity. A man to their left sold garden implements like trowels and rakes and several types of a more foreign variety that Desmond couldn't identify. Someone else held a bundle of leashes attached to animals she was selling, strange, goat creatures with horse faces. They bleated and pulled against their leashes, snouts fully engaged in smelling whatever the breeze carried their direction.

At the top of the steps, four guards, a pair on each side, hauled open a set of two-story-tall wooden doors. Jacquess went through without acknowledging their presence.

"Welcome to Pandresian Palace!" He held his arms over his head. "You are honored to be here."

The ceiling of the grand hall was made of the same colorful glass as the windows Desmond had seen earlier. Light streaming onto the tile floor was a warm blend of color that gave the place a rosy tint. Set in rows on either side of their path, enormous statues of cranes glowered down on them.

"We have the finest of everything the realms have to offer. Food. Art and entertainment. Protection." He cast a sidelong look at Gwen. "Baths."

A second set of guards hauled open a second, smaller set of doors. They received the same level of inattention as the first, as did the many ladies and gentlemen of the king's court.

In fine, silken dress, they waited patiently in rows on the left and the right sides of the throne room. No one moved or spoke. They remained perfectly still, perfectly silent as they gave their king's entrance their full attention. They might've been little more than decorations in his mind because Jacquess didn't acknowledge them in the least. He made a direct line for the throne, the back of which was decorated in many carved birds.

The guards and the women with the baskets separated and filed dutifully to what must have been their assigned positions near the king, while Desmond and the others gathered at the foot of the throne. He and his friends made a pitiable sight, he decided, all dirty, ragged, and bruised.

Jacquess frowned. "You look worse in here where everything is clean. Roshan!"

A bald man in a purple robe shuffled into the room from a side door. He cut a wide arc around the front of the throne and bowed.

"Yes, Highness?"

"Roshan, please remove these ragamuffins and have the stylists scrub them pretty. Dress them so they're presentable. I'll be taking afternoon supper with the lot of them."

"Right away, Gracious Leader of the People." Roshan herded them toward the side door through which he'd entered.

CHAPTER 29

Roshan led them down a narrow corridor with pale walls and doors. "We have the finest facilities available and the finest products. When we finish with you, you'll look better than you ever have." He clapped as he walked, almost a song, and the doors opened, releasing into their midst several younger people dressed in robes similar to Roshan's, only not as ornate.

Gwen whispered into Desmond's ear, "This is weird."

He agreed.

They ascended a wide flight of stairs that made a turn, and on the second floor, they found another corridor, similar to the first, except the doors there were fancier. These were taller and painted deep burgundy with ornate, golden trim.

Roshan waited until everyone caught up, and once they did, he grasped a pair of knobs, and swept the double doors open with a dramatic flourish. He spun around to face them as he stepped inside.

He bowed. "Welcome to the Pandresian Palace Royal Salon. Shall we get to work?"

High above, hanging from the cathedral ceiling was a golden sculpture of glacier jungle tree branches with vines draping and reptiles lounging, feathered squirrels frozen in mid-flight between. Below it, a wall divided the two halves of the room. Shining bath tubs and salon chairs waited on either side.

Charlotte's eyes sparkled. Breathless, she clasped her hands beneath her chin, about to burst with excitement. Desmond had never seen her so happy. This was her dream come true.

Roshan directed them. "Boys to the left. Girls to the right."

A woman came to lead Charlotte away, but there was no need. She practically skipped ahead. Gwen, while not as ecstatic as her cousin, did seem significantly happier about a bath than usual.

Desmond found himself caught up in the excitement as well. The accommodations were luxurious beyond any he had seen. All things metal were polished with an attention to the smallest detail, down to the shining combs and scissors arranged on the counters. Overstuffed chairs and sofas looked inviting after a long day of hiking.

Only the idea that getting cleaned up would lead to a meal kept him moving toward the line of copper tubs. They were set up as bathing stations, separated from one another by tall, sheer curtains. Each was equipped with an enormous rug, a chair, an array of scrubbing implements, a rack of towels, and a tray of colorful bottles.

Despite all the tools at the disposal of the salon staff, no one, including Roshan, knew what to do with Elm. Desmond watched the scene through the sheer curtain between them. At first, the tree stag glared at the bathtub with his arms crossed. He snarled at a woman who tried to coax him in.

"Come on, Elm," Vincent teased from the other side. "Surely a big guy like you isn't afraid of some soap."

Elm grunted. "Mind your business."

Water splashed as he flopped clumsily into the suds. He growled at an assistant who approached with a scrub brush, sending her scurrying away.

In a bath of his own, Desmond hung the vessel on the faucet to keep close watch over it as he soaked. The bottle was so small, so unassuming that if he didn't know what it was for, he never would've guessed it was capable of holding starlight. A couple of the assistants eyed it when they came to refresh his bath water, and he wondered how safe he and his friends really were in the palace of King Jacquess.

Afterward, with his skin scrubbed clean, mirrors everywhere revealed the physical toll their adventures had taken. His arms and legs looked like they'd been through a battle. He even had some marks on his back. To his surprise, he smiled. He looked like he'd been somewhere, done something real.

The palace staff fussed and trimmed and brushed. They took away the soiled clothing and brought new pants and shirts.

Roshan said, "We tried to judge your taste based on what you wore into the palace, the colors, at least, except for you, Elm, and Charlotte, who came in wearing what looked like a potato sack. We didn't have anything comparable available."

Elm received a band-collared shirt that buttoned in the front so he didn't have to worry about fitting it over his antlers. The palace staff had paired it with loose-fitting, dark pants, giving the outfit a pajama look. Desmond doubted very much that this was what he wanted to wear.

Desmond's and Vincent's outfits were closer to what they'd come in with. The trousers were similar, plain and dark. Vincent's shirt was a silvery gray, Desmond's a deep blue. The fabric was smooth but sturdy, thicker than most of his clothes back home. He couldn't shake the feeling that he was wearing some kind of uniform. He rolled up the sleeves, looked over, and saw Vincent doing the same.

Charlotte and Gwen came around the wall just as the boys were finishing up. Their hair was pinned up in elaborate looping styles, smaller versions of what the women with the baskets of food had worn. Their long shirts were feminine, flaring at the bottom, almost like dresses. The palace staff had put Charlotte in a red and cream color scheme. Gwen's was purple and gray. Their pants, like Elm's, had a satin, pajama-like quality to them, which Gwen seemed to like, despite her natural inclination toward tomboyish things.

"I can't handle the smell of the food coming from out there. It's like torture," she said with her mouth full of lavender candies she ate from a dish in her hand.

"Where did you get those?" Rasq was ready to snatch it from her. "Can I have some?"

She held the dish closer to herself and gave him a coy grin. "Only if you tell me how pretty I look."

"Absolutely gorgeous." He lunged.

She dodged and squeaked and giggled, hiding behind Charlotte and then Desmond.

Roshan eased the candy dish from Gwen's hand. "We're going to the dining hall now. Plenty of food is waiting, so let's leave this dish where it belongs."

As they left the salon to head for the dining hall and Desmond's hunger washed over him again, he considered the way the king had treated them. Desmond and the others had come in from the jungle, hungry and tired, and the king hadn't let them eat yet because they weren't clean. King Jacquess didn't welcome them into the palace because he was concerned about their well-being. He knew they had the vessel, and he wanted it for himself. Desmond would have to be very, very careful.

On the first floor, the dining hall was even grander than the salon, bigger than any other room they'd seen so far in the palace. Walls were smooth and metallic with stripes of what looked like iridescent white stone embedded throughout. Beneath the highest of high ceilings, two rows of thick columns molded into a spiral shape ran the full length of the room.

Between them, a table stretched long enough to accommodate fifty people, but only half the seats were set for the meal. The king's court, the same people who had waited for him in the throne room, now sat on either side, with Jacquess at the head, of course. They had already started eating.

"I'm going to jump on that table." Gwen wiped her mouth with the back of her hand.

"Down, girl. Let me announce you and seat you, and then you can eat yourself sick." Roshan smiled at her and signaled for a nearby horn player to sound.

The rumble of conversation in the room ceased. The crowd turned to them.

CHAPTER 30

Roshan stepped forward and bowed. "Highness, I present to you our guests, Gwen and Charlotte, Rasq, Desmond, and the two Keepers, Elm and Vincent."

"My young friends." Jacquess rose, and his fellow diners rose with him. "You will all sit next to me. Desmond, you especially, so that I can hear this delightful story of yours."

There was something vaguely threatening about the invitation. *Tell me your story or else.* Or perhaps the unsettling feeling was due to the multitude of stares directed at them.

Two of Roshan's underlings escorted Desmond and company to their seats. They followed close behind, polite but unwavering in their urgency, giving little pushes when they perceived potential hesitation. Desmond, Vincent, and Rasq were seated to the king's right. Gwen, Charlotte, and Elm sat across the table from them.

The feast seemed to offer healthier fare than that which filled the fairy queen's table. Meat was present, but vegetables dominated the table space. Peppered and smelling buttery, they packed bowls and platters. A plate of some green, mashed substance passed into Desmond's hand as soon as he sat down, and he scooped a large portion directly onto his plate, his appetite overruling any curiosity about what the food might actually be.

Gwen, despite her usual revulsion at many types of vegetables, did the same, grabbing whatever was in her reach, as did the others. None of them were particularly interested in impressing anyone with manners.

"My, we are hungry." Jacquess clasped his hands and watched their frenzy with an amused smile. "Eat all you like. Eat the whole table if you need it. I'll have the chef prepare more."

When Desmond had eaten enough for his brain to stop spinning, he said, "Thank you for finding us."

"You are quite welcome. Though, I don't get all the credit. Pandresian City has the best empaths of all the realms." He motioned to a group of women down the table, the same ones who had presented them with food and water at the edge of the jungle.

Vincent glanced down the table, and as his gaze traveled back along the guests seated between him and them, he gasped and began choking on his food. Rasq smacked him on the back, and a chunk of an orange vegetable flew from his mouth to land in a dish of sauce.

"Well, that was dramatic." The king waved for the nearest servant to take the dish away. "As I was saying, we have the best empaths in the realms. They come in handy for tasks like finding a person or telling me if someone is lying."

Elm said, "You knew we were coming."

The tree stag looked like an entirely different creature with the white fuzz on his hard skin so clean it caught the warm light in glimmers. He'd regained a piece of his nobility, his pride, and he sat up straight in his chair, the Keeper medal now on the outside of his shirt and shining.

"I did." This fact pleased the king. "Now, that was my story. Let's hear yours, Mr. Winters. How do three and a half human children end up in the glacier jungle with two Keepers and one of the most valuable relics in the realms? Begin."

Desmond looked to his companions for some sort of assistance, but he saw only fear. *Don't tell him too much,* they seemed to say. But what was too much? His worry was that he'd say the wrong thing, and the king would find an excuse to take the vessel from them.

What information put them in the least danger, if there was, indeed, danger? He guessed there was, judging by the armed guards at the edges of the room. He had no real choice in the matter, especially with the full attention of the king's team of empaths.

"It started in the bookshop." He told them everything, building steam and enthusiasm in the retelling of his adventures: the Authors Unknown, dinner with the fairy queen, Bensai, and the molebat. He lost himself, nearly forgetting to stop when he reached the point in the story in which they'd met up with the king, and he realized that his friends were gawking at him. They hadn't expected him to go so far.

"That is a long story, young man." Jacquess approved. His face darkened, ever so slightly. He bent toward Desmond. "Now, I would like to hear how a simple shopkeeper is a worthy use of starlight."

Rasq's face reddened. "We don't need your approval."

Elm shook his head at the halfling to silence him.

"Actually, you do need my approval. The supply tunnel lies within Pandresian borders, which means I either grant you access or you take your chances with another point of entry. Tell me why I shouldn't keep the vessel for myself."

Desmond said, "Castle keeps the archive for all the realms. He's important—"

"Important for what? Storing books? I can do that just as easily. Bring them to me. They would be safe here."

"Lucinda..." He wanted to use her name but wasn't sure how to do so in this instance. "He was Lucinda's husband."

A woman with periwinkle skin and hair the color of rust interjected, "If I may, Your Majesty."

"Of course, Lady Holly. You may speak."

Vincent lowered his gaze to his plate.

She was astonishingly beautiful, with finer features than the rest of the Pandresians. In spite of her odd coloring, she looked more human. She also didn't seem as formal as the other ladies with her hair falling loose past her shoulders and an understated, white dress.

Lady Holly said, "We owe Lucinda a great debt, one which can never be repaid. She has given us all life in exchange for her own. That is a sacrifice, everyone agrees, but in giving her life for us, she broke Castle's heart. Saving Cosalis cost him the love of his life. We owe him a debt as well."

The king fell back in his chair like an angry child. He scowled at the food on the table for several moments, during which Desmond and company held their collective breath. The man who could destroy almost all hope for Castle's life was throwing a silent temper tantrum.

Jacquess finally conceded. "Very well."

The dining hall door burst open, jolting everyone in the room. A burly bear of a man with dark hair and a tunic made of stitched animal skins sauntered in. At the first plate he came to, he reached past a painfully thin man wearing a monocle to grab a leg of meat from a plate and promptly went to work on it. He made a racket, chewing, the metal necklaces around his neck clinking together as he continued toward the head of the table.

CHAPTER 31

"We have no appointment," Jacquess said to the stranger.

Roshan practically fell through the dining hall door. He barely had the breath to utter the words, "I present King Tarashet."

"I'm aware of who he is, but thank you, Roshan."

Tarashet grabbed an unoccupied chair from the nearest wall. He dragged it over and jammed it between Jacquess and Desmond. He plunked down and proceeded to gnaw on the greasy leg like an animal.

Jacquess asked, "What do you want, Tarashet? Your rude entrance makes my guests uncomfortable."

He harrumphed. "Since when do you care about the comfort of your guests? All of you, leave," he ordered the royal court.

Their frightened expressions spoke of willingness, but they awaited permission from their king. He waved them off. The stampede for the exit shook the floor.

Tarashet howled with laughter. "What worthless people you have. Except for this one. Lady Holly." He nodded to her.

She hadn't moved from her seat. "I would like to remain, if it pleases both kings."

"Yes, of course. Have you given any more thought to moving to Brimsage? The offer still stands. I could use someone like you."

"No thank you, Your Majesty. As always, I appreciate your invitation."

"I'll never understand your loyalty to this weak brother of mine, but I respect it." He took a large bite from the meat in his hand. He chewed until Desmond met his gaze, then he smiled with his mouth full and grease glistening on his beard. "I've come to see you."

It was the most terrifying thing Desmond had heard all day.

"How did you know he was here?" Jacquess asked.

"I have informants," Tarashet replied without taking his hard eyes off Desmond. "They told me the grandson of Allos was here, and he had the vessel. What an interesting situation, says I. How does the grandson of a thief come by a treasure like that?"

"Allos Winters?" Jacquess said, his mouth dropping open.

"You let him into your palace, and you don't know who he is? Fool." He turned back to Desmond. "Did my brother tell you about me? I don't suppose he did. That's because he has no appreciation for all this glass and stone and steel. As if my kingdom played no part in anything." He moved closer. "I make the world go round, boy, and I've come for the vessel."

Across the table, Elm snapped, "It's not yours to take."

Tarashet saw him for the first time. "You're a rare one. How about you come along home with me, big cow? You'd make a great addition to our circus."

Elm began to climb over the table. A voice from behind stopped him.

"Halt." A soldier appeared, seemingly from nowhere. He held a leash with a snarling hyena at the end.

They'd filed in through the kitchen door, four of them dressed in matching black uniforms, all with slobbering hyenas of their own. They were neater than their king, more disciplined.

"Allow me to reiterate." The king returned his attention to the vessel. "I'll even use manners. Please. Hand over the vessel if you and your friends would like to leave in the same condition in which you arrived."

Desmond felt everyone in the room looking at him. Just days before, he would've handed it over with little to no argument, maybe because some part of him *had* been cowardly (though he would never admit it to Gwen), maybe because the man was so large or the obstacles seemed impossible. But no. Not this time, not this version of Desmond. Keeper medal or no, he had become a protector of the realms, and the realms wanted him to save Castle.

"No."

The king drew back in his chair with a look of incredulity on his grease-streaked face. "No? Who are you to tell me no?" Laughter erupted from him. "Somebody come take it from him."

"Wait." Vincent raised his hand. "The vessel is nothing without the light of Cosalis inside. Can you honestly say that you are one hundred percent certain you or your people can draw light from the star?"

"Why couldn't I?"

Holly offered an explanation. "The light of Cosalis blinds. The sun deafens and burns. Only those with selfless intentions may approach the star."

"That can't be true."

"The monks who tended the gate were only able to do so because of their devotion. Since they had no notions of using its light for themselves, Cosalis allowed them access."

"Then you'll fill the vessel and bring it back for me." He tossed the greasy bird leg he'd been eating to the nearest hyena, and it snatched the meat from the air. "I'll come back in the morning. My guards will escort you." He slapped his hands onto the table, rose from his seat, and left the room as casually as he'd come in, like he owned the place.

"That was unpleasant." Having lost his appetite, Jacquess pushed his chair back from the table. He mumbled the words, "Roshan will return for you," and he departed with several guards in tow.

Only Desmond's group and Holly remained at the table while servants cleared the dishes.

Holly said, "It's good to see you, Vincent. How are you?"

He cleared his throat. "Fine, and you?"

"I'm happy to be here. May I speak with you privately?"

"Of course."

They exited through the kitchen door with Vincent looking nervous on the way out.

Roshan appeared behind Desmond. "That's a long overdue conversation."

"They know each other," Charlotte said in a wistful voice. "Was he her boyfriend?"

"Yes, sweet child. Long ago and not so far away."

For some strange reason, she smiled at Desmond. "They make a cute couple. Don't you think?"

He shrugged. "I guess so."

Roshan showed them to accommodations at the far side of the palace on the second floor. "You can stay here overnight. The king doesn't want you wandering far, especially with Tarashet's hyenas around. Revolting creatures. I assume Vincent will join you shortly."

Their sleeping quarters consisted of one large room. At the center was a round sitting area with a firepot, a small table, chairs, a sofa, and fancy cushions scattered throughout. Four sleeping areas separated from one another by partitions were situated at the outer edge of the room. Each had a bed with a nightstand, and its own blend of colors: teal and gold, emerald green and gold, sapphire blue and gold, and silver and gold.

"I bet I can guess what the king's favorite color is," Gwen said.

"At least they aren't burgundy." Charlotte pretended to gag.

Roshan told them, "I'll have a late dinner delivered to your room in a while. I have a feeling the king may no longer be in the mood to receive guests."

"I'll bet." Rasq chuckled.

"What was the deal with that whole brotherly love thing, anyway?" Gwen asked.

"When one is king and has a king as a brother, disputes can arise. Their power should be equal, a city to each brother, as their father decreed, but every so often, one of them...oversteps."

Rasq said, "No wonder Jacquess wants so many Keepers around."

"Our Royal Highness sees the value in surrounding himself with good people. You should know that just because he refrained from vocal opposition doesn't mean he has rolled over."

"Are you saying he could protect us from Tarashet?" Desmond asked.

"I'm saying you should take heart. Situations aren't always as hopeless as they might appear." He gave a wink. On the way out, he paused in the doorway. "I wouldn't wander if I were you. Tarashet hasn't left the grounds, and please trust me when I tell you that he isn't opposed to taking hostages."

"Got it," Gwen answered for the group.

They went straight for the beds, Charlotte and Gwen to a room, Desmond and Rasq to the next. Elm lumbered off to the silver one.

"I can't remember the last time I slept in a real bed." It creaked under the tree stag's weight. "Ugh, of course, it's too short. Pandresians."

Desmond lay back, laced his fingers behind his head, and thought of the kings, both hungry for the possibility of extending their lives. He tried to formulate a strategy in which he might use their greed against them, perhaps as some kind of distraction, but just then, his mind wouldn't cooperate. Just then, he needed to rest. He clutched the vessel, rolled over, and fell asleep.

CHAPTER 32

The sky outside the colored glass was dark when Desmond woke. Warm, flickering light told him that a fire burned in the sitting area in the middle of the room. He sat up, feeling groggy as if he'd slept for a week, and staggered over to where Rasq, Charlotte, Gwen, Elm, Vincent, and Holly sat in a circle on the floor, lounging on the cushions.

Holly said, "You're just in time. I'm going to tell everyone the story of Lucinda and Castle. You should know who you're saving, why he deserves to go on. Few people have the capacity to love and accept others the way he did. The kings might think he's just some lowly bookshop clerk, but he is so much more." Holly blinked away tears. "Lucinda, my sister, was born with a connection to the star, an extraordinary gift. The rest of us empaths can read emotion and sometimes thought. She is the only person we know of who could hear the will of Cosalis."

Gwen asked, "How can a star have a will?"

"How does any creature have a will? A mind? A heart? A lack of understanding on our part doesn't make a thing impossible. Lucinda knew this better than anyone. She wanted to see as much of our world as possible, wanted to touch every part she could. That's what led her through the realms, eventually to the junction and over the aqueduct, to a passage that opened to a field of golden wheat."

Rasq said, "That sounds like the way we came in, only there's a bookshop there now, not a field."

"Lots of shops, actually," Charlotte added. "It's quite a nice place, the street, I mean, not so much the bookshop."

Holly shook her head. "Never judge a place by its outward appearance. A building can have a soul as well when endowed with the right kind of magic. We'll get to that in a moment. Frederick Castle was the first human Lucinda met when she wandered into the field. He had fallen asleep while reading in the warm sunshine, and when he woke, she was there. The two of them were smitten with one another at first sight, and that night, at her insistence, he took her home to meet his parents."

"Awfully fast." Elm grunted.

"I think it's sweet," Charlotte said.

Holly laughed. "It was very fast, even faster under the influence of his mother and father. Frederick and Lucinda saw each other for a while, with her returning every night to the passage in the side of the hill. She stayed with the Authors Unknown."

Rasq said with more than a little sympathy, "Poor lady. Those people are weird."

"And loud." Gwen nodded.

"The books they'd written were beginning to stack up around them like walls; there were so many. Lucinda convinced Frederick that they should build a library to house and protect the collection, only when they presented the idea to Frederick's father (who owned the land), the senior Mr. Castle changed the plan to a bookshop. Frederick needed to make a living, and since the elder Castles were eager to see their son take a wife, they also put forth the stipulation that he marry Lucinda, a stipulation with which she and Frederick were only too happy to comply. Once the bookshop was finished, in the same field in which they met, beneath a starry night sky, with both humans and people from our world in attendance, they wed."

"Wait, so people, creatures, or whatever from the realms visited the human realm?" Desmond asked.

"Yes. They do so more often than you might think."

"I never saw any fairies or frog people before coming here," Gwen said.

"The frog," he offered, "with the pink stripe. Do you remember? And the bird?"

"Those aren't the same. I would have liked to see something really good. Like him." She gestured at Elm. "Could you imagine seeing him stroll down the sidewalk?"

Elm grimaced at her.

Holly went on. "We try to keep interaction with the human realm to a minimum for the safety of all involved. The wedding was an exception to this general rule, as was the bookshop construction, which was done by Cavern Realm goblins."

"I'm glad we haven't seen any of those," Charlotte said. "They must be hideous."

"They are and not very cordial either," Elm confirmed and then asked Holly, "Lucinda convinced them to help?"

"They had a supply problem. A neighboring realm interrupted shipments of rope. Before she reached the human realm, she resolved the conflict for them. Goblins may not be the prettiest creatures, but they are very good engineers, geniuses, really. Their buildings aren't just buildings. They're machines."

"We noticed. The shop shuttered itself when Castle collapsed," Desmond said.

"The bookshop was designed to protect the archive at all costs."

"Well, it didn't do anything to protect Castle himself," Rasq said bitterly. "We could've called an ambulance for him."

"Doctors wouldn't have been able to save him. Since he took on the responsibility of protecting the collection, he isn't like ordinary human beings anymore. The magic linking him to the shop protects him from illness. He's actually over a hundred years old."

"Looks about a hundred and fifty. What's wrong with him, then?" Gwen asked.

"The magic weakened over the years. He isn't dead, but he isn't alive, either. He needs a fresh infusion."

Rasq said, "He knew it was going to happen. He gave me instructions to go to the Authors Unknown."

"Yes, he knew. Lucinda told him long ago, just after the construction, and she tried to warn him about what might happen to her as well, but he never wanted to hear any of it. From the age she could comprehend her place in the world, she understood her responsibility. She approached every person, every creature in every realm, with a kind of wonder because she realized she might have to give herself, one day, in order to save them. They were all her people, and she told Castle this often, but in his mind, the two of them were forever."

"He couldn't bear the thought of losing her," Charlotte said.

Gwen poked her. "Stop being a baby."

"You stop it."

"They were inseparable for many years." Holly sighed. "Until the light of Cosalis faltered. Lucinda sensed the star was dying. Knowing that her husband would never let her do what she needed to do, she sent him into town on an errand, telling him that she didn't feel well and that she needed medicine. There was a winter storm that night, but he went anyway, into driving snow for her. Hours later, when he returned, all he found was a note apologizing and explaining what she had to do. By then, she was too far ahead for him to catch her before she reached the star."

"That's so sad. No wonder he's such a crabapple."

"Though his heart still beat, he lost his life, and despite it all, he continues to fulfill his promise. You didn't choose this quest, but I want you to know that this man, this beleaguered soul, is worth your efforts."

They sat listening to the crackle of the firepot while the gravity sank in.

Holly rose. "I should go. We all have a big day tomorrow, and you need your rest. Rasq, may I speak with you alone?"

He agreed and went with her into the hallway. She closed the door behind them.

"What did she want?" Desmond asked when he returned.

He quietly cleared his throat. "To tell me that I was a gift for Castle. My mother didn't abandon me. She left me for him in an effort to give him new life."

"Big sacrifice."

"Yeah, I guess nymphs aren't so bad, after all."

CHAPTER 33

The next morning, clean clothes and breakfast awaited them in the common area.

"I'm beginning to like this place." Gwen needed no invitation. She bypassed the clothes for the food and dug in.

Everyone else followed her lead. They sat at the table and ate while Roshan stood nearby. He kept watch over them, though Desmond wasn't sure why. Was he sticking around to make sure none of them ran off or was he there in case the hyena guards showed up to take hostages?

Roshan said, "The kings will meet us on the palace stairs in time to see you off. King Jacquess hopes gratitude for what he has provided inspires loyalty. If you'll excuse me, I need to check on some staff members." He bowed as he exited.

"I don't trust these people." Elm inspected his food as if he expected it to find something bad in it.

Vincent sat next to Desmond. "Stay close to me when we leave. I'll do my best to protect you if necessary."

"Really?" Elm asked. "You haven't done anything but make goo-goo eyes at that empath since we arrived. You're distracted. The boy is better off sticking with me."

"Why? So you can make off with the vessel once he's filled it with starlight? Not likely."

"Stop fighting," Desmond said calmly. "We'll stay together. All of us."

Rasq said in a voice almost too low for him to hear, "The kings aren't going to let us leave with the vessel once it's full."

"I know. I think we'll have to run."

Gwen sighed. "I wish we had Henry. He'd get us away in a jiff."

"Who's Henry?" Vincent asked.

"A hare from the fairy realm. He's very fast. He saved our lives."

"Then, I wish we had Henry, too."

They dressed in the clothes Roshan left for them. Vincent informed them that the matching outfits (dark shirts, dark pants with plenty of pockets, and boots) were, in fact, Keeper training uniforms.

"Haven't worn one of these in a while. Not much of a fashion statement, but they're easy to move in."

Elm's shirt wouldn't fit over his antlers. He tried to pull it on anyway, and it tangled. He shook free, eliciting laughter from everyone in the room.

He chuckled. "I need to have a talk with the tailor."

Vincent showed him a zipper, and they were eventually able to get it on him. His was a sleeveless version of the shirt, made of the same stretchy material.

Minutes later, Roshan and a company of armed guards arrived to escort them outside, and he seemed nervous. He tried to keep all of them in sight as they moved into the hall.

The guards surrounded the group on all sides, looking even more rigid than before. Desmond guessed that meant Tarashet was still around, not that he'd really expected the king of Brimsage to give up on stealing the vessel for himself.

A crowd awaited them on the palace steps. To their right, King Jacquess stood at the front of rows of troops. To their left, King Tarashet stood before rows of his own troops and their hyenas.

At the bottom of the steps, in a more cheerful part of the scene, citizens had assembled. They waved colorful flags and scattered flower petals in the path the procession would take to the supply tunnel.

Tarashet stepped in front of Desmond. Jacquess did the same.

The king of Brimsage waved over five soldiers from his side. "My guards will accompany you to ensure all goes smoothly." He patted one of them, a spike-haired, muscular guy with orange skin and deep-set eyes, and said, "Grel here is the captain, so don't think you can get away. However quick you think you are, be assured that he is much quicker." Tarashet leaned closer to Desmond. "Your grandfather stole precious metals from me. Were you aware of that?"

"I didn't know him."

"Regardless, as far as I'm concerned, you owe me."

Desmond stood up straighter. "The vessel doesn't belong to me."

"That fact does not absolve you from debt. I expect payment."

Jacquess said, "I offer my own troops as well."

And so the group of six became a group of sixteen plus five smelly hyenas that sniffed them all a bit too intently. Everyone going to the tunnel lined up with Desmond and the kings at the front.

Horns loosely resembling trumpets blared, and the group moved forward, into a crowd of people waving or crying with joy. Pandresian citizens close enough to touch them did, only to have the guards urge them back.

The kings led the way through town, turning left on a street that crossed over the canal. The waterway was several feet below, but people had gathered there as well and were waving up at them.

Desmond asked Jacquess, "What do they think we're going to do?"

He shrugged. "They don't know. They break out this fanfare for anything involving me. They get annoying, sometimes, when they forget their boundaries."

Desmond saw the emotion in their faces, the hope in their eyes when they were close. This wasn't flattery for their king. It was reverence as if they knew the true importance of the mission.

"Yes, yes." Jacquess waved. "Your king is among you."

Tarashet snapped, "Stop behaving like a fool."

Desmond rolled his eyes. He would be happy when he didn't have to deal with either of those men anymore. He would take a cannibal fairy queen over them any day of the week.

The tall gate barring entrance to the supply tunnel loomed over them. It was a black model topped with spikes, the points of which nearly touched the copper ceiling. Light shone from somewhere deep inside, flickering along the walls like a flame.

"Roshan!" Jacquess called him forward.

"Yes, Highness. I have the key." He trotted forward and unlocked the gate, heaved it open. The hinges squealed.

"Let go of me!" Gwen shouted.

Desmond spun around to see her thrashing, a hunk of her hair in the grip of Tarashet. He pulled her closer to him and grinned.

"I've found that collateral is the best motivator. Keeps men honest. She stays with me until you return with the vessel."

Jacquess stepped toward him, and the nearest hyenas growled. "We did not discuss this. The guards are with them. A prisoner isn't necessary."

Gwen squirmed. She hauled back one leg to give him a hard kick in the shin. He growled and let her go. Three hyenas approached, snarling.

Elm shot her an approving glance as he put himself between her and them. He said to the king, "Stop this."

Tarashet's face went red with rage. "You've just committed a crime, human, punishable by execution. What do you think of that?"

Emboldened by the sizable Keeper protecting her, she retorted, "I think you stink of day-old fish, and you have the manners of a rabid wolverine."

Tarashet showed his teeth. "You will see the interior of our lowest dungeon; I swear it. Bring her to me," he commanded his guards.

"Wait!" Rasq said. "Take me instead of her. I'll go willingly."

Vincent put a hand his shoulder. "No one is going with him. We're staying together, remember?"

"No. It should be me." Charlotte's voice was quiet, but her tone was resolute.

They all looked at her.

She said to Tarashet, "Please excuse me for a moment, so I can speak with my friends?" Her politeness defused his temper.

"Very well."

She pulled them into a huddle. "He isn't going to let you leave without one of us staying behind. He's had this planned from the beginning. I can get him to let his guard down and then escape. They won't see me as a threat."

Desmond agreed. "I hate to admit it, but she's right. They would guard Rasq, Elm, or Vincent heavily. Gwen hasn't exactly made a friend of him. He might do something to her."

"This is taking too long." Tarashet raised his voice.

"We'll come back for you," he assured her.

"You'd better."

They broke the huddle.

"Who's it going to be? The halfling, the rude girl, or the other one?"

Charlotte replied, "The other one," and moved forward, away from the group.

Desmond didn't like seeing her apart from the rest of them. They made a pretty good team, despite their differences, and he wasn't sure they could've made it that far without her.

"Trusting a Winters with your freedom, eh?" Tarashet prodded. "Probably not the smartest choice."

She looked at Desmond. "I would trust that Winters with my life."

CHAPTER 34

They lined up at the mouth of the supply tunnel: Vincent, Elm, Gwen, Rasq, Desmond, and all ten of their armed escorts. Everyone was quiet, save the hyenas bickering and snapping at one another with all the manners of stray dogs.

"Wait!" a voice in the crowd shouted.

Lady Holly pushed through. She ran by the kings and their guards, to Vincent, and threw her arms around him.

"Be careful," she told him.

He rested his forehead against hers. "I'll be fine. We'll come back."

She whispered, "That's what I'm afraid of."

"Lady Holly." Jacquess urged her back. "The sooner they leave, the sooner they return. Please join me."

She kissed Vincent, and then pulled away, her reluctance to do so apparent. She positioned herself at her king's side.

Desmond took a last look at Charlotte with King Tarashet as they entered the tunnel. She was braver than he would've guessed before they'd begun their journey. They all were.

The group proceeded in rows of four people, shoulder-to-shoulder, with the guards at the outer edges. Desmond and Vincent were first, with a guard from each king on either side. Next came Gwen and Rasq, then Elm, with the remaining guards in the back.

"Is Lady Holly your girlfriend?" Gwen asked Vincent.

"No. We had something special once, but that was years ago."

"Looks like she wants to get back together."

Vincent smiled.

175

"Be quiet," Tarashet's captain of the guard, Grel, commanded. The hyena at the end of the leash he held gave a shrill yip of a warning.

"I will not be quiet. Your king isn't here," Gwen said.

"I was granted the authority to use whatever means necessary to ensure the success of the mission."

"That includes picking on little girls, does it? Sounds about right."

"Only obnoxious ones."

Vincent intervened. "Alright. No need for everyone to fall apart. We just have to get along for a short while."

Desmond changed the subject. "What are the figures etched into the walls?"

The primitive drawings had begun several yards into the tunnel. At first, they consisted of writing like hieroglyphics. Further into the tunnel, they became larger, more detailed renderings of what looked like farm animals and people caring for them. The scene that arrested Desmond's attention featured several men with plain clothes and long braids at the tops of their heads. They carried baskets of food and supplies toward the star.

He stopped to touch the grooves in the copper. The metal was warm like skin, like a living thing with blood moving through its veins.

"The monks," Vincent told him.

"Move along," Grel said.

Desmond did not move along. "I want to look at these first."

Vincent explained further, "The Order of the Caged Sun devoted their lives to worshiping Cosalis and feeding their life energy into it through meditation. When the star began to falter, they realized they weren't strong enough."

"It needed Lucinda."

"That's enough," Grel nagged again.

Desmond complied but insisted on staying close to the wall. The daily routines of the monks passed before his eyes in a series of scenes. The monks prayed and made offerings of fire and held ceremonies.

The Order of the Caged Sun had lived on a network of platforms and catwalks built around the primary cage. Their rooms were bare, no real walls between them and no furniture inside. He couldn't imagine living that way, in the constant heat and light, but the Order seemed to view these challenges as honors, not hardships.

The temperature of the tunnel climbed as they descended. The soldiers were the first to sweat. Drops formed on their foreheads and ran down the sides of their faces, their necks. It soaked their hair and the parts of their uniforms that weren't made of metal.

"The light of Cosalis blinds. It deafens and burns. Only those with selfless intentions may approach the star." Holly's warning echoed in his mind.

Desmond felt heat but not as badly. He wondered what they expected in return for completing their mission. A promotion? Money? They wouldn't be able to complete the journey. He said nothing but smiled to himself.

Then he had another thought. What if one of the people who were with him before Pandresian City couldn't go on? He worried most about Elm, who had stolen the vessel in an effort to revive Arbolettis, but was that selfish? And Gwen. Did she care more about unlocking the doors to the bookshop than she cared about saving Castle's life? Even Desmond had his own reasons for wanting to go home. He hadn't seen his parents in what felt like an eternity.

They kept going, and the starlight dancing on copper walls grew brighter. It illuminated the etchings of the monks until every scene was ablaze. Then the gate leading into the cage came into view.

A soldier belonging to Jacquess fell to his knees. He gasped for breath.

"Get up," his captain commanded.

"Sorry, sir. I can't...I can't breathe."

Another soldier helped him back to his feet. "The heat is burning my throat. I can't go on, either."

"We have orders. Do not turn back," their leader insisted.

One by one, Jacquess' guards backed down. They ignored continued pleas from their captain and retreated back the way they came, their heads hanging with shame.

Tarashet's soldiers looked longingly after them but stayed. The consequences for abandoning their mission would be much harsher. Desmond was willing to bet that Tarashet didn't take failure lightly.

The group, now significantly smaller, pressed on while the temperature continued to increase. Desmond was sweating, his pulse beating in his ear, his heart laboring. The tunnel became an oven with the smell of hot metal permeating the air.

Gwen coughed. Elm moved more slowly than before. Sweat soaked Rasq's chest. Vincent kept wiping his face with the back of his arm. They couldn't all have selfish intentions. Yet, the star threatened to cook them alive, just like the soldiers and the hyenas that were ready to pass out at any moment.

Desmond refused to fail this far into the game, so close to the star. He grasped the vessel in his hand tightly and plowed ahead of the group. He picked up the pace, into the heat. He pulled ahead of everyone else.

"Halt," Grel called after him and then stumbled.

The faces etched into the walls seemed to move as they grew brighter, and the gate rose above Desmond, a shadow against the brilliance of Cosalis. He would do this or die trying.

The iron gate was hot, and the latch resisted when he pushed. He wiped sweat from his brow, drew back, and kicked the gate open. It gave with a groan of its warped hinges. He removed the vessel from around his neck to loop the strap around his wrist.

"They can't come any closer," Elm said behind him.

Desmond turned. Rasq, Vincent, and Gwen were with him. Several feet back, the remaining soldiers and hyenas had stopped, some of them collapsing to the metal floor.

"Should we help them?" Rasq shouted to be heard over the roar of the star. He mopped his face with the bottom of his shirt.

Other soldiers, with the help of the hyenas, were pulling their unconscious comrades back. They would retreat, perhaps to a cooler part of the tunnel to wait for Desmond and the rest of his crew to return with the prize.

Desmond said, "They'll be fine." He turned back to Cosalis. "I wish I could say the same for us."

CHAPTER 35

Cosalis raged far below in a swirl of blinding energy. Columns of light shot up from the surface to the mouths of conduits in the earthen ceiling. Solar flares. Desmond had read about them before. His science book hadn't done them justice.

The chaos of the place surprised him. For some reason, despite Lady Holly's warning, he'd expected some benevolent orb or he expected it to be that way for him. He expected physics to fall by the wayside because he carried the vessel. But the star was a beast of a thing, so unlike the person he'd thought Lucinda was that he wondered if her energy was really inside. What did a person have to be in order to stoke the fire of a star?

The network of platforms once used by the monks was falling apart. Long ago, the structure had been orderly, but now it hung in ruins, catwalks dangling at haphazard angles in places where chains had broken free. Folded blankets on the floor and baskets like the ones he'd seen etched on the copper tunnel walls lay abandoned.

Amid the emptiness, spider sentries made their rounds. The clicks of their joints and jets of steam they emitted weren't audible over the roar of the star, but Desmond swore he could hear them in his head, the memory of the sounds. As he stood at the gate, taking in the scene, he counted twenty of them in the immediate area with many more further out.

Rasq said, "This is hopeless. They'll be on us in no time."

"Tarashet insisted on putting the spiders in here after the monks left. They were supposed to protect access to Cosalis, which I guess they do," Vincent explained. "They kind of took on a mind of their own."

"Remind me to thank him later," Elm grumbled.

Gwen said, "I'm going to try something," and before anyone could stop her, she ran out onto a catwalk to the left.

The spiders sprang into action. They closed in from all directions, their legs switching back and forth in a mechanical scurry. They leaped over gaps and slid down chains. Ten of them surrounded her.

She stopped running.

The spiders kept coming as long as the platform beneath her feet swung, but the moment it slowed to a stop, the spider bots froze in their tracks. They remained there, as if someone switched them off, for several seconds, and then they slowly turned to head the opposite direction, away from Gwen.

"They sense vibration," Desmond said, "just like real spiders on a web."

Vincent cupped his hands around his mouth to yell, "Good job, Gwen!" He told Desmond, "You run; we'll distract them. Whenever they get close, stop running until they go after someone else."

"This is too easy." Elm shook his head.

"Such a pessimist."

Desmond stared at the star, wondering how he was going to get the light into the bottle. Even if he did get down there, even if he managed to get past the spiders, the heat wouldn't allow him to get close.

"Desmond?" Vincent's voice reached him. "Are you ready?"

"What if I can't draw the light?"

He put a hand on Desmond's shoulder. "You've come this far. You're meant to do this."

"I just don't see how. I mean, look at that thing."

As if in reply, a trio of fiery flares erupted from the surface, one right after the other, shaking the catwalks.

"Don't worry about what it looks like. Focus on the task you came here to do. Think about freeing Charlotte and saving a man's life."

He nodded.

Vincent clapped his hands together. "Okay, the three of us will fan out. Rasq, you go that way." He pointed slightly lower than where Gwen stood. "Elm, take the high road to the right and I'll take the lower. Desmond, you're on direct center, the path to the star. When the bots get too close, just stop moving. Then the others pick up to lead them away, so on and so forth. Have we all got it?"

Without reply, Elm launched into action. He ran and jumped to swing on a chain, causing as much of a ruckus as he could.

"I'll take that as a yes." Vincent went next, followed by Rasq. Gwen figured out what they were doing and joined right in.

Desmond waited until the bots gave chase. They scattered until none remained between him and the star. He surveyed the path ahead, the gaps between the rails. He couldn't make a perfectly straight line down, but he would manage.

He closed his eyes, took a deep breath, and ran. With the chains jingling around him and the metal rumbling beneath his feet, he made a jagged line toward the star. Still with the vessel in his hand, the strap wrapped around his wrist, and the air growing hotter, he jogged to a gap, jumped across to the next platform, which swung.

Rasq was forced to stop first. He cringed as the bots closed in. They abandoned their quarry and diverted to join the group after Vincent. They moved as if of one mind, like a school of fish, never managing to zero in on Desmond. The plan was working.

Desmond made his way closer and closer and the heat, sound, and radiance bore down on him. It weighed his arms and his legs and seemed to push him back. He was only a few rows away from Cosalis when he missed his footing. He fell, and as he landed, his hands hit the metal hard. He got back up, focusing half of his energy into his grip on the vessel. The other half went to his legs. He tried to stand, but the platform seemed to spin away from beneath him. He fell again.

A great shadow appeared over him. He made out unnatural lines, grappling claws on hinges. It reached for him.

Blinding light replaced it. A mechanical screech rose over the sound of the star, receding as the bot fell into the vast abyss below. Then Desmond was being hauled upright by a large hand on his shirt.

It was Elm. The tips of his antlers were singed, and his eyes were wide with desperation. He grabbed the next spider to fling it aside.

"Go!" He shoved Desmond toward Cosalis.

CHAPTER 36

The spider bots swarmed, so many more, perhaps a hundred coming in from all sides. They'd caught on to the game.

Vincent, Rasq, and Gwen hastened toward the star as well, jumping from row to row in pursuit. None of them would be fast enough to help Desmond.

His head still spinning from the heat, he leaped for the next platform, but he didn't land on metal. The catwalks had vanished, the spiders, his friends. He was alone in the light.

A face, that of a woman with flowing hair, emerged. She was made of fire, but he no longer felt any heat. He thrust the vessel toward her.

"Castle needs your help." The heavy air around him swallowed his voice. He had spoken; he was sure, but no sound came.

What he did hear was Lucinda's panicked breathing, running, her footsteps echoing down the copper tunnel. Against a current of monks making a mournful exit, she pushed toward the dying star, closer to the anguished cry of the thing, the shrillness with a grating undercurrent of rock against rock. Cosalis brightened and dimmed as it struggled to hold onto existence.

Lucinda's entire life led to that moment. She stood on a platform, looking down on the giver of light to so many. A piece of it rested in her soul. She was sister to a star, and the only being in the realms who could save everything. Her heart ached for Frederick. He would never understand.

"I'm sorry, my love." She conjured one last memory of him, the day they met in a field of golden wheat, and she held onto it as she gave herself to Cosalis.

The weight of the vessel in Desmond's hand had changed. "Desmond!"

He opened his eyes to Vincent shaking him. He looked down at the vessel. It glowed a brilliant gold. He no longer felt the intense heat of the star.

"We're surrounded."

Desmond looked up to find an army of spider bots looking about as angry as any robots could look. There was no escape.

He asked, "What are we going to do?"

"One way left." Vincent nodded toward the abyss beneath him. The only thing visible, aside from the brilliance consuming almost everything, was a bundle of chains hanging from the lower level of the star cage. "They won't let you leave with the starlight."

"Are you crazy? There's nothing down there," Rasq said.

Desmond told him, "I'll go. Just let them kick you out. We can meet up later, somehow."

The ring of spiders constricted. Like a mass of ants on a hill, they climbed over each other. They moved along the tops of the rails and leaped from chain to chain in a disorderly wave.

"I'll go with you. Someone has to," Vincent said.

Rasq stood his ground as well. "I'm not letting those things throw me out again."

Rather than take the time to voice an opinion, Elm snatched Desmond by the waist and said, "Enough talking," and stepped off the catwalk.

He dropped through the air, his arm reaching for the first chain he found. He struggled to grab hold of the links slipping through his fingers. Falling, falling, they plummeted away from the star.

The others were shadows against the churning bright, Rasq alone, Vincent carrying Gwen. Spiders jumped after them, flailing.

Cosalis reached with a flare of its light. Desmond blinked, and they were no longer hanging by the chain. They were no longer underground or surrounded.

He was sitting in rain and mud. In fact, all five of them sat in mud. They were in a field, the outer edge of it, with the towers of Pandresian City visible in the distance.

"How did we get here?" Rasq was the first to speak.

Desmond stared at the bottle in his hand. Starlight shone within the amber glass, potent and swirling just like the surface of the star itself.

He said, "I think it was Lucinda."

Vincent bellowed into the sky, "Thank you, Lucinda! That was fantastic."

"Quiet down before you draw attention to us." Elm brushed himself off as he stood.

"There's nobody here," Gwen said.

"They don't know where we are. They don't even know if we're alive." Vincent grinned. "What a great feeling."

Desmond said, "Yeah, except they still have Charlotte."

"Right." Vincent's excitement deflated. "Probably should get busy walking back then."

"Ugh. It's so far." Gwen groaned.

The city was far, but Desmond was glad they'd ended up with an advantage. Now that they were free of the kings and the guards, they might stand a chance of getting out of there with the vessel. He smiled as he tucked it into his shirt, and he thanked Lucinda for saving them.

CHAPTER 37

"How did all the realms get here?" Gwen asked as they walked back toward Pandresian City.

No one replied at first.

Elm grumbled, "Why do you ask such questions?"

"I just want to know how all of this came about. There has to be some kind of story. In the human realm, we have stories. Different people have different ideas, and they argue. This world just seems so...patchwork, and how is your sun underground? It makes no sense."

Vincent said, "When I was a kid, the grownups told me that miners found it when they dug too deep, and then they built the conduits to harness the energy."

Elm offered his own version. "Our elders told us that in ancient times, the star lived in the sky, and some greedy realm buried it so they could keep the strongest light for themselves."

"That's preposterous. Who could handle a star? Let alone bury it?"

"Mmhmm." Gwen nodded to herself. "So the arguing is universal."

After a few beats, Rasq chimed in. "The Authors Unknown say the realms are pieces of worlds that were destroyed. Cosalis deemed them worthy of survival, so it drew them near. It keeps them alive."

They all fell silent, perhaps pondering this idea that seemed to make so much sense. Dying worlds. Desmond couldn't imagine the death of an entire world, every living thing falling into oblivion. And he thought of Elm's Arbolettis, the world that might have died twice.

Several minutes later, he looked up to see a vehicle speeding toward them. It slid to the left down a hill, then corrected its path.

"What is that?" He pointed.

Vincent squinted. "Wish I had a telescope, not that it would do that much good in this weather. I'd say it's....probably either really good or really bad. Someone on a mudrunner."

Elm looked with him. "Lady Holly."

She drove a long chariot pulled by an iguana creature with the speed and agility of a much smaller, lighter animal. As she arrived, she coaxed the lizard and chariot to a sliding stop several feet from their group.

Though the mudrunner had a short windshield and a leather top like an umbrella over her head, her face and hair were wet in the rain. She had abandoned the formality of the king's court, trading her flowing dress for a pair of goggles and a fitted shirt and pants similar to the Keeper training uniforms Jacquess had given them for their trip to the star.

She asked, "You got it, didn't you?"

"Yes," Desmond said.

"I knew it. May I see?"

He started forward. Elm stopped him with an arm across his chest.

"What are you doing?" Vincent asked.

"Why is she alone?"

"Does it matter? Would you rather she have guards with her?"

"It does matter. We don't know her."

Vincent stepped toward him. "Holly is one of the most good-hearted people I've ever met."

"I'd like to offer an explanation if I might interrupt." She hopped down from the mudrunner. "I've recruited some retired Keepers to shelter you until we can rescue Charlotte. They've agreed to help. I've also arranged for transportation out of the city."

Elm remained skeptical. "What kind of transportation?"

"Showing you will probably be better. Now, may I please see the vessel?"

Desmond put a hand on Elm's arm. "It's okay." He pulled the bottle from beneath his shirt, and it dazzled in the gray day.

With the reflection of starlight dancing in her eyes, she cradled the bottle in both hands. "Lucy." Tears welled in her eyes. "I can feel her presence."

Vincent put his arm around her shoulder, pulled her close, and kissed her on the forehead. "She's in there, alright."

"I know you'll keep this safe." She let it go, then addressed them all. "I have the beginning of a plan, or more like the end. Your shelter and escape are covered. We have until tonight to free Charlotte from the palace."

"What do you have in mind?" Vincent asked.

"You'll see." She gave a mischievous grin. "I'll show you on the way back."

They crowded onto the mudrunner, which wasn't built to hold so many passengers. The wheels creaked as the iguana turned the thing around.

Over the first hill, they gained momentum and soon, they were off and running at full speed through the rain. They splashed into puddles in the ditches and flew up rises between rows of sprouting plants.

To the right of and beyond the city, smoke rose from a range of black mountains. The glow of fires burning throughout permeated the dreariness.

"That's Brimsage," Vincent told Desmond. "Chirpy would be right at home. In fact, she probably came from there. They use molebats in mining operations. I've been, once. It didn't seem like a nice place to live. Everything has a fine layer of soot over it, even the air."

They veered to the left of Pandresian City, cutting a wide arc around the wall and then continuing through a field of short, yellow plants. As they neared the stone edge of the canal, Holly pulled back on the reins. They were still outside the city, near a tunnel leading in. Above that, Pandresian City towered high above them, reaching for the clouds.

CHAPTER 38

"The city looks so much bigger from down here." Gwen shielded her eyes from the rain as she looked at the wall and the towers above them.

"It's a wonderful place," Holly said. "I'm sorry you're experiencing it in such a way. The kings can make a mess of things when they want to."

"They certainly can," Vincent said sadly. He stepped down from the mudrunner onto the edge of the canal and winced. He rested a hand on his left side, on his ribs.

The others climbed down and assembled in a group. They were a mess, every one of them, dirty and exhausted.

Holly asked, "Are you injured?"

He shook his head no. "We ran into some trouble down below. We're probably all a little battered and bruised. I'll be fine once I have a rest. I just got too comfortable is all." He patted the iguana and told Holly, "You're still a much better driver than I am."

"I know. I remember your run-in with the city wall."

He laughed. "These big lizards have too much of a mind of their own. Mechanical things and I get along better."

"I'm sure the poor iguana you were with would agree. His nose hasn't been the same since." She adjusted the reins and spoke to the lizard. "Back to the stable with you, good boy." She slapped his haunches, and he took off, further down the canal to a bridge, then crossed over, making his way toward the other side of the city like a responsible lizard.

The canal wasn't guarded, but it was soaked from the persistent drizzle, and the conditions made for a miserable march to the tunnel. Considerably more energetic than the rest of them, Holly moved into the lead.

"If it's rest you need, you'll be pleased with your accommodations. It's a lovely home. My friends who live there are absolutely thrilled for the opportunity to help out." She was more relaxed than she was in the palace. Desmond decided this was more her element - Keeper business out in the world.

"Are you sure we can trust them?" Elm asked.

"Oh yes. They're practically parents to me."

"Don't tell me you've gotten the Fairlaces involved," Vincent guessed. "I really hope you didn't rope them into this."

"I didn't *rope* them into anything. They saw the drama at the supply tunnel and asked how they could help."

Gwen stuck to the outer edge of the stone walkway, as far as she could get from the canal without tromping through mud. The water was placid the last time they saw it. Fed by the storm, it had become angry, its waves lashing the stone. Rasq walked between her and the canal.

Desmond might've been the person to do that for her before they came to the realms. He couldn't help but feel a pang of jealousy. He'd never had a crush on Gwen. She was always more like a sister, but to see someone else so close to her bugged him.

A cold breeze from the tunnel, from deep within the city, carried a concentrated smell of rain and something like rotten meat. It was bad but not bad enough to keep them out in the rain. Once inside, they took a few moments to wring out their shirttails. Gwen squeezed water from her hair. Elm did a dog shake.

Rasq didn't seem to mind being wet. His attention was focused on something further in. He left Gwen's side to stare.

Desmond saw it, too. Among shafts of light coming through the grates overhead, a large shadow bobbed atop the current. He couldn't quite make out a shape.

"What is it?" he asked.

Holly joined them. "That, my young friends, is your mode of escape. Come on. I'll show you."

They left the entrance and went deeper into the tunnel, where faint reflections of ripples flashed along the ceiling, and the sound of rushing water echoed around them. The place was cold and dark, but they were safe from the guards that likely patrolled overhead.

A wooden dragon head came into full view first. Like some dark demon, it peered out with painted eyes and a toothy grin, nodding in the turbulence. The head was attached to the front of a black boat, the hull of which was as long as Desmond's parents' sedan. It reminded him of Viking ships, only much smaller.

Gwen backed away from it. "Why does it look like a monster?"

"Aw, it's not that bad, is it? I thought it was kind of pretty. We got it from Brimsage on trade. Tough as nails but light as air. All you need is a good push." Holly put her hands on her hips and looked up at it admiringly.

"Oh no. You don't mean...we can't ride that out." Vincent crinkled his nose. "It smells too awful."

"Fastest getaway in the city, love."

"What smells awful?" Desmond asked.

Vincent explained, "They have a fertilization ceremony for the crops. Heavy rains come on the same day every year. At the far end of the city, workers set up a network of rain catchers and chutes that drain into a kind of balloon made of livestock skins and filled with a noxious mix of, well, you don't want to know what. When the rain stops, there's a speech, and the king breaks the balloon. The canal channels that wave of nastiness into the lerecane fields as fertilization for the crops."

"We'll ride the wave out," Rasq said.

"It should carry us pretty far, actually. The ride won't be pleasant, but it should be effective enough. Good plan." He directed the compliment at Holly.

She nodded, then proceeded down the tunnel. "Charlotte is being held in a room on the third floor of the palace. Guards from both cities watch over the door. That's all I know so far."

Vincent asked, "What about the other empaths? Are they going to tell Jacquess we're here?"

"They won't tell him or Tarashet. They know how important this mission is."

Holly led them down a long corridor, around a couple of corners, into a section of the tunnel that was more open to the street above. The grates came more frequently, letting in shadows of people at street-level. The scent of grilled meat from the market traveled down to Desmond, making his stomach growl. He tried not to think about how good breakfast at the palace had tasted.

They came to a break in the tunnel, a spot where the canal was completely exposed to the street above. Holly motioned for them to remain in the shadows and then went out into the rain. She scanned the railing above them and ducked back into the tunnel.

"Stay here. I'll signal when the alley is clear. Up there." She pointed to a section of railing. "Watch for me, and move quickly." She put up the hood on the back of her shirt and took a nearby flight of steps to street-level. At the top, she leaned on the railing, pretending to take in the view.

Desmond watched from the shadow of the tunnel. A Pandresian soldier tipped his helmet in greeting. A woman offered to sell her some bread. A pair of kids across the canal climbed on the edge, and she scolded them for their carelessness.

The rain swooped in for a round of intense downpour that pounded the walkway next to the canal and the surface of the water. It must've sent whoever lingered on the street scurrying for shelter because that was when Holly finally signaled with a frantic wave.

The five of them bolted up the steps to the street, where Desmond suddenly felt very exposed. They entered an alley too shady and narrow for the residents to grow their city gardens, and they hurried up a cracked, concrete hill to a door painted the same color as the stone wall.

Holly knocked four times. The door cracked open just enough for a head to poke out. It was a tall man, very old with big, dark eyes and a wrinkled face.

"You made it. Come in."

They filed into the dark room, and the stranger closed the door behind them.

CHAPTER 39

"Are you certain you weren't followed?" the old man asked as he put one of his big ears to the door. His hair, a wisp of gray fluff, stuck out in all directions, and the edges of his overalls were frayed.

"Of course, Zandelane. You taught me well." Holly put back her hood.

Desmond and the others crammed into the tiny entryway, their clothes dripping onto the wooden floor.

Holly introduced the man. "This is Zandelane Fairlace. He and his wife, Addy, are Keepers of the realm."

Zandelane eyed Elm. "You're a big one."

"Like a walking alarm bell." A petite woman as equally aged as the man entered from an adjacent room. She wore her silver hair pulled back in a ponytail and a Keeper medal around her neck. Her gray dress had a set of four pockets sewn onto the front. Her feet were bare. "I'm surprised you made it with him in tow." She went closer to get a better look at him. "Arbolettis?"

"Yes," he answered sadly.

"Sorry, dear." She patted him on the arm. "I was fortunate to see it. Beautiful, beautiful." She shook her head. "Let's go into the next room, see what we've got."

Holly said, "His name is Elm. You remember Vincent, of course."

"Yes, yes."

They followed her into a cramped living room with no windows. The woman turned a brass knob on the wall to brighten the light hanging from the middle of the ceiling. The illumination it cast was a shade of whitish blue that chased shadows into the deepest corners.

A pair of sofas faced each other from the walls to their left and right. The furniture was nice but odd looking, a disorderly mix of wood with what appeared to be rugs as upholstery. At the far wall sat a small white table and two chairs.

She said, "I apologize for the lack of space. We don't usually have so many guests. Usually, just the two of us are puttering around the place. You must be Desmond."

"Yes, ma'am."

"May I see the vessel?"

"Addy, let them get settled before you go prodding about." Zandelane crossed the room to sit in a chair at the table.

"I'm not prodding." She smiled at Desmond, an unnervingly eager expression. "It's not every day someone walks into my sitting room with an elixir of immortality."

He looked to Vincent, who nodded his approval. Desmond pulled it from beneath his shirt as he'd done for Holly. It shone with swirls of white, yellow, and fiery orange. Hands shaking, Addy pulled it close for inspection.

"It's warm," she reported to Zandelane. "Like a liquid miracle. Lucinda?" She directed the name to Holly as a question.

"Her presence is there. Her spirit lives within the light of Cosalis."

"It always did. Marvelous." She released the vessel and pointed. "You are Gwen, and you are Rasq."

They nodded.

"I've heard good things about all of you. Everyone have a seat and rest. Are you hungry?" The enthusiasm with which their group replied caused her to chuckle. "Well, then, I'd better get on it before you start chewing the furniture."

They arranged themselves on the sofas, Desmond between Vincent and Elm. Rasq and Gwen sat on the other couch, looking comfortable together. Holly remained standing.

Zandelane took a pipe from the table next to him and lit it. "So tell me, young Desmond, did you touch the star?"

He'd had no opportunity to reflect on the experience. What did he remember of it? Everyone waited for his answer, including Addy, who paused in the open doorway.

"I remember brightness and heat, and," he drew a sharp breath as the vision came flooding back to him. "I saw her. Lucinda and Cosalis as it was dying."

Addy clasped her hands together.

Holly went to her knee and took Desmond's hand into her own. "You saw her?"

The sound of her running into the supply tunnel echoed in his memory, the vision of her pressing through the crowd of monks. He had witnessed her give herself to the star.

Holly studied him for several moments, reading him, he thought, and he let her. This way was easier. This way, he wouldn't have to talk about what he'd seen.

Her brow furrowed. "She showed him her sacrifice." Holly shook her head. "She meant no harm by giving this memory to you. She was alone in this for so long, and to her, sharing it is joyous."

"It doesn't feel like joy."

"Cosalis has always been her purpose. That's part of what she was trying to tell you. The other part is that her spirit still lives. She wants Castle to know. She wants everyone who loves her to know. Deep within the star, she is alive." Holly withdrew her hand and stood. "I must return to the palace before they notice I've been gone so long." She wiped tears from her face.

Vincent rose from the sofa to walk her to the door. When they'd left the room, Addy grinned at Zandelane.

"Seeing them together again is nice. I do wish they'd come to their senses more quickly. They should be married by now."

Zandelane spoke around the pipe. "You're old-fashioned. If they wanted to be married, they'd be married."

"You're old-fashioned." With a swirl of her skirt, she disappeared into the next room.

Desmond listened to the conversation between Vincent and Holly.

Vincent said, "Come with us."

"You know I can't. Pandresian City is my place."

"It's just...you know I won't be able to come back. I'll be an outlaw."

Desmond hadn't considered what Vincent was sacrificing by siding with them. What kind of punishment did a betrayal of both kings warrant?

"Jacquess and Tarashet will probably put a price on my head."

She said, "In which the Keepers will have no interest."

"Still, I won't be able to return. I won't be able to come back to you."

She soothed him in the same tone she used with the kings. "We were apart for so long before, and we've managed to find one another again. If we are supposed to be together, destiny will find a way. For now, we must finish walking the paths we're on."

His voice quieter, Vincent told her to be careful. When he returned, he was alone and somehow wearier than before.

He cleared his throat. "So, what's for lunch?"

CHAPTER 40

While Addy cooked, they talked about the realms they'd visited. Rasq told everyone about Castle and about growing up in the bookshop, how he wanted to be a Keeper as soon as he discovered them in the pages of a book about the realms.

Zandelane said, "The role sometimes finds you, as I would say it did in this case."

"Not me. The Authors Unknown entrusted the vessel to Des."

The old man laughed. "Why does that matter? All of you are working toward the same goal. Who wears the bauble around his or her neck makes no difference."

"He's right," Vincent agreed. "The vessel doesn't make anyone more important than anyone else."

Desmond asked, "How do the Keepers get appointed? Who hands out the medals?"

Vincent fielded the question. "I know we seem like a disorganized bunch, but we do have a hierarchy. The elders train us, and the council bestows the title to those who are worthy."

Addy's face appeared in the kitchen doorway. "Zane, set up the guest table, would you, please?"

With Rasq's assistance, Zandelane removed a long, folding table from behind one of the sofas. Legs they extended from the bottom were a foot tall, propping the top up just high enough for people sitting on the floor to eat. The next part of the setup, their seating, involved the arranging of couch cushions on the floor.

Desmond helped Addy serve bowls of meat, unidentified steamed vegetables with multiple stems, and some sort of pale pink grain that crunched like dry cereal. Over lunch, they discussed their plan for entering the place.

Addy said, "I've been talking to a friend of mine in the stable about getting you inside. The drains in the palace connect with the drains in the stalls. You can sneak into the palace that way."

Vincent groaned. "Not the lizards."

"Yes, the lizards. No guards would go into the sewer, even if they were ordered. I'll go along for that part, but once you're underground, you'll be on your own, until it's time to get back out, of course. I'll help you with that. We'll finish eating. You all can have a nap and get cleaned up, whichever order you like, and then this evening, we'll embark." She cocked an eyebrow at Elm. "Except for you, big boy. I can overcome many...obstacles, but I can't work miracles. You'll probably have to sit the whole operation out."

His mouth fell open. "All due respect, but you are not my elder. I go where I please."

Zandelane snapped, "You're a giant white tree deer. I could hang my entire collection of hats on your antlers. What shall we disguise you as? A parade float?"

Gwen smothered a giggle with her hand.

Vincent intervened. "I think, maybe, in this instance, we could find a different sort of role for you, one outside the palace."

Addy said, "If you will all allow me to finish, Elm will wait with that horrid boat and make sure nothing prevents your escape once the rest of you are down there."

They finished eating and took turns cleaning themselves up in the tiny, upstairs bathroom and resting. With no time for proper laundry, their borrowed Keeper uniforms received a quick wipe down with a wet rag. It was no palace salon, but Desmond was happy for it, just the same.

When Desmond returned to the first floor, Addy was putting a dark cloak over Gwen's shoulders. She reminded him of Mrs. Dunwiler, the way she fretted over them.

Zandelane chewed on the mouthpiece of his pipe, supervising. "I still think you should wait until the rain lets up. The king's guard gets testy when they're stuck out in the weather."

"True. They will be testy, which is why we will be extra cautious. However, the rain makes for excellent cover when you consider how many other people will have their heads covered to stay dry. A sunny, hot day would make disguises much more difficult."

She finished outfitting the lot of them with cloaks in varying shades of brown or gray, and then it was Zandelane's turn to offer his contribution to the rescue. He left and came back with an armful of stuff that he dropped onto his table. He showed the objects one at a time, first holding up a necklace with a rock pendant.

"These are air stones infused with the scent of Brimsage, boiling lava and sulfur, a touch of campfire." He placed one around each of their necks. "They'll disguise your scent so the hyenas won't be able to smell you. I should've given them to you earlier. We're lucky no patrols came around. Nasty mongrels. If you smell like their home, they'll be more likely to ignore you."

Gwen sniffed the necklace. "I hope this smell doesn't stick after I take this thing off. Gross."

"Better than dealing with the hyenas," Desmond said.

Zandelane nodded and continued. "Can't go anywhere without a good length of rope. For climbing, for rappelling, for tying up guards, if need be." The loops of rope he handed out were shiny, the fibers densely woven together. "This blend is imported from a friend of mine who lives in the next realm over. It's lightweight but super strong. No matter what you do to this rope, it won't fray or unravel, and it's nearly impossible to cut. Just clip those on your belts."

"Hopefully we don't get tied up with it." Rasq held his up to study it, first tugging on a small section twisting it as if trying to figure out how he might escape from it.

"Next up, we have self-igniting fireworks." Zandelane chuckled. "I see your faces lighting up. What is it about fire and small explosives that's so darn entertaining? These are more sound than light." He passed out three to each person. "They're waterproof until you break the seal. Just twist the cap and toss."

He demonstrated as he spoke, dropping the small canister to the floor, inches from his feet, and while he reached for the next object on the table, the firework let a shrill whistle, followed by a series of pops far too loud for the space they were in. Everyone else's hands flew to their ears for the duration of the assault, which lasted ten very long seconds.

"Now, these are the things you have to be careful with." He held up a contraption for them to see. It was small and made of thin pieces of wood, one of them bent into a bow shape. Below that, mounted off to the side, was a wooden ring. Zandelane fastened the leather strap around his wrist.

"A crossbow," Rasq said.

"Yes, a mini-crossbow. Each of them is equipped with three quarrels. They're like darts. The tips are dressed with a con-coction Addy cooked up in the kitchen. It should put a guard to sleep in a matter of seconds, and he or she should have some lovely dreams." He slid a lever, and a quarrel notched into place. "Shall I demonstrate?" He swung his hand around the room. Everyone gasped and ducked. "Only joking. See this ring? It's the trigger. You stick your thumb up and through." He aimed at the sofa to his right. "Pull down and toward your palm." The quarrel released with a click.

"I love it." Gwen practically drooled. "I wish we had those since the beginning. We could've shot all sorts of nasty things."

"Well, you only get three shots, so all the nasty things outside of the palace will have to wait."

Arms crossed over his sizable chest, Elm brooded in a corner near the entryway while the rest of them finished getting ready. He seemed more irritated than usual, moodier. Desmond could tell he didn't appreciate being left out of the action. He perked up when the time for him to go down to the boat arrived.

He and Zandelane left in early evening. They threw a dark blanket over Elm, which wasn't the best disguise because it made him look like a covered coatrack. However, it was good enough to enable him to blend in with the shadows better than his white, fuzzy exterior otherwise would have. As Desmond watched them leave, he hoped it wouldn't be the last time he saw them.

CHAPTER 41

Addy had, at a distance, followed Elm and Zandelane until they reached the edge of the canal. She returned to the apartment with good news.

"They made it with no trouble. If alarm bell can keep himself out of sight, they should be fine."

"Hope we'll be able to say the same for us," Gwen said.

Addy ruffled her hair. "You'll likely have no trouble if you follow a few simple rules, which I will share with you momentarily."

Outside, the air had cooled with the onset of night, and the shower had waned, somewhat. The street they'd crossed earlier was brightly lit and packed with people. Desmond and the others paused near the door to the Fairlace apartment, reluctant to venture out from the safety of the dark alley.

Addy said, "Oh, come on. It's not as scary as all that. Look here, the palace is down this street, turn left, cross over the canal, turn right. Curlao Seed Shop will be on your left, the kitchen door on your right. Pass those, and near the rear side of the palace will be the stable."

All except Vincent gave an uncomfortable nod of agreement. He had the same gleam in his eye as she did. They lived for adventure.

She continued, "Now, for the rules. Follow these, and you'll be in and out before you know it. Ready? Rule one, act as if you belong. Guards look for suspicious behavior, so don't slink about the festival like you're afraid of getting caught. Rule two, don't run unless you absolutely must. Should one of the guards spot you, remove yourself from their line of sight and duck into some dark corner. Most importantly, never panic. A panicked mind is a clouded mind. There is always a solution. All you have to do is find it."

"Got it." Desmond forced himself calm.

"For your additional information, the Pandresian guards have blind spots in those pretty helmets of theirs. The edges block their periphery." She held up a finger to the left and right of her head. "Use that to your advantage if you can."

"What about the Keepers?" Vincent asked.

"Oh, they don't have helmets," she answered quickly.

"Not what I meant. What should they do if they encounter one?"

"Most of them would be on our side. However, a few are loyal to Jacquess. I would be wary of anyone who gives you more than a passing glance. Bid them good evening if they speak to you and move with haste but not too much haste."

Flustered, Rasq put down his hood. "This is too much - the route, blind spots in the helmets? How are we supposed to remember all this and watch our backs?"

Addy said matter-of-factly, "It's like riding a bicycle, dear. Do you have those in the human realm? Once you get the hang of it, you never forget. Find a sense of balance and flow with the crowd. Go."

Gwen asked, "Now?"

"Yes, now. Go." She shooed them on with a two-handed wave.

The three younger ones reached the end of the alley and hesitated at the border between darkness and bright lights. Beneath the stark glare of torches and large lanterns carried on sticks, a party had sprung up. The throng packed the street, pedestrians moving this way and that, getting in the way, getting out of the way with little concern about order or civility, and the music, the heavy beat of drums seemed to encourage the discord. The sound reached into Desmond's chest, threatening to override the natural rhythm of his pulse.

"Desmond should stay here," Rasq blurted out suddenly.

The rest of them stared at him.

"I won't."

"If they catch you, our work is for nothing. Castle will die. The starlight is too important, and we can't risk them getting it."

"We've made it this far because we stuck together. Charlotte needs all of us. I need all of you to make it back. How far do you think I would get by myself with this thing around my neck?"

Disarmed by this sensible response, Rasq backed off. "Fine, but you have to promise me something. Promise me that if we don't all get out that you'll go ahead, that you'll find a way to get back to him. If any one of us escapes, it's you. Got it?"

Desmond nodded reluctantly, though he wasn't certain how sincere a promise he'd made. He didn't want to leave without anyone.

Addy spoke to them all in a hushed voice. "Since they're looking for a group, we'll separate and meet up inside the stables. I will get there first and alert my contact that you're coming. Do you remember where I told you to go?"

Rasq said, "Down this street, left, over the canal, right. After Curlao Seed Shop and the palace kitchen door comes the stable."

"Good boy. Give me a thirty-second head start." She put up her hood and vanished into the crowd.

"Are you nervous?" Gwen asked Desmond as they waited.

"Yeah."

"Me, too."

"We'll be okay. Just hold steady." He wasn't sure what he meant by those words, exactly, but they seemed to calm her.

Vincent said, "We should space ourselves out, so we aren't seen leaving together."

Rasq volunteered. "I'll go first."

"Good, then Desmond." Vincent pointed. "I'll stay here with Gwen and go last."

When his turn arrived, Desmond put up his hood. He merged into the street traffic, keeping his head down to avoid eye contact. The rules Addy had given him played over and over in his mind like a mantra while the energy of the place pulsed around him, a beat of its own, drummed by footsteps, propelled by the movement of the crowd. He saw what she meant by flow, and he gave himself over to it, even enjoying some of the sights when he felt safe enough.

Lady Holly was right. Pandresian City *was* a great place. Colorful and loud. Beings had come from several realms. He could tell by the variety of their forms, some looking as alien as Elm with their animal faces and strange clothes.

A four-legged man in a tuxedo waved propellers on sticks out of reach of children with feathered wings in place of arms. A clown peddled toy ducks to tall, slim creatures that didn't appear to have any mouths. Desmond took in these details, nearly losing himself in the effort to ingrain them in his memory. He wanted to remember it all, the men with torches burning in their hats, the women with candy-colored hair that looked hard like molded plastic.

He reached a densely packed area, where people had gathered to watch a baritone-voiced magician perform tricks, and Desmond cut left, away from the canal, toward fenced gardens in front of what looked like residential towers. Guards from both kingdoms and hyenas from one congregated there. The latter had grown impatient at the ends of their leashes, and they leaned toward the crowd to sniff intently at passing pant legs, growling on occasion.

Desmond's hand went to his neck, to the necklace Zand-elane had given him to keep them from smelling him. It was there. Still, as he moved within snapping distance, he held his breath, kept his head down, and concentrated on the beat of the drums. On he forced his trembling legs, unwavering. He would not run. He would not cry out.

A nose pushed onto his pants, then a second. Not just one hyena, but a line of them, sniffed him, and their throats rumbled with a sound that threatened to become a growl. But it didn't. He reached the end and nearly collapsed to his knees with relief.

CHAPTER 42

At the foot of the palace steps, the energy of the festival intensified. Pedestrians crowded closer, shoulder to shoulder in narrow aisles. Vendors pushed their wares, yelling at passersby and thrusting merchandise into their midst. Overhead, acrobatic performers suspended from wires flipped through the air among fireworks that fizzed by, dangerously close.

The painted sign for Curlao Seed Shop rose over the crowd ahead of Desmond, and then the kitchen door appeared to his right. The crowd thinned there, so he moved into the shadow of the palace. He continued toward the back of the building, where uniformed staff worked in the greenery on the royal grounds, hanging garlands, barking orders, or carrying boxes. It was a madhouse with the deadline fast approaching. No one wanted to be the unfortunate soul who disappointed the king, so much so that they paid no attention to Desmond.

The stable was a wooden building connected to the palace by a covered corridor. As he neared the main door, a guard on a mudrunner nearly ran him down. The driver yanked on the reins too hard, causing the iguana at the front let a strange cry, and then they trotted off toward a side street.

Desmond decided that the front entrance probably wasn't the sneakiest. He crossed over the muddy tracks left by claws and wheels. He rounded the corner of the building, and the tall stacks of hay bales there made excellent cover.

The sets of shutters on that side of the stable were closed, except one. He stayed close to the wall as he crept toward the open window, and when he got there, he crouched beneath it, listening for anyone who might be inside.

"What are you waiting for?" A voice from behind nearly made him jump out of his skin. Gwen was standing over him.

"Don't do that," he whispered.

"We're going to get caught while you're looking before you leap." She stepped sideways onto a bale of hay to get around him. She sat on the sill, then threw her legs over, and dropped inside.

He went after her, landing on the earthen floor on his rear. He dusted himself off.

Addy, Rasq, and Vincent were already there, as was another man dressed in dirty coveralls and a slouchy hat made of loosely knitted yarn. His deeply creased face lifted in a smile.

"This is him?" he asked of Desmond.

"Yes. Desmond, meet Lysander, master of all creatures tamed. No time for autographs. Hurry, now." Addy started toward the main aisle down the center of the stable, stopping short to check for guards.

Lysander put out his hand for a shake. "I'm pleased to meet you, young man. We owe Castle a debt. I'm proud to help in any way I can."

Desmond detected the familiar heat of Rasq's glare and ignored it. "Thank you, sir."

"I'll show you to the access hatch. This way." He went deeper into the stable, past several empty stalls. "A guard just took our last mudrunner, so no one should be in for a while," he said with no apparent fear of anyone hearing him. They seemed to have the building to themselves. "The only iguana left is Waslen. She's an old girl, arthritis in the knees." He motioned to an open stall door. Inside, a large iguana with scales faded to watercolor shades of green slept, curled up like an oversize cat.

"She's so pretty." Gwen lingered near the stall door.

Lysander heaved open the sliding door to the last stall on their left. Tools, bridles, and saddles hung on the walls. At the center of the floor sat a round rug, red with golden tassels at the border, an oddly fine decoration for a place they kept livestock. He moved it with his shoe, revealing the edge of a metal hatch, and Vincent bent down to do the rest.

He flung the rug aside and reached for the handle, pulled it up, and gave it a twist. The groan of the hinges filled the stable. Desmond winced at the volume.

The hatch opened to a ladder descending into darkness. A horrid smell drifted out, making everyone cover their noses with their sleeves.

"Well, no one said the walk would be pleasant." Lysander didn't seem to mind the smell much, probably because he didn't have to go with them.

Gwen complained through her sleeve. "We get any of that stuff on us, and they'll smell us coming."

"The walkway is nice and wide. Just stick to that."

"Vincent, you remember what we talked about? How you're going to get out of the palace?" Addy asked.

"Yes. Grappling hook and line from the next building."

"What does that mean?" Gwen asked.

Desmond answered for them. "It means you'd better not be afraid of heights."

Addy patted her on the head. "Be good, and take care of each other. Remember what I taught you. Make me proud."

Vincent went down first to confirm they were in the clear. He offered a thumbs-up to the rest of them, and they climbed down. When they were at the bottom, Lysander waved from overhead.

"Good luck." He shut the lid with a slam that echoed in the tunnel.

"Not a very stealthy entrance," Rasq grumbled.

"Stealthy enough. We haven't been arrested yet." Vincent started in the direction of the palace.

"Yet."

They moved among patches of light from grates overhead and shadows of the palace staff. Between those and the movement of the water, the lap of small waves against the edge, the tunnel seemed a living thing, all too willing to amplify the sound of every movement.

Desmond caught snippets of conversation from above, gossip about who was courting who, schedules for festivities, comments on the quality of the food being prepared for the feast. No one mentioned Charlotte. No one talked about the fact that she was being held against her will. This angered him for some inexplicable reason, as if her captivity was merely incorporated into their routine.

Desmond and the others arrived at a ladder leading far higher than the first, and they climbed for what seemed like a long time. Where the stench from the sewer dissipated, the sound of running water began, coming from somewhere behind the wall.

"Where does this lead?" Gwen asked Vincent.

"To a floor between floors, a utility room where pipes from the upper levels join those from the first."

They finally reached the top and a hatch that opened to a dimly lit, stone chamber the size of a large closet. A pair of gas lanterns illuminated a network of pipes and small waterfalls leading down through openings in the floor, to the sewer from which they'd just come.

"Doesn't smell as bad up here." Gwen smoothed the front of her cloak.

Vincent hushed her with a finger to his lips. He went to the door, turned the handle slowly, and cracked it open.

He reported, "We're alone for the moment. This is an emergency exit stairwell. It shouldn't be too heavily guarded. If we see a soldier, I'll take care of them. Desmond and Gwen - in the middle. Rasq, you're in charge of covering us from the back."

He nodded and adjusted the wrist crossbow into a better position for firing. He held his arm out as they crept up the spiral stairs.

CHAPTER 43

Desmond disliked the feel of the place, so like a dungeon with its stone walls. They could be trapped there easily if guards approached from above and below.

At the edge of an open doorway, Vincent held up a hand, a signal for them to stop. He cocked his head to listen and then ventured a look. A couple of hasty steps later, he was on the other side of the doorway, urging them on and casting wary glances at the next turn in the staircase.

Gwen and Desmond went together. Rasq, who refused to turn his attention forward even for a few seconds, stumbled backward, nearly falling into the rest of the group. They rounded the bend and saw light spilling from the next doorway.

From behind them came a click followed by a series of thumps as a guard rolled down the stairs.

Gwen pushed by Desmond to get to Rasq. "What did you do?"

He was equally shocked by his own action. "I was supposed to."

Vincent reached back to pull him forward. "Yes, you were supposed to. He'll be fine. Come on."

"But he fell down the stairs," Gwen said pityingly.

"He'd probably get a reward for knocking *you* down. We have to go," Desmond told her.

They stole past the next doorway, encountering no one else on the turning staircase as they went. At the edge of the third floor, they stopped to assess the situation.

Determining which room Charlotte was in required no guesswork. They could see it from the staircase, past a junction of hallways. Guards, men from Jacquess, men with hyenas from

Tarashet, lounged on the floor or leaned against the walls, none of them looking particularly pleased about their station.

Desmond ducked back out of sight. "There's too many of them." He had a sinking sensation in his gut. They didn't have enough darts for all the guards and the hyenas.

"Can we go in another way?" Gwen asked.

Vincent said, "There is no other way. This is as close as we could get. Where's Rasq?"

He was gone. Another series of thumps reached them from below. He jogged back up to them.

"A second guard found the first. I only have one quarrel left."

Vincent nodded. "We're running out of time."

"Look." Gwen tugged his sleeve. "That door."

The first door on the right side of the hallway had opened a crack. Was it that way before?

"We don't know who's in there," Desmond whispered.

"Anyone hungry?" A woman approaching from one side of the hallway junction carried a box.

"No one is allowed here," a guard barked at her.

"Oh, too bad. I guess I'll just deliver these sandwiches to the salon staff."

She was dressed like an empath. Fancy dress, rosy hair pulled back in a long ponytail. She continued on her way.

One of Tarashet's men jumped to his feet. "Hold on, there."

She disappeared from view, but her voice was still audible. "Nope, you heard the captain. Rules are rules."

Rules may have been rules, but the men were hungry. Despite their captain's protests, they trailed after the woman like a pack of dogs, the hyenas bringing enough drool for the lot of them, and after seconds of deliberation, the captain went, too.

Roshan appeared in the door that had opened. "Come." He waved at Desmond and the others.

"Wait." Rasq stopped Gwen with a hand on her arm. "Do you think he can be trusted?"

"Do we have a choice?"

They entered a posh room carpeted in burgundy velvet. Bottles, towels, and soaps wrapped in decorative papers lined shelves on every wall. A chandelier above them twinkled.

"Nice." Gwen took in the scene as someone shoved a robe into her hands.

Roshan clapped twice. "Come, come. We are hurrying."

His assistants pulled the drab cloaks from the shoulders of Vincent, Rasq, and Gwen. On went the salon staff robes. Next, they went to work on vivid makeup and a white wig for Vincent. Desmond received different instruction.

Roshan led him to a large cart laden with toiletry supplies and pulled back a curtain in the lower portion. "You, my friend, are far too popular to pass for one of my lovely assistants. In here." He slid a panel on the bottom of the cart open. Underneath was a small chamber, part of which hung between the bottom shelf and the floor, in the center of the wheels. In a sing-song voice, he said, "Crouch in, crouch in." He pushed gently.

"I can't fit in there."

"Crouch in, crouch in." Roshan put a hand on Desmond's head to help cram him.

Desmond curled into a ball on his knees. Because of the way his back stuck up, they couldn't slide the panel shut again.

Roshan handed the panel off. "Hide this, please. Thank you. Elisma, please stack as many folded towels in there as will fit." He addressed Gwen, Rasq, and Vincent, "You are salon staff trainees. You will hold your heads high, so you can look down your nose. No matter what we do, we are better. Guards are dirty. Guards are beneath you. Gwendolyn, darling, please tuck that crossbow into your sleeve. I will do the talking."

With no further conversation, the cart was rolling. Enveloped in fluffy towels and a scent like floral perfume, Desmond could see nothing outside.

"Halt," a man's voice said. "No staff is permitted in this section of the palace."

Roshan kept his tone light but firm. "We're stocking rooms for guests the king has invited. Shall I inform him you forbade me from making them comfortable?"

"I haven't heard about any guests."

The curtain on the bottom of the cart skated open. Desmond clenched his fists, channeling the fear in order to keep the cart as still as possible. Towels moved. A sniffing hyena poked its nose into the cart from the other direction.

"I must request that you remove your filthy hands and your filthy dog from my clean towels."

"You must request, huh." The guard was skeptical. "And who are they?"

"My trainees."

"Why are they made up like clowns?"

"Tradition dictates that entry-level salon staff must be enhanced to reflect our standards until they reach them in a more natural way."

"You're awfully tall for a lady," the guard said.

Vincent made no effort to hide his manly voice. "I'm not a lady."

"How very ill-mannered of you, sir," Roshan snapped at the guard. "I need to proceed. Now, will you allow us to pass or shall I alert the king of the delayed availability of these rooms?"

Hushed voices consulted one another far too long for Desmond's taste. All seeming to talk at once, they debated the merits of cooperation versus denial and shared desires to avoid punishment. One man told the rest he'd heard of someone ending up in shackles for disobeying an order from the chef, an action which resulted in undercooked fish being served. In the end, they decided.

"Every room but that one."

"Why?" Roshan pressed.

"Don't worry about it. Leave the doors open when you're inside. Maybe I should have a couple of men escort you."

Without missing a beat, Roshan countered, "And maybe I should send for a member of the staff to clean up the mud you'll track in with those clunky boots of yours."

"Just go about your business, and get out."

CHAPTER 44

The cart rolled again, and Roshan launched into a lesson. "The first thing we do upon entering a room is inspect the decor for flaws. Of course, the maid service should do so beforehand. We are merely a secondary line of quality control. The king has entrusted us with this duty because we understand the value of appearance. It is everything when one has visitors."

A heavy object dropped to the floor. The door slammed, men shouted, and banging on the outside of the door commenced. Then hands were digging, throwing towels aside, yanking Desmond from the cubby in the bottom of the cart. He stumbled, legs stiff from the lack of circulation.

Rasq and Gwen threw off their robes. Vincent, white wig askew, shoved a spear he'd taken from the unconscious guard into the door handles to hold it closed. He went to the nearest piece of furniture, a chest of drawers, and began to push. Desmond helped him barricade the doors with it.

Roshan dashed across the room, opened the stained glass windows. "This is as close as you'll get. She's in the next room."

"Wait, you want us to reach her from outside?" Gwen asked incredulously.

Not inclined to argue, Roshan pushed her that direction. "Unless you know of some convenient secret passage, this is your option."

Tossing his wig on his way to the window, Vincent said, "Desmond, you and Rasq get Charlotte. Gwen and I will set up the line for our escape. Addy is probably waiting for us."

Rasq hopped up to the window ledge with no hesitation. Desmond went next, onto the wet stone. They had two floors between them and the ground, the crowd moving like a river. Dizzy, he flattened himself against the wall.

"Don't look down," Rasq advised.

"Too late."

The simple architecture of the palace meant they had no statues to grab onto. They had a wall and the ledge on which to stand. That was all.

"Don't think about the distance. Concentrate on your feet on the ledge. It's the only thing that matters."

"Okay."

They edged over and found the window open. Charlotte was standing just inside, arms crossed, foot tapping.

"About time." She wore a dress similar to what the empaths wore in sunny shades of orange and yellow.

"You knew we were here?" Desmond dropped into the room.

"I heard the conversation in the hallway between Roshan and the guards. They aren't very bright, are they?"

The guards beat on her door, the handles of which were secured by a length of gilded cord. It stretched as the men pushed.

"Uh-oh." Charlotte backed toward the window.

Rasq told them, "Go," and held up his arm with the crossbow.

Charlotte asked, "What is that?"

"Crossbow with sleep darts." Desmond returned to the ledge and offered her his hand. He said to Rasq, "You only have one quarrel left."

"Hurry up, and I won't have to use it."

Then he and Charlotte were out the window, back on the ledge with Rasq climbing up after them. The rain ceased suddenly, and with it, the festival went quiet.

"What happened?" Rasq looked to the sky.

She said, "The rain stops like this every year." She prodded Desmond. "Go on. It's alright. The rain stops like someone shut off a faucet. The king gives a speech, and then he opens some bag thing to let disgusting water into the channel. Silly, if you ask me."

Rasq started, "That means..."

"We're going to miss our boat," Desmond finished.

A shiny object toting a red line sailed into the window ahead of them.

Desmond looked over at a neighboring building, the direction from which the silvery object had traveled, to see Addy Fairlace holding a telescope to one eye and waving from a window on a floor lower than theirs. She'd draped a rug over the sill to cushion their landing.

When Rasq, Desmond, and Charlotte got back to the first room, Vincent was securing the end of Addy's rope around a support column.

He said, "There you are. We're all set. Go ahead."

"Wait." Roshan stopped Vincent. "Someone shoot me with one of those darts you used on the guard."

"What on earth for?"

The doors banged hard into the chest of drawers, snapping the spear in the handle in two.

"I need to look like you coerced me. Come on. Hurry."

"Okay." Vincent nodded. "Thank you for your help. We are forever in your debt."

Roshan put his hands together and bowed as the door swung in again, wider, and moved the chest of drawers. Vincent's quarrel sailed through the air and met its mark, a spot on Roshan's shoulder. He collapsed to the floor.

Vincent said, "Use the rope Zandelane gave you to slide. Go."

"What about Charlotte?" Desmond asked. They only had four ropes.

"She'll come with me."

Gwen took the rope from her belt, threw one side over the line, and put her hands inside the loops to hold on. She let a squeal as she dropped. Desmond used the rope the same way and went flying over the crowd, kicking his legs.

Addy lifted Gwen by the back of her pants to move her before Desmond hit the rug with bone-jarring force. With her help, he scrambled over the sill and inside to make room for Rasq and then Vincent carrying Charlotte.

They had landed in a second-floor apartment with goldenrod-colored walls and furniture made of dark wood. The only decoration consisted of framed pictures of iguanas and award ribbons.

"Is this where Lysander lives?" Gwen asked.

Addy answered, "Yes, and he's risked far too much by letting us in here."

She led them through to the next room and the next, to a stairway, where they nearly collided with a woman carrying a basket of clothes.

Charlotte gathered the front of her long skirt up to move more easily. "Who's Lysander?"

"Explanation is best left to a less hectic time." Addy passed the front door and moved toward the back of the building. "I'm Addy Fairlace, by the way. Nice to meet you." Before Charlotte could reply, they were running through a narrow, rain-soaked alley.

CHAPTER 45

The king's voice boomed from the front of the palace. "And so, with this, we begin a productive year of cultivating crops and trading with our friends and neighbors. As is customary, we offer gratitude for the people and the leadership that keep Pandresian City great. The council, the Keepers. We are all imperative in this golden machine."

Desmond would've rolled his eyes if he weren't afraid of tumbling down the sloping alley. With most of the crowd in audience at the king's speech, their path was clear of resistance. There was no need to sneak, no need to look casual. Their escape was an all-out dash for the boat, past a pair of children splashing in puddles and an animal that looked like a cross between a chameleon and a goat, toward the canal.

The king's voice reached them again. "To this next harvest, we offer richness. May it be lush. May it feed our families and fuel our trade."

Out of breath, Addy was starting to slow. She stopped at the top of the canal stairs to lean on the rail for support. "Go on. This is where we part ways."

"Guards will be here any second," Vincent said.

"I'll be home before they get here." She gave a weary grin. "Get on, now. The floodwater is coming."

Gwen hugged her and went down the stairs. The rest of them did so as well, sparing a couple of seconds to tell her goodbye, and again, they were running, through the dark tunnel, where the water had gone eerily placid. Elm waited alone at the boat.

"Zandelane?" Vincent asked Elm.

"I sent him home after we loaded the supplies."

"Good. Did you have any trouble?"

"A couple of patrols in an adjacent tunnel. They didn't come down far enough to notice the boat."

They piled onto the dragon, taking seats on the long bench down the center so that they all faced front. Leather handles were mounted down both sides of the interior of the boat.

Vincent nodded to them. "You might want to hang onto those."

Gwen made the mistake of looking behind them. She turned back to the front, looking stricken.

Rasq patted her on the back. "It's okay. We're all here."

Oars lying on the floor of the boat rattled as a roar filled the tunnel. The net holding supplies Elm and Zandelane had loaded swung on its hook at the back of the boat. The canal gave a warning swell.

Then the wave hit, a wall of murky water rushing at them from behind, propelling the boat into a sudden acceleration that lifted it. Elm ducked to save his antlers and his head as the wooden dragon splintered against the roof of the tunnel.

"Stay down!" An adult male voice (Desmond couldn't tell whose) shouted over the noise.

Into the night, the headless dragon rocketed them away from Pandresian City, away from guards gathering at the very last bit of railing to throw spears. The boat continued into the open fields, past channels diverting some of the water for the budding crops.

More guards, these on mudrunners drawn by Lysander's iguanas, approached from both sides. They pulled up alongside the water, closer and closer, and just when Desmond thought the headless dragon might not have enough momentum to get full away, the sound of falling water reached him.

"Was this part of your plan?" Elm asked Vincent.

"Wasn't really my plan."

The guards on mudrunners gave up the chase. They skidded to a halt, wheels sliding on the wet ground.

Rasq released one of the handles to put his arm around Gwen. "I've got you."

Desmond couldn't see what lay before them. He wasn't sure he wanted to.

"Hold onto me," Elm said over his shoulder, "tight as you can."

Desmond did what he was told. He shut his eyes, felt the warmth of the vessel full of starlight against his chest.

Help us, he silently implored Cosalis, Lucinda, whoever would listen.

The front of the boat dipped, and they were descending on rapids, bobbing, swinging wildly as the current tossed them where it pleased. They struck a rock on their right. The wood emitted a crack that seemed to echo.

"It's leaking!" Charlotte yelled from the back.

The headless dragon tilted forward at a dangerous angle, then hard to the left, even faster than before. A boulder rose into view, a hulking monster of a thing.

"Lean!" Still holding onto the handle, Elm threw his weight the other direction, and everyone in the boat did the same.

The tail of the dragon grew a mind of its own and began to come around. They were going into a spin.

Another crack of wood against stone came from the front of the boat, a wave of dark water, and the river, his friends, all whirled into darkness.

CHAPTER 46

Fog. Desmond smelled it before he opened his eyes. Like chilly mornings at his house, when Gwen would coax him to the outdoors and show him the animals that preferred that strange version of nature, that border between night and day. He remembered the owls most of all, peering at them from the thick of the veil like spirits.

His clothes were wet. He felt sand beneath him and shallow water, the gentle lap of ripples reaching their end.

"Grandson of Allos Winters." A gruff-voiced shadow spoke overhead. It was a bulky creature, wide head, torso of a muscular man.

He blinked the shadow into focus. A lion man. That's what the stranger was, and he had a Keeper medal around his neck, which reminded Desmond of the starlight he was carrying. In a sudden fit of panic, he felt his shirt, found the vessel there.

Desmond propped himself up on his elbows to take stock. He wasn't injured, aside from some fresh bumps and scrapes. The crossbow on his wrist had broken to pieces. He ripped the remains of the leather strap from his arm.

A warm breeze eroded the edges of the haze at the riverbank into thin wisps. The evening light had a strange stark quality, the day refusing to surrender the sky to dusk. They must have crossed into another realm because they'd come from night. Time had shifted, ever so slightly.

Shattered bits of their dragon boat floated. He spotted Elm lying nearby.

"Where are we?" Desmond rose, felt the sand tilt beneath his feet, and rested his hands on his knees to steady himself.

Other lion men accompanied the first. Their breastplates were a regal blue, their metal helmets simple with decorative nose guards down the center. They walked the bank of the river, searching.

Elm stirred as he was nudged. He coughed onto the sand.

"The Kelosian Veld. I'm here to escort you back to Nola Junction."

Kelosian Veld. Nola Junction. These words meant something to him a few realms ago. The Authors Unknown had planned to send him to the veld, where he would meet a lion, a Keeper named...what was it?

He guessed, "Haelo?"

The man grunted. "You're late."

A body crashed into Desmond from behind, wrapped arms around him. It was Charlotte. Her dress was in tatters, her curls tangled, and a scratch marred her cheek, but she was alright. Gwen came next, hugging him with equal enthusiasm. Rasq was with her, looking more disheveled than ever. From the other direction, Vincent came limping out of the dwindling fog.

"Keeper Elm of Arbolettis, by order of Queen Illifernet Fassunae of Fairy Realm and by order of the Council of Elders, we place you under arrest."

Elm sat in the sand and water, glaring up at the trio of lions in front of him. He made no move to defend himself or escape.

The soldiers, who had not expected this passive reaction stood at the ready, two with swords poised, the center armed with a set of irons.

"Wait. What are you doing?" Desmond ran to them.

Haelo followed at a much slower pace. "Elm is to be charged for the theft of the vessel and hindering a mission to preserve the realms, thereby breaking his oath to serve as a protector.

He will be taken before the Council of Elders. They will hold him responsible for his actions."

Elm stood and presented his wrists for the irons. With a quick yank, a soldier removed the Keeper medallion from the tree stag's neck. He handed it over to Haelo, who placed it in a pouch on his belt.

"But he helped us. Take those off." Gwen moved toward them.

Haelo put his arm out to keep her from interfering. "This isn't your decision."

Desmond began to protest, but Vincent leaned down to say, "It's okay for now. Let it go."

Haelo put a hand on Desmond's shoulder and turned him toward the land. "Come, starkeeper. We've set camp over that ridge."

"Starkeeper." He repeated the word, unsure of whether he wanted anyone to call him that.

Rasq trotted up next to them. "What about the king's guard? Jacquess and Tarashet?"

The other lions joined in a chorus of growls and grumbling.

"Let them come. We'll send them scurrying like rodents."

His troops agreed heartily.

Exhaustion settled over Desmond as they plodded up the ridge in the fading daylight. He began to feel every scratch, scrape, and bruise dragging him down in the heat. His arms swung at his sides like lead weights.

Their bleak surroundings didn't help matters. The ridge, which was actually more of a sand dune, served as a border between the edge of the water and the rest of the place. The arid landscape was flat as far as he could see. Low grasses and brush grew in long runs, dividing the ground into jagged patches.

Lamps were coming on in the mass of white tents pitched several meters out. Desmond estimated they had about fifty, all filled with lion warriors dressed in armor. Guards at the edge of camp held bows at their sides and wore scabbards complete with swords. They saluted as Haelo arrived.

"We've set up a tent for you at the center of camp," Haelo announced to Desmond's group. "Anyone trying to get to you will have to go through every one of us."

Despite Elm's predicament, Desmond was glad for the protection. He wondered how their quest might've gone if they hadn't gotten sidetracked by the theft of the vessel.

"How did you know we were coming?" he asked.

Haelo grinned down at him, fangs showing. "Keepers work in cooperation more often than not, and the city is full of them."

Boisterous conversations between the lion men went quiet as they came through. Staring ensued. Desmond was getting used to those looks, though, the curiosity.

"Here." Haelo stopped at a tent with its flap door tacked open. "Get some sleep. We have a full day planned for tomorrow."

Charlotte asked, "How far is the junction from here?"

"Less than a day's ride. I would take you now, but the council has insisted we wait for their representatives to take Elm into custody. The crime he committed is a dire one, and they take the arrest of enemies of the realms very seriously. He's a danger."

"Where are you going to keep him?"

Haelo sighed, obviously annoyed with the concern for the well-being of a creature he had already written off as delinquent. "We have arranged his confinement near my tent. He will not be harmed while in our charge. Your concern is admirable but uncalled for. He's a criminal."

Elm chimed in without looking up from the ground. "Let me go, little one. All that matters is that they get you home safely. I have nowhere else to go, anyway. What's a Keeper without a realm?"

Haelo shot him a glare. He motioned for the others to go into the tent.

The interior was comfortable. Colorful cushions were arranged at the edges, grouped like beds for them to sleep on, and a rug covered the ground at the center. There, too, a table with meat, bread, and a decanter filled with an orange beverage beckoned.

"Eat up. Rest. Guards will watch over you. Please let me know if you need anything else." He put his hand on his chest, tilted forward in a bow, and left them.

CHAPTER 47

Desmond, Gwen, Charlotte, Vincent, and Rasq sat around the table on the floor. Their meal, while welcome and tasty, was eaten in somber silence for several minutes. They had lost one of their own.

Charlotte finally piped up. "So, what have I missed?"

This initiated a round of stories, the control of which bounced from Desmond to Gwen to Rasq and back again. They told her about their visit to the star, Addy and Zandelane and sneaking through the festival. They told her about Lysander and his iguanas and the sewer.

Knowing the guards were likely hanging on every word, they were careful about what they said. There was one unspoken certainty. No one planned to leave Elm behind. Just like they wouldn't leave Charlotte or any of the others. It was all or nothing, and no one would offer debate on the subject, not even Rasq. They'd come too far together.

After they'd eaten and the sky had darkened to night, Vincent stood up. "I'm going to go get the lay of the land."

"I'll go with you," Rasq offered.

They weren't gone long when Desmond became restless and got up to leave.

"Where're you off to?" Gwen asked.

"I'm going to talk to Haelo. Maybe I can get him to let Elm go."

She snorted with laughter. "Good luck with that."

Desmond took a path between small cooking fires and lion soldiers standing around. One of them with his shirt off gave himself a shower with a bucket behind one tent. Further down, a tight circle of four of them sharpened swords with flat pieces of dark rock.

A pair of lionesses (he guessed their gender by lack of mane) practiced hand-to-hand combat. The larger of the two lifted the smaller into the air and slammed her onto her back in the dry dirt. He cringed at the thump of flesh against the ground.

Haelo's tent was easy to identify in the crowd. It stood taller than the rest with regal banners billowing in the hot breeze.

Desmond needed to decide how to approach Haelo. He had two goals for the conversation. He would try to talk the Keeper out of turning Elm over to the council. If that didn't work, he would gather as much information about the situation as possible. He waited until all the lion visitors left and then peered in.

"Hello?"

"Come in, Desmond." Haelo, sitting in an armchair behind a desk, looked up from a piece of animal hide with a map drawn on it. "I trust you found your accommodations acceptable."

"Very much, thank you."

The Keeper's tent was nicer than Desmond's, more decorated with fancy swords, spears, and other weaponry arranged on racks. The furniture, while simple, was more than a stack of floor cushions. A low, wooden cot in the corner, the chest serving as a nightstand, and the stack of books on top made this tent a home away from home for a man who appeared to have considerable power.

"I suspect you're eager to get back."

"I am." Desmond studied the map on the desk. "I was hoping I could see Elm before we leave."

Start with a small request.

"I would think that a person charged with the protection of an object as precious as starlight would be less eager to converse with a thief."

"He isn't what you think he is."

"He didn't steal the vessel?"

"He did...take it for a while. He wanted to use it to restore his realm."

A criminal but with noble intentions.

Haelo laughed. "Arbolettis? A tiny bottle of starlight can't raise an entire realm. What a fool."

Desmond bristled but kept his tone even. "Maybe." He touched the map, a spot near a squiggle of blue he supposed was the river. "We're here?"

"Yes. Very good. We plan to go this direction, around the village of Raseftic. The portal to the junction, the one you should've come through days ago, is here." He pointed to a box.

Desmond tried to memorize the map, the approximate direction they would have to travel, and then he brought the conversation back to the reason for his visit. "Elm saved my life. I can't move on without thanking him for that."

"He saved you to get close to the starlight. On that riverbank, if we hadn't shown up when we did, he would've snatched the vessel and fled. The grandson of a thief the likes of Allos should know to proceed in a more cautious manner. More than anyone else here, you should be familiar with the workings of a criminal mind."

Desmond unclenched the fist he felt his hand forming at his side. "I never met my grandfather." He had grown tired of people insulting his family. Regardless of whether the allegations were true, they were rude.

"Some traits are genetic. I, for one, don't see how the Authors could justify entrusting the vessel to you. This duty should've fallen to someone like me, an experienced Keeper. My family has been honorable for generations. My father was a Keeper, my mother and grandmother."

"I'm not Allos, and I'm not a thief."

"Perhaps." Haelo stroked his chin. "Still, you should know better than to trust the tree stag. Obviously, your time with him has blinded you to the potential for betrayal."

Desmond said, "He put himself in danger for us. If I say nothing, if I don't acknowledge him, the lack of closure will weigh on my conscience. It's the right thing to do."

Appeal to his sense of right.

Haelo considered the request before answering. "Very well. He's under lock and key in the cart behind my tent."

Desmond sensed a reluctance to discuss the subject further. He was fortunate to have gotten as much as he did. Luckily, he had the rest of the night to work on Elm's liberation.

"Thank you." He turned to walk away but stopped. "I also want to thank you for the protection you've offered us. I've never felt safer. I wish we could've come to you in the beginning as we'd planned."

Flattery might just get you everywhere.

Haelo puffed up his chest. "We take great pride in the skill of our soldiers. Since the tree stag means so much to you, I won't stop you from talking to him whenever you like between now and when you leave our company. At least two guards will be with him at all times. Just don't get too close."

"Yes, sir." Desmond saluted on the way out.

Access. It wasn't freedom, but it was a step in the right direction.

Desmond went around the side of the tent, to the back. Elm was there, shackled to a metal rack between him and where the driver of the cart would sit once their caravan moved. One wrist was bound behind him and linked to a chain leading down from the back of a metal collar. His back was to Desmond.

"Stop right there." A guard towered, several inches taller than any human man Desmond had ever seen.

Elm stirred at the voice but didn't turn around.

"Haelo gave me permission to speak to him."

"*General* Haelo didn't share this information with me." Apparently, failure to use the proper rank designation was enough to rankle him.

"He just gave me permission." Desmond nodded toward the tent.

"Verify." He ordered a nearby and much shorter comrade who scurried off.

Horses were penned nearby, massive, hardy creatures that reminded Desmond of Clydesdales, only with less hair. They had no manes, and their narrow tails were twisted like rope.

A soldier inside the corral gave a command to one of the horses, "Poleshnidek," and the great beast lowered itself to the ground for him to get on.

"Poleshnidek." It sounded German to Desmond as he repeated it to himself under his breath. Getting the horse to rise again required a pat on its head.

The lion returned moments later to report that Desmond did, in fact, have authorization to visit the prisoner. They allowed him to approach the cart.

"Elm?" When he received no reply, Desmond walked to the other side.

The tree stag was awake. Within his reach, food and water sat untouched. They'd freed one of his arms so he could eat.

"Are you okay?"

"Fine." Elm didn't look at him. "Just go."

"Why aren't you eating?"

"Doesn't matter."

"It matters to me." Desmond nudged the food tray closer to him. "You need to eat to keep your strength up." He tried to communicate, with a look, that escape was on the agenda, and for an instant, their eyes met.

Elm understood. He began eating.

CHAPTER 48

On his way back to the tent, Desmond found Vincent and Rasq. They joined his walk from the side, almost as if someone had choreographed their meeting. All involved kept their voices low.

"I saw a map," Desmond said. "The path to Nola Junction is a straight shot." Unspoken communication lay beneath his words. They could find their way home without the assistance of the lions. "General Haelo says I can talk to Elm up until the council comes to get him."

"Good," Vincent said. "We're well-guarded. I don't think the Pandresian soldiers will be a problem for us. They won't get inside the perimeter."

Translation: Security was tight.

"The horses look strong," Desmond said.

"Strong enough for all of us?"

"Yes."

A plan was forming between them. They would free Elm and ride out of the camp. All they needed was a very good beginning, a series of events or a particular circumstance that would allow them an opportunity.

Back in their tent, they had an all but silent conversation between the five of them involving a combination of charades and whispering. They needed a distraction to draw the attention of the lions away from Elm and the horses.

Rasq started off by producing the waterproof fireworks Zandelane had given him. He placed them on the table.

Desmond had one as well. Vincent had a couple, and Gwen had none.

Next came the pointing of fingers as they decided who would facilitate the distraction. Desmond pointed to himself. The vote of no was unanimous.

Rasq silently suggested Gwen, who nodded enthusiastically and gathered up the fireworks to stuff them into her pocket. Vincent suggested that she set them off at the edge of camp. Charlotte would be responsible for picking her up.

A while later, Haelo sent a soldier to retrieve his guests. The good general had invited them to a bonfire at river's edge.

There, the lion men exchanged stories about their strength. They told of competitions, battles, prowess with weapons, each story more boastful than the last. Most of them exaggerated; Desmond could tell. Their personalities seemed to lie at various points on a wide spectrum ranging from animal to human. Some of them, the brutish ones in particular, seemed more naturally inclined to use their tales to intimidate their fellow lions.

Then, last of all, was Haelo. He sat at the center of a log, with his soldiers on either side.

"I have a story." His booming voice cut through the rumble of conversation between storytellers. "The story of the time I met Allos Winters."

Everyone fell silent. Desmond went numb.

"He was a human unlike any other I've met, slippery as an eel, and he could talk his way out of anything." Haelo paused to see if Desmond was listening. "Many years ago, I was tasked, as I often am, with delivering a prisoner. A woman named Jez was accused of kidnapping the son of a nobleman for ransom. She'd had a change of heart and let the boy go. We found her in the next realm, west of the veld. She had taken a ship to evade capture for her crimes. When we apprehended her, she fed us this story that the boy was lying, that he had run away and accused her of kidnapping so he wouldn't get in trouble." Haelo laughed like he'd told some kind of joke, and the lions laughed with him. "Our party crossed paths with Allos toting what was likely a sack of stolen goods. I should've known he was trouble by the level of interest he took in our cargo. A crying woman in a cage." He gave a contemptuous snort. "Allos asked if he could share our dinner. His contribution to the meal was a bottle of Pandresian tulip nectar. We ate. We fell asleep because he'd laced the nectar with shade berries. And that thief, that slithering snake of a human male, made off with our prisoner, a jug of ale, and half our gold." He kicked the dirt in front of him into the fire. "We are considerably less trusting now." He snarled and locked eyes with Desmond. "How does it feel to be the grandson of a thief?"

The story was a warning. *We're watching.*

"The same as I imagine being the grandson of anyone feels," he shot back.

Perhaps he and his grandfather were more alike than he'd realized. He decided he was okay with that.

With story time finished, the soldiers dispersed. Desmond was the first of his party to rise. He noticed, as they walked back to their tent, four guards followed. Executing their plan was going to be trickier than he'd thought.

CHAPTER 49

Vincent closed the tent flap behind them and ran his hand through his hair. He said nothing. No one said anything, at first. They simply stood in a circle, swapping looks of anger or worry. Rasq broke away from the group.

He got low to the ground, on his hands and knees to feel along the place where the canvas walls met the floor. It was stitched together. Desmond realized what he was doing and grabbed a knife from the table.

The two of them waited until the guard's shadow moved away. They poked the blade into the stitching and cut. One by one, the stitches popped open. Whenever the guard came back around, they waited until he left to begin again. They made a hole in the back wall and then moved to the next wall to make another exit.

In a hushed voice, Vincent asked Gwen, "You remember how to ignite the fireworks?"

She nodded and crouched next to the hole.

Vincent motioned for Desmond and Charlotte to wait by the second hole they'd made in the tent. He directed Rasq to stand with him.

Vincent would go out first, draw the attention of the guards in the immediate vicinity long enough for Gwen to make a dash for the other side of camp. He held up four fingers to Desmond and Charlotte to signal he wanted four horses.

Charlotte's mouth fell open. "I don't know how we'd manage that with only two of us."

Desmond reminded her to be quiet.

Vincent sent Rasq over to them. He would free Elm by himself. He slipped out of the tent flap, into the camp of lions that would become their enemies in the coming minutes. Voices came from outside.

He said, "Hey, all. I need to visit the bush for a quick minute, if you don't mind."

"Back in your tent."

"Shall I relieve myself in the corner, then?"

Shadows on the other sides of the tent moved his direction, including, after a brief hesitation, the soldier near Gwen. Once he was away, she ducked under the tent, making a shadow of her own as she ran off.

Desmond held his breath. He listened for angry voices to stop her. Charlotte took hold of his arm. Rasq held fists at his sides. They heard nothing but Vincent's debate.

"Well, then, don't expect this tent to ever smell the same. I'll recommend the good general put you on laundry duty." Vincent stumbled back in, evidently pushed.

They waited for what seemed like forever.

Desmond became aware of every sound and movement, the slight swell of the tent with the breeze, every smell, vibrations in the ground. He waited for the signal that would launch everything into motion. He thought of the layout of the tents, the main avenues in front and the narrower spaces behind them, where stakes and lines would slow any attempt to run. They would slow the soldiers more, the clunky oafs in heavy armor.

Desmond reached for the future, a vision or some sign that would tell him how their attempt at escape would pan out. Win or lose, he would've felt better knowing. Too much time, too many minutes had passed.

Poleshnidek. He brought the word to command the horses to the forefront of his mind. He would need it.

The first firecracker was like the starting pistol at the beginning of a race. He, Charlotte, and Rasq didn't wait to see if the guards would leave to investigate. By the time the gunpowder cracks had really started, the three of them were running behind the tents, hurdling the lines connected to the stakes.

Seconds became precious, dissolving away faster than they could make good use of them. They reached the horse pen and found the guard there distracted by the rush of the other soldiers toward the sound of yet another firework.

The three of them ducked under a rail, into the side of the pen opposite of where the guard stood watch. Horses, the equine giants, were agitated, snorting and grunting. They wore no saddles.

"No." Charlotte moved from horse to horse. "We can't ride them like this."

Rasq powered ahead, searching. "There." He broke into a jog, and Desmond lost sight of him.

"Wait!" He held Charlotte's hand, and they chased after him. They squeezed between long legs and hooves.

"Poleshnidek." Rasq practically shouted. Three horses with saddles kneeled before him, and he grinned at Desmond and Charlotte.

They mounted the horses, and the beasts obeyed commands, rising with a quick lurch, despite the surrounding chaos.

Charlotte patted her horse, a blue-black brute, on the neck. "Easy."

Desmond felt high above the world. "Vincent wanted four."

A great roar cut across the noise, the sound of it driving a chill into Desmond's veins. Haelo. His eyes wild with fury, the Keeper stood next to the guard tasked with watching over the pen.

"We'll have to make do." Rasq turned to Charlotte. "Find Gwen, and go straight to Nola Junction. We'll meet you there."

As if in reply, another round of fireworks went off. She rode in the direction of the sound, skillfully guiding the horse to leap over the rail of the pen.

"Can you do that?" Rasq raised an eyebrow at Desmond.

"I guess we'll find out."

He dredged up memories of Charlotte's riding competitions, the way she and the horse moved as one. He silently thanked his parents for making him go. He was no expert, but he had an idea of what to do.

His horse also had an idea. It galloped full out and leaped, landed expertly on the other side.

Desmond looked back to see Haelo attempting to mount a horse with no saddle. His underlings did the same, and the pen fell into chaos. They shoved each other and growled, which frightened the horses, causing some to rear up.

Outside the rail, several lions surrounded Desmond and Rasq. The circle constricted, but, intimidated by the horses, they refused to get too close.

Rasq turned in the direction of Elm and the cart and forged straight through their line. Desmond went after him, along the edge of the pen, through flying projectiles from all around, knives, an arrow or two when someone managed to get one nocked. He kept an eye out for Haelo, but the general was lost in the crowd of horses and soldiers.

In the commotion, they had forgotten all about their prisoner. Near the cart, a pair of guards lay unconscious on the ground. Vincent and Elm threw their weight into the u-shaped rack to which they'd chained Elm, struggling to uproot it from the wooden floor. Rasq pulled his horse alongside the cart and hopped down to help them, and the bolts broke free. Elm flung the rack aside with a disgusted growl.

Vincent got onto Rasq's horse as angry men rushed toward them. They fled without looking back.

Elm mounted Desmond's horse in an awkward jump. Confused by the sudden heft, the horse threatened to buck. Desmond managed to coax it into a run.

Elm gave a breathless laugh. "They look mad."

In their rage, the lions at the edge of the camp dropped to all fours. They became predators like their more animal cousins in pursuit of prey, but they were no match for the massive horses. They and the camp shrank into the distance.

CHAPTER 50

The horses gained speed, seeming to relish the wide open veld. They'd crossed miles before Desmond stopped looking behind him to see if the lions were closing in.

"Are you okay?" he asked Elm.

The tree stag pulled at the shackles. "Uncomfortable. Staying on this horse would be much easier if I could use my arms properly."

"Do you want me to stop?"

"No! Ride like our lives depend on it, because they do. Mine does, anyway. Where are the girls?"

"They're supposed to meet us at the junction."

Elm seemed to sense his worry. "They'll be there."

Desmond and Elm caught up with Vincent and Rasq, and the four of them rode until the horses began to tire. They slowed to a canter.

"They probably need water," Rasq said. "Did anyone bring water?"

No one did. In fact, no one brought anything but the clothes they wore, so they pressed on until they came to a creek (if it could be called such) that was barely more than a trickle across the dry land. The water ran around four inches wide.

"It isn't much, is it?" Desmond asked.

The massive horses didn't seem to mind, however. As if trained to so, they lowered themselves to the ground in unison and proceeded to drink, pausing when the trickle waned.

"How much further do you think we have to go?" Rasq fiddled with Elm's shackles.

Vincent said, "Probably not far. Give me a go at that."

Desmond kept his eye on the horizon behind them. "They're coming after us." He squinted in the darkness, unable to tell if the movement he detected was real or his paranoia playing tricks on him. "We should go."

With a clank and a squeal, the shackles at Elm's wrists opened. He threw them away and rubbed his wrists. Vincent reached for the collar but Elm stopped him.

"No. Desmond is right. They're coming, and they won't stop for their horses to drink."

"Maybe that will help us. We'll be able to outrun them if we can move faster," Rasq said.

They mounted the horses and were off again. With the animals refreshed, they returned to their initial speed.

The uncertainty that Gwen and Charlotte would be at the junction nagged at Desmond. They were moving so quickly, they should've caught up with them or at least spotted them in the distance; he thought. What would he do if they hadn't made it? What if they lost their way in the desert? What if they hadn't even escaped the camp?

But as they neared a great stone archway, what could only be a portal to Nola Junction, figures awaited them there - two girls and a giant horse. He laughed and looked over to Rasq to see his relief mirrored on his friend's face.

Gwen and Charlotte jumped up and down, waving wildly, but not out of joy. Desmond turned to see Haelo and his small army charging toward them.

Vincent motioned for the girls to go through the portal, and they did so, leaving the horse behind.

Desmond barely got his horse to a stop before commanding it to kneel. He and Elm barreled through the portal with Vincent and Rasq close on their heels. After a brief flash between realm and junction, they were in the dim light, the oppressive quiet, and the multitude of dark portals on stair-step walkways.

Gwen backed away from the portal. "Can they come through?"

"Yes." Vincent was already trying to decide which portal would make the best exit for him. He grasped Desmond's shoulders and bent down. "You've all been very brave. You've done fantastic things other people could only dream of. Good work. This is where we part ways."

"Where's your Keeper medal?" Desmond noticed it was missing.

Vincent let him go. "I left it back at camp, in the tent. I've gone against the council's wishes." He walked away. "Come on, Elm. I guess we're on our own from here. Where do you want to go?"

"After that desert? Somewhere nice and cold." He bowed to Desmond and the others. "I'm honored to have helped you and Mr. Castle. I am sorry for the trouble I caused in the beginning."

Charlotte burst into tears. "This can't be goodbye."

The great, white beast gently lifted a tear from her cheek. "I won't forget you. You won't forget me. We'll always be together that way."

Gwen sniffed. "It's the dumbest thing I've ever heard."

He laughed. "Until we meet again."

Vincent paused to wave. "Farewell! Good luck raising the old man. Tell him I said hi." He gave a grin and passed into darkness.

"That goodbye was too fast." Charlotte started down the stairs.

Rasq said, "I can't believe they're gone."

"They'll be okay, won't they?"

"They have each other," Desmond replied.

They'd just reached the bottom of the stairs when Haelo plus five soldiers burst through the portal.

He bellowed, "Desmond Winters!"

"Run," he told Gwen, Charlotte, and Rasq. "They won't take me."

They fled for the exit - the door leading out of the junction. It opened easily for them, and they disappeared.

Desmond planted himself between his friends and Haelo and his men with their spears ready to skewer.

"A thief, just like your grandfather!" The general loomed, appearing even taller than before and displaying sharp teeth in a snarl.

"We're going home, now. If you want to keep your oath to protect the realms you won't try and stop us."

Haelo roared, the sound of it echoing in the vast junction. He reeled in the animal temper well enough to speak. "What did you do with my prisoner?"

Desmond pretended to think in a dramatic fashion, tapping his chin and squinting. "He went..." He raised a finger to point. He swept right. Lion heads swiveled. He swept left. Lion heads swiveled again. "I believe they went through that one." The portal was, of course, nowhere near the portal through which Elm and Vincent had escaped.

Haelo narrowed his golden eyes. "Why would you care what happened to someone who stole from you?"

"Because he made up for it. He did the right thing, eventually."

Desmond looked over at the pile of rags in which they'd found Elm that first day in the junction. He was glad they could leave him in the hands of Vincent, the man who had sacrificed almost everything to help save them all, including Castle.

Haelo puffed himself up. "You'll go free today. I have no choice in that matter, but know this. Your presence is no longer welcome in the Kelosian Veld. Like your grandfather, you've dishonored my people and stolen from us. Should I find you in our territory, you will be arrested and put on trial for your crimes and, if I can persuade the council, the crimes of your grandfather. Have I made myself clear?"

Desmond shrugged. "I didn't like your realm, anyway. It was too hot, and the scenery was boring."

The vessel warmed against his chest, and he imagined he heard Lucinda laugh.

Haelo recoiled indignantly. He glared down at Desmond, while Desmond glared back up at him, then, without another word, he turned to leave. He passed through the line of soldiers gawking.

It was over. They were free. Elm was free and Vincent. Elation surged through Desmond, and it gained strength as he opened the door and heard the rush of the river.

CHAPTER 51

His friends waited for him on the bridge. Gwen had all but forgotten her fear of the river.

"After that boat ride, a bridge is nothing. I can't believe I missed this the first time through. It's so pretty," she said of the fish decoration on the wall.

Back in the tunnel, Charlotte complained, "Ugh, I can barely walk. Those horses did a number on my legs."

Gwen said, "At least you had some experience riding. I had no idea it would hurt this much. My whole body is killing me."

Desmond agreed. "I hope I don't see another horse for a long time."

"How long do you think we've been gone?" Charlotte asked.

"Hard to say," he said, "Seems like a month."

Rasq pushed open the door leading into the bookshop office. The light there was on. Castle remained on the cot, looking a little grayer than before. Desmond removed the vessel and handed it over to Rasq.

Gwen chewed her thumbnail. "What if it doesn't work?"

"It will work." Desmond stepped back.

Rasq inspected the golden fire swirling in the bottle. "What do I do? Is he supposed to drink it?"

"I am not prying his mouth open." Gwen held up her hands.

Charlotte shook her head. "I don't think I can do that either. Maybe we can pour it on him, and the heat will do the trick. Try a couple of drops to start."

Rasq nodded. He drew a breath to steel himself and popped the cork.

The light of Cosalis rose into the air by itself. It swirled like glittering smoke, gathering into a mass before floating over to Castle's prone form. It stretched the length of the old man's body, hovering there for a moment. As if all at once gripped by gravity, the light dropped onto him like water. It soaked into his clothes, his skin and hair.

He gasped awake and shot straight up on the cot, seemingly bewildered by the children cheering and hugging one another at his bedside. He touched his chest, his face, ran his fingers over the thin patch of hair on his head. His expression soured.

"What is this?" His voice came hoarse. "What did you do to me? Wretched creatures. Get out of my store." He swung his legs over the side of the bed to get up but thought better of it.

Rasq kneeled beside him. "It's okay. They helped me save you."

Castle touched his chest again. "My heart is warm. I haven't felt like this since..."

"Since Lucinda," Charlotte finished for him.

"Yes. Lucinda." He looked at the vessel still in Rasq's hand. "How?"

"We've been to the realms." As Rasq spoke, the machine that had locked down the bookshop let a great clunk that shook the floor.

Everyone turned their eyes to the ceiling, listening to the series of squeals and whirs and clicks emanating from the walls.

"The doors are opening," Gwen said.

She, Desmond, and Charlotte dashed from the office for the main area of the shop. Lights flickered on. Shutters on the windows flew up to reveal a clear night, peaceful as far as they could tell.

Rasq helped Castle out to the stool behind the counter, then joined the others. They seemed riveted there, close to the end of the ordeal and, somehow, unable to leave.

"Seems a jolt, doesn't it? Coming back. All of a sudden, it's over." Gwen sighed.

All of a sudden, just like the way their friends, Vincent and Elm, had escaped into the portal, they, too, were moving on.

"You all can go. I'll take the vessel back to the Authors Unknown. They'll be expecting their story." He laughed. "That'll probably take a while." He looked at the floor. "You won't forget about me, right? I've never really had any friends before and..."

Before he could finish, Gwen threw her arms around him in a hug. "What sort of people do you think we are?"

Charlotte joined them. "We'll visit all the time. I'll bring you pants that fit."

Behind the counter, Castle said, "Given that they have stolen from me, from my shop, I am the only person who can grant them permission to return. Young Mr. Winters, I want to talk to you before you take your leave."

Desmond returned to the counter. The others followed.

"I expect Rasq will fill me in on what happened while I was out of commission. Am I to understand you had a role in returning me to the land of the living?"

"We all did."

The old man nodded, thoughtfully. "I suppose this redeems all of you, somewhat."

"Somewhat?"

In no happier a tone, Castle announced, "The three of you are free to return to the bookshop during regular business hours. Given that you have seen the realms firsthand, you may borrow one book at a time from the collection. Damage to any of the volumes there or another theft will result in a lifetime ban from the premises. Do I make myself clear?"

Desmond stifled a smile to reply, "Yes, sir."

"You are still a Winters, and you have a long way to go to prove you're worthy of any level of trust."

"I understand."

Castle reluctantly added, "Thank you."

"You're welcome."

They said a quick round of goodbyes, with promises to return made by Desmond, Charlotte, and Gwen. Rasq turned the sign to closed and waved from the other side of the door as they left.

"Our bikes are gone." Gwen put her hands on her hips. "Now what?"

Charlotte patted her on the back. "We walk."

Desmond swore the air in town smelled sweeter than before. Lights on the fronts of the buildings, window displays with their mannequins and baked treats were for them alone. No cars cruised the streets, not in new downtown or anywhere along the road. The three of them lingered on the bridge, so Gwen could admire the view for the first time.

They reached Charlotte's house first. Every lamp in the house was on.

Gwen asked, "Do you think it's weird no one was waiting for us outside the bookshop? I mean, three children were missing. Not to sound self-centered or anything, but shouldn't there be a fuss?"

"What if we've been gone for years?" Fear crept into Charlotte's voice.

"We haven't been gone that long. Branches from that big tree were still lying at the edge of the road, at the fork," Desmond said.

"True. I guess my house does look exactly the same." She looked at Desmond. "Is it weird that I'm nervous about going in? How do I explain?"

"I have a feeling our parents already know about the realms, or at least my parents do. How could they not?"

After another round of hugs, she set off down the sidewalk. Gwen and Desmond waited until the front door opened and Charlotte's parents scooped her up before moving on.

"You know they're probably phoning your mom and dad right now," Gwen told him.

His parents. They seemed far-off, pleasant people in a pleasant dream. They'd been gone so long; he'd been through so much, what if none of them were the same?

Gwen and Desmond went around to the back door of the house, perhaps wanting to prolong this last step of their adventure just a few seconds longer. Mrs. Dunwiler, upon seeing them enter the kitchen, dropped the pot in her hand, and before it could clang on the floor, she had both Gwen and Desmond in her arms.

She called Mr. and Mrs. Winters into the room and then blubbered into her daughter's hair. "Gwennie, where have you been for three days? Are you hurt?"

"We're fine, Mom."

Then his own mother was there, beautiful as ever. She placed the phone she'd been holding on the table and stared at him as if she could barely believe her eyes. His father came in behind her. Desmond pried himself from Mrs. Dunwiler's grasp to run to them.

"My boy," his mother said through tears. "I knew you would make it back."

Tyler Winters grinned down at his son. "Of course, he did. I told you he'd be just fine. He's a Winters, after all. The realms are no match for our stock."

Desmond pulled away. "You do know."

"Yeah. When we found your bikes outside the bookshop, we knew where you'd gone, and I knew you could handle whatever the realms tossed in your direction. Mrs. Dunwiler took some convincing, though. It was all I could do to keep her and Charlotte's parents from tearing into the place. Is the old man alright?"

"He's alive. We saved him."

He ruffled Desmond's hair. "Good boy."

His mother said, "I won't lose you again."

She didn't have to worry. Desmond was home. They were together, and he had a story to tell them, for once.

Here's a sneak peek at the second Desmond Winters book, *Desmond Winters and the Ghosts of Arbolettis.*

CHAPTER 1

"Look." Charlotte pointed to the newspaper on the counter in front of an unreceptive Mr. Castle. "Other stores advertise. That's how they get customers to come in and buy things."

Desmond, Rasq, and Gwen were in the rafters near the back of the store, building a set of shelves to house the collection of books by the Authors Unknown. The current home, the gated enclosure at the center of the bookshop, wasn't secure enough to keep them safe, and the old man had grown tired of people asking him about the books. It seemed like the less available something was, the more people wanted it.

"I get enough hooligans in here as it is with all these new stores. We don't need their money."

After they'd returned from their last adventure in the realms, Charlotte decided that things around the bookshop needed a change. Not only did the store need a makeover, so did the two guys who lived there. She told them it was all too depressing, and she was going to fix the situation no matter what it took.

Castle thought he might get rid of her by handing over money for her to buy a few things and letting her have her way. He actually had plenty of money in the form of a heaping pile of gold stashed in the closet. People from the realms brought him offerings every so often, and he kept almost all of it, spending only what was needed to keep Rasq and himself fed and the lights on and the water running.

Charlotte said, "Yes, you make it a little too obvious that you don't need customers with the way you chase them all out.

Most stores need money to stay in operation, and it looks suspicious that you're able to stay open when almost no one buys anything. Do you want them to start asking questions?"

His shoulders slumped. "No, but I'm not buying advertising."

"Then let someone buy a book."

He scratched behind his ear, thinking, and then sighed. "Fine. Maybe one."

Gwen hammered a last nail into a piece of wood for the floor they were installing in the rafters of the shop.

She said, "What a handful. I feel sorry for whatever sucker ends up married to her, which will probably be you." She grinned up at Desmond. "Can you imagine her as a wife?" She scrunched up her nose and imitated Charlotte's voice. "Don't wear that. Wear this. Don't do that; it's bad business. Your driving is horrid."

"I don't plan to marry anyone."

"That's what they all say."

Rasq paused his sanding of one of the shelves and said, "I like the clothes she brought me. They actually fit."

"That's just because you don't know any better."

"What's wrong with them?"

Gwen rolled her eyes. "Nothing. Just...pick your own clothes next time. Boys don't usually let girls choose for them. What does she know about what boys should wear, anyway?"

Desmond and Rasq looked at each other and then got back to work, sanding the shelves. Desmond thought the clothes she picked for Rasq were fine. They looked much better than the rags he wore when they first met. The other pants, shirt, and boots were filthy and torn, and they didn't even fit. Now, he dressed like the rest of them, jeans and t-shirts. No one walking down the street would've even noticed that he wasn't quite one hundred percent human.

Behind the counter and behind Castle, the office door flew open, slamming against the wall and startling everyone in the room. A figure in a purple cloak rushed in, saw Castle and stopped in its tracks, gasping.

Everyone in the shop stopped what they were doing to stare.

"You shouldn't be here," said Castle. "Go back the way you came." He motioned toward the office and the door leading to the tunnel. Whoever, whatever it was had come from Nola Junction and the realms.

Charlotte dashed to the front door of the shop, turned the sign to closed, and locked the door. She reached up and pulled down the shade so no one outside would see what was happening.

Rasq dropped from the rafters to the bookshelf below, and then ran, leaping from shelf to shelf until he reached the one closest to the counter.

"Show-off," Gwen muttered as she climbed down the ladder.

"You could try if you want," Desmond said.

"And break my leg? No thanks."

They joined Castle, Charlotte, and Rasq already at the counter. The five of them gathered around the hooded figure, who remained in the office door, seemingly unable to move from that spot.

"Go back the way you came," Castle said again.

"I can't," said an accented, feminine voice. She put up her hands to show she meant no harm.

Fur. Claws. Desmond should've been accustomed to seeing such things, but months had passed since their last jaunt into the realms, and this unexpected visitor had caught them all off guard.

She held up an object the size and shape of a compass, the top of which glowed with a white light.

"I've come for the starkeeper. We need his help."

Someone had addressed Desmond that way before. He didn't like it, because it set him apart from his friends, as if he'd done something more than they had. The truth was that they'd all saved Castle.

"Stay back," Rasq told Desmond.

"I don't need you to protect me." He stepped forward to speak with the stranger. "We don't have the vessel anymore. After we were done with it, we put it back where it belongs. If that's what you're here for, you won't get it."

She pulled back her hood. Her face was feline, long white whiskers, fur gray with black stripes. Her golden eyes were wide with what looked like fear. "I'm not here for the vessel. I'm here for you." She came forward slowly, leading with the thing in her hand. Castle raised the gate on the counter to let her through.

She approached Desmond. Rasq moved to stop her, but Desmond motioned for him to stay back. She lifted the object toward him, and it dimmed. She frowned.

"I don't understand." She tapped the top of it and lifted it once more, turning to Rasq. As she faced Gwen, it lit up.

Gwen glanced warily around at her friends but let the cat girl approach. The object brightened until it bathed everything around it in a stark and glaring light, and it sang, a distinct tinkling sound like a tiny bell ringing over and over again.

"What is that thing?" Gwen asked, her fear evident.

The girl stashed the object in a pocket. "Adelmar was wrong. Close but wrong. You must come with me."

Desmond Winters and the Ghosts of Arbolettis

Available now on Amazon.

ABOUT THE AUTHOR

Lea Ryan writes about the strange and the dark, as well as the light and love, and strives to immerse readers in vivid fictional worlds. She currently lives in Indiana with various family members and assorted pets.